WELCOME BACK TO PIE TOWN

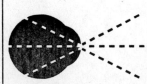

This Large Print Book carries the
Seal of Approval of N.A.V.H.

WELCOME BACK TO PIE TOWN

WITHDRAWN

LYNNE HINTON

WHEELER PUBLISHING
A part of Gale, Cengage Learning

GALE
CENGAGE Learning

Detroit • New York • San Francisco • New Haven, Conn • Waterville, Maine • London

GALE
CENGAGE Learning®

Wheeler Publishing Large Print Hardcover.
The text of this Large Print edition is unabridged.
Other aspects of the book may vary from the original edition.
Set in 16 pt. Plantin.

LIBRARY OF CONGRESS CATALOGING-IN-PUBLICATION DATA

Hinton, J. Lynne.
  Welcome back to Pie Town / by Lynne Hinton.
    pages ; cm. (Wheeler publishing large print hardcover)
  ISBN-13: 978-1-4104-5514-7 (hardcover)
  ISBN-10: 1-4104-5514-9 (hardcover)
  1. Veterans—Fiction. 2. Post-traumatic stress disorder—Fiction. 3. City and town life—Fiction. 4. New Mexico—Fiction. 5. Domestic fiction. 6. Large type books. I. Title.
PS3558.I457W45 2013
813'.54—dc23   2012040956

Published in 2013 by arrangement with William Morrow, an imprint of HarperCollins Publishers

Printed in Mexico
1 2 3 4 5 6 7 17 16 15 14 13

*This book is dedicated to
the women and men
who serve our country and to
their families and communities
who welcome them home*

ACKNOWLEDGMENTS

I gratefully acknowledge my friends and loved ones who continue to encourage and support me and my writing. I am especially thankful for my husband, Bob Branard, who has never left my corner. Sally McMillan is more than an agent; she is my dear friend. Special thanks go to editor Wendy Lee and publicist Lauren Cook, and hats off once again to Carolyn Marino, who first said yes.

Keith Cochran, Deputy Sheriff of Stevens County, wonderful father, husband, and friend, helped me out a great deal with issues of the law. Thank you, Keith, Sara, Isaac, and Jessica, for being such a fabulous family. And thank you to the Creekside Writers in Chewelah, Washington, for your continued love and support.

I am rich with the best things in life: good friends, a loving family, beauty and grace all around, and a never-ending confidence that I am not alone. I am truly blessed.

With the zigzag lightning flung out on high on the ends of your wings, come to us soaring.
With the rainbow hanging high on the ends of your wings, come to us soaring.
With the near darkness made of the dark cloud, of the he-rain, of the dark mist and of the she-rain, come to us.
With the darkness on the earth, come to us.
With these I wish the foam floating on the flowing water over the roots of the great corn.
I have made your sacrifice.
— from the Navajo Night Chant, as translated by Washington Matthews

PROLOGUE

The old man stopped and rested as he came near the top of Techado Mountain. The wind whipped around him as he took a few deep breaths, leaning on the walking stick he brought with him. He stood for only a few minutes, nodded, and continued moving up the narrow path. It was a difficult walk for him and one he wasn't sure he would make many more times.

When he finally arrived at the peak, he rested again and then headed to the center of the plateau. He glanced around at his surroundings, looked up at the sky. Then, using his stick, he drew a large circle around himself. When he finished he tapped his wooden stick, and a long narrow piece of metal fell from inside it. He leaned the metal pole beside his leg and dropped his walking stick outside the circle.

He then bowed in the four directions, honoring the four sacred mountains that provided powers of protection and blessing to the Navajo people: Blanca to the east, Mount Taylor to the south, San Francisco Peaks to the west, and Hesperus to the north. He reached inside the sack he carried on his shoulder and pulled out a small leather bag of corn pollen. He held a handful of pollen in his fist, uncurled his fingers, and watched as his offering danced in the air all around him. He waited.

The sky was dark, stars and moon hidden by the storm clouds of the early summer season. He felt the charge in the air and knew he had picked the right evening to prepare his herbs for the necessary properties of healing. He reached again into his shoulder bag and removed a bundle of leaves and pods and seeds tied in a small rectangular piece of cloth. He untied the cloth, opened it, and placed it on the ground. Then he drove the metal pole that had been inside his walking stick into the middle of the bundle of herbs and into the earth. He bowed once more, stepped outside the circle, picked up his cane, and headed behind an outcropping of large stones located at the northeastern edge of the mountain.

He sat down, dropping the bag and walking stick by his side. He looked up and watched the movement of the clouds, the unsettled way the storm was pulling together and gaining strength. He studied the formations above his head, the direction of the wind, and thought of Sun Bearer, the father of Changing Woman's twin sons. He remembered the story he had been told as a child, the story of the twins who killed Big God with supernatural weapons given to them by their father. He thought of how the twins defeated Big God and tossed away his head, which eventually became the famed Cabezon Peak, the mountain east of the San Mateo Mountains and north of the Cañoncito Navajo.

He remembered his grandfather telling him that the twins, Monster Slayer and Born for Water, became faint and dizzy after defeating Big God, sick from the effects of war, the ghost of their nemesis, Big God, still clinging to them. The story goes that Kingbird and Chickadee aided their friend Changing Woman by shooting pine and spruce arrows over the twins and then treated them with herbs struck by the lightning from a storm.

The old man smiled when he recalled his grandfather explaining that this was the first Enemy Way ceremony, the first ceremony used to cure a Navajo from the effects of war. He leaned back against the rock and thought of all the things his grandfather had taught him, the offerings needed for each blessing, the songs, the assigned times when the rituals were to be used. He had learned so much in his early life and in his many years as a diagnostician for his people. He was grateful for his lessons, for his role, for his place.

He looked around and noticed the speed of the wind, the movement of the slender blades of grass beside him, the push and pull of a small piece of tumbleweed caught in the branches of a nearby piñon tree. He could smell the coming of rain. He could see the clouds tighten above him, and he felt the ground under him and knew the time had arrived. He stood up and could feel the charge all around him. He smiled. He had chosen the right evening. He waited as the electricity built up and was watching the top of the mountain just as a single crack of lightning discharged from the cloud above and hit the metal pole and then ran down until it hit the bundle he had placed in the center of the circle.

He waited a few minutes, nodded his head in approval and acceptance, and then slowly walked over to retrieve both the bundle of herbs and the lightning rod. He replaced

14

them all where they had been stored when he arrived on the mountain. Using his foot, he carefully erased the circle he had drawn, wanting to leave everything as it had been before he arrived, and bowed once more to the four directions, north, west, south, and then east. As he finished he turned once again to the south, his eyes falling upon the small village below him, and he felt a sudden shiver. The large bolt of lightning that would push the town into darkness had not yet fallen, but the old man could sense it would soon come.

He reached into his sack again, pulled out the small bag of corn pollen, and emptied the contents in the direction he faced. He dropped his head and said a few words, a prayer to the gods, and turned to walk away, heading down the mountain and back across the desert to his home.

The old medicine man hoped his blessing would protect the people in the small village below him. He hoped but could not promise that no harm from the lightning or the storm brewing around them would come to the people of Pie Town.

PART ONE

ONE

Everybody in Pie Town knew exactly where they were and what they were doing when the bolt of lightning struck the transformer at a substation near the edge of town, cutting off power for half of Catron County for more than two hours. It was late, about nine o'clock in the evening, and most everyone was home for the evening, and a few were in some stage of preparing for bed.

Oris Whitsett was standing at the bathroom sink. He was shaving, something he liked to do at night after his shower. He found that the hot water, the steam, the clean way he felt, the freshness of a newly shaved face relaxed him and made it easier for him to fall asleep.

Previously a person who enjoyed a morning shower and shave, he began this nightly ritual when Alice, his wife, got sick and came home from the hospital. He found that he had so much to do in the mornings getting her up and ready that he never had time until evening to think about himself and his own needs. She also seemed to appreciate his smooth face and his warm body when he would curl in bed around her at night before falling asleep. It became a part of his pattern of caregiving and intimacy, but even years after she had died, he found he liked a late night shower. He enjoyed an evening shave.

He had a towel wrapped around his waist and another around his shoulders, and his face was covered in a white, thick, foamy cream. He was getting ready to place the razor just at the top of his cheek when the power went out. He waited. Oris was used to the flickering of lights that often happened in Catron County, New Mexico, during the seasons of spring and summer. High winds sometimes made for power surges in the area. Usually, there were only flickers, no real outages.

He had noticed the signs of an evening storm earlier when he went over to visit his neighbor, Millie Watson, who had taken a serious fall a few weeks earlier and had just returned from the long-term care facility in town. Her daughter had come home with her, planning to stay a couple of weeks until Millie was able to take care of herself, and

Oris had stopped over with two takeout enchilada dinners prepared especially for them by Fred and Bea at Pie Town Diner.

He had stayed for only a short time, maybe twenty minutes, and was walking home about seven P.M. when he noticed the stirring of the wind and tight clouds bunching overhead. He considered then that he should take his shower and shave before it got dark, but then he had gotten home and turned on the television and become interested in some show about ghosts and haunted houses. Before he knew it, he had sat through two hours of programming, and when he finally got up to take his shower, he thought the storm had actually come and gone.

Oris stood at the sink in darkness and wondered if he could shave himself without looking. With one hand he touched his face, and with the other he slowly pulled the razor down. It was harder than he expected, and after the second cut, his chin burning, he stopped, wiped his face clean with the wet cloth he found in the sink, and dried with the towel around his shoulders. He then tried to make his way from the bathroom to the den. He felt around for his favorite chair, sat down, and waited.

He knew he had candles and a couple of

lanterns, but for a few minutes, an hour even, he sat in darkness. He was a bit chilled, wearing only a towel, but except for the burning from the cuts on his face, he was not uncomfortable. He actually enjoyed the darkness. He closed his eyes and leaned back.

He thought about the television show he had just watched. He thought about ghosts and haunted houses, and he thought about Alice and wondered if the clouds and the night winds and the storm might bring her back to him, wondered if this might be the thing she needed to return. He wondered if a cover of darkness could bring her to him, if she had been waiting for just this occasion to visit.

It had been over a year since his last visit from his dead wife. Oris remembered how it felt when her presence was suddenly and completely gone after Alex, his great-grandson, passed away. And since that death, that horrible and grievous death, there had been no sign, no communication, no vision of his beloved, but he didn't care. Every night he waited and he hoped. And even though he sat that night in complete darkness, his face burning from the blind shave, his body wrapped in a towel, he could not give up believing that the light, his light, might once again one day, one night, this night, come.

Two

Roger and Malene had just gotten into bed, though it was early for them both to be getting ready for sleep. Roger had been up since four o'clock that morning, responding to a call from the FBI about a drug bust north of Datil, a small village just southeast of Pie Town. They had waited until the last minute to let the sheriff of Catron County know about the raid and request navigational assistance to an address somewhere close to Socorro County over on the Alamo Navajo land. They had called just after four o'clock and expected him to meet them on Highway 60 at the Broken Arrow Motel in Datil by four-thirty. When he arrived, they showed him the address and wanted him to drive them to the location via the most direct, and yet hidden, route.

Roger knew the federal officer supervising the raid, having assisted him before in a couple of sting operations in Catron and

Socorro Counties. He had never particularly cared for the man. He was brash and arrogant and usually ill prepared for the stings and busts he liked to organize. This one had been no different. The federal lawman had decided on a particular house and an alleged perpetrator based on a very unreliable informant. That was soon revealed when eight FBI cars and two DEA vans barreled down the driveway to a small ranch house just before sunrise and at least twenty officers surrounded it with guns raised and orders to fire on command, only to find out they were on the property of the new elementary school principal. Living alone and still in bed, sixty-four-year-old Maria Begay had to be taken to the hospital in Socorro because the raid had shocked and upset her to the point of a fairly significant heart attack.

There were no drug dealers at that location, no drugs other than a few bottles of aspirin and stool softeners, and no apologies offered to the hospitalized school employee or to the sheriff, who had tried to explain to the federal officer before they sped up to Field's Place, thirty-five miles north of Magdalena, that there were no drugs in the vicinity of the Alamo Navajo people. He had tried to explain that more than likely the officers were searching for the drug-running operation he had informed the bureau in Albuquerque about a couple of weeks earlier, an operation that he suspected had taken over one of the old sheep ranches south of Datil, near Old Horse Springs.

Once all the commotion had taken place near Alamo — with the arrival of police vehicles, ambulances, and eventually even Albuquerque news helicopters — the sheep ranch off Highway 12 that Roger had suspected was a hideout for drug runners was completely abandoned and wiped clean. They arrived too late.

It was well after lunchtime before he was excused from the wild goose chase and could finally respond to his own calls, which included investigating a burglary in Quemado and serving an eviction notice near Reserve. He didn't make it home until after seven o'clock in the evening, only to discover his wife, Malene, asleep on the couch.

She had had her own grueling day. She was at work by five-thirty in the morning, having agreed to relieve the third-shift nursing assistant, who needed to drive her husband to the National Guard Training Center in Santa Fe. She had completed that shift and then worked her own until she was finally able to leave at four o'clock in the afternoon. After work she drove to Socorro to do some grocery shopping, and she had just gotten home at six-thirty, sat down on the sofa, and quickly and easily fallen asleep.

She awoke to her husband's kiss on the cheek, and the two of them ate a quick dinner, read the paper, completed a few chores, and finally decided to go to bed when neither of them could keep their eyes open even though it was only eight-thirty. When the lights flickered and finally went out, Roger awoke and considered getting up, getting dressed, and heading out to the station to see if he was needed. But then, remembering that Danny White, a capable, smart deputy, was on duty, he rolled over, pulling the covers over his wife and himself. He placed his arm around Malene and fell back to sleep.

THREE

Francine Mueller was just finishing up at the diner. She had come in late that evening to make the weekly pies. After baking six in the afternoon — two lemon meringues, two chocolates, and two custards — she had decided she wanted to try a new recipe, Tri-Berry Pie, that she read about in her *New Mexico* magazine. She had driven down to Magdalena and picked up the few ingredients that Bea and Fred didn't have on hand and then stopped at her house and eaten a sandwich before walking back to the diner and baking three of the pies.

Francine had become a very good baker in the last year. After winning the first annual pie contest at the church celebration the previous spring, she had taken a cooking class at the community college, and Fred and Bea had given her free rein in the diner kitchen in the late afternoons to practice her art. They were happy to get out of her way and let her create any kind of dessert she felt inclined to try.

Bernie King had taken a particular interest in Francine's baking skills: he had ordered two pies a week, every week, for a year. Nobody understood how the Catron County rancher was eating two pies a week all by himself, but no one ever said anything because in reality everybody was eating more desserts once Francine switched from being a waitress to being the sous chef at Pie Town Diner.

Francine had turned off the oven and left the pies on the counter to cool, and she was thinking about Trina Lockhart, the young mother who had stopped by the diner for a couple of slices of pie earlier in the day. Trina had worked at the diner while she was pregnant, and Francine thought of the girl as a very special friend. Trina was smart and funny, and even though there was an age difference of almost forty years between the two, they had become close. Francine was happy that both of them had found love, Trina with Raymond and she with Bernie, and they often teased each other about how love had suddenly and easily come to them both in Pie Town.

Although there had been others interested in a match between Francine and Bernie,

Trina had actually been the one to fan the flame between the two, pushing Bernie to ask Francine out. And once he did Trina's bidding — Bernie took Francine down to Silver City for a movie and dinner — the rest, Francine thought with a smile, was history.

She glanced out at the parking lot and saw the familiar vehicle pull in. She smiled and waved at Bernie. Just as he slid out of the truck, the lights in the diner went out. Francine waited for a second, hoping it was just a flicker, and then stumbled out of the kitchen, around the tables, trying to feel her way through the darkness. She was standing at one of the booths when she heard the front door open.

"Francie," Bernie called out and shone a flashlight in her direction. "You okay?" he asked.

"Just fine," she replied, making her way closer to him, glad to know he was there, glad he kept a flashlight in his truck.

"Looks like the power got knocked out all over town. I hope you're ready to lock up and leave."

Francine waved away the light he still had shining in her direction and nodded, moving carefully through the diner to the door. "Let me get my purse," she said while she walked back to the kitchen, the light following her every step. She stopped. "I can't remember which ones I turned on," she said, sliding her hand along the wall to the plate of light switches. "What if I don't get the right ones turned off?"

"Just turn off what you can," Bernie instructed. "If there's any left on in the kitchen, it won't be the worst thing for Fred and Bea to pay a little extra on their power bill. They should be happy that you're willing to work so late."

Francine smiled. She loved the way Bernie had taken to looking after her. She loved the thought that he cared for her, worried about her.

"Smells good," he noted. "What's the special this week?"

"Tri-berry," she answered. "I saved you a slice." And she patted the bag she had tucked inside her arms and walked past Bernie and out the door.

"Sounds perfect."

He followed, and she turned to lock the dead bolt. "Wonder how long the power will be out," she said. "I'm not sure I remember where my candles are. And it's been a while," she added, "since I checked the batteries in my flashlight. I hope it still works."

"No need to worry about that," Bernie

said, taking Francine by the arm. "I have a generator at the ranch, and I think you should just come out and stay with me tonight."

"Well, Bernie King," she said with a grin as she turned to face him, "what will the folks of Pie Town say to that?"

He blushed, cleared his throat, and held open the door on the passenger side of his truck. "I'm sixty-five years old, Francine, and I don't rightly concern myself with the thoughts of others. Do you?"

Francine's face reddened as well. "I suppose I do not," she replied, still standing at the door.

And the two of them got in, heading out of the parking lot and in the direction of the King ranch just a few miles out of town.

FOUR

Father George Morris was reading scripture when the power went out. The tea kettle was whistling, and he had put his Bible down and was preparing to get up from his desk and walk into the kitchen to have a cup of tea.

"Ah, Lord, the storms of summertime." He sighed. He reached into one of the desk drawers, found a flashlight, turned it on, and made his way into the kitchen. After pouring himself a cup of tea, he began feeling his way through the cabinets for the candles he knew were kept above the stove.

He found a few votive candles and placed them on small plates, lighting them with the matches he had collected from his desk drawer. He set the candles around the front room of the rectory and sat back down at his desk, the cup of tea beside his Bible. He thought about the scripture he was reading, the Gospel of Mark, and particularly the story of Jesus walking on the water, the story of high winds and fear, a storm experienced by the disciples. He thought of the irony of his reading about a storm, considering what was happening all around him, and had to smile. He opened his Bible to read more but then, realizing that he would not be able to read with so little light, closed the book and considered just going to bed, even though he wasn't actually sleepy.

He thought of the events of the day, the meeting of the education committee and the decision to start a nursery for the worship hour on Sunday mornings. He thought about his visit to the parish in Quemado and his conversation with Father Quy, the priest serving the two other churches in the vicinity. He recalled the man's cynical comment that Father George had a cushy job serving only the Holy Family Church in Pie Town, not being responsible to the diocese in Gallup, and how it seemed that Father George had taken to radical ways by not wearing his collar and allowing Protestants to share in regular worship.

George had chosen not to engage with the other priest once he made those remarks. He knew that the other parish priests in New Mexico and the entire Southwest thought the arrangement in Pie Town with the diocese in Gallup was inappropriate and out of line. He knew that Holy Family Church was a kind of renegade organization that even seemed close to breaking ties with the Catholic Church. He understood that once he and the citizens of Pie Town chose to build their own church, without supervision or assistance from the diocese in Gallup, he and the Church were moving into uncharted territory. Father George still referred to himself as a Catholic priest, but he was not in full standing with the Church. It was a unique and precarious relationship, and many other priests were not happy about it.

George had tried to build a friendship with the new priest in Catron County when he arrived, but the orthodox young man, trained in his home country of Vietnam, could never understand the role of the priest in Pie Town. George had decided after this last visit that he would make no further attempts at being friends. He was, after all, deeply involved in the lives of his parishioners, in the events of the community, and happily, he noted to himself, had more than enough friends. If Father Quy wanted to make a connection with George, he knew how to contact him. Pie Town wasn't that far from Quemado.

George looked at his watch, trying to make out the time, and took a sip of tea. He thought about his afternoon, his visit to Frank Twinhorse's garage. He had taken in the station wagon he had been driving for the entire time he had been in Catron County. It had not been a reliable vehicle when it was given to him by the Monsignor in Gallup, and now it was simply falling apart.

That afternoon, George had taken his car in because the brakes were squealing. Since he didn't know a drum from a pedal, and since he needed his car the rest of the week, he was hoping that Trina or Frank would be able to tighten something or oil a part and take care of the problem quickly. He was hopeful that he wouldn't have to leave it with them for any length of time.

Trina, the young woman who had arrived in Pie Town at the same time that Father George had, was working at the garage. She was good at what she did, loved working on engines, and had learned a lot about auto mechanics while serving an apprenticeship with Frank. She had, in fact, replaced more parts in the station wagon than George could count and had practically rebuilt the transmission earlier in the year. She was quite skilled at her work and very happy in her new job.

When he arrived at the garage, Trina and Frank were nowhere to be found. He called out for them, walked around the bays and into the office, but neither of them answered or showed up. Finally, just as he was getting into the station wagon to leave, Frank pulled up in his tow truck, explaining briefly that Trina was home with Raymond and that she had called Frank over to handle a situation.

Father George knew that Raymond, Frank's son and Trina's boyfriend, had been in Pie Town for only about five weeks. The church had thrown a big "welcome home" party for the wounded soldier when he was released from the Veterans Hospital in Albuquerque, and even though the young man seemed a bit uncomfortable with the attention from his hometown, he acted like he enjoyed the gathering. He was quiet but did not seem troubled, shy but not necessarily withdrawn.

George had visited Raymond while he was hospitalized and had seen the physical wounds of war. The young soldier had been in a vehicle that exploded because of a roadside bomb. He was the only one who had survived. His left knee was shattered. Both lungs were punctured. There was significant hearing loss, a fractured skull, brain trauma, and more than eight or nine other broken bones. Raymond had come through numerous surgeries and had been sent home after lengthy stays at medical clinics and hospitals in Afghanistan, Germany, North Carolina, and finally Albuquerque.

Father George had concluded, even though there had been no real cause for his suspicions, that Raymond had suffered as much, if not more, emotionally as physically during his short time of service in war, and after his visit in Albuquerque he had suggested to Trina and Frank that the young man might benefit from support services offered to returning veterans. Both the boy's father and his girlfriend had explained that they mentioned this to Raymond, but that he seemed unwilling to consider talking about his experience with anyone.

Once Raymond had been home a few weeks, he became increasingly withdrawn, and Father George started paying closer attention. He checked on the young man every couple of days, and even though Raymond wouldn't look George in the eye and seemed unable to sit still for any length of time, the priest thought everything was going as well as could be expected. He had not seen signs of real trauma for the soldier.

"What kind of situation?" George remembered asking Frank.

The father wouldn't answer any questions about his son. He had checked the station wagon and announced that the priest would need new brake liners on the rear wheels. He could leave the car at the garage until the parts arrived and were installed, he was informed, or it was probably safe to drive around town if he wanted to return later in the week. George had decided just to keep the car until the parts were delivered.

"Would it help if I visited?" he had asked Frank before driving off. He knew where Trina and Raymond lived. He knew they had moved out of the little garage apartment and into Roger's house, since the sheriff had moved in with Malene once they got married. "I can drop by, offer to talk to Raymond, offer to drive him to Albuquerque to talk to someone there."

And George, sipping some more of his tea, recalled how Frank appeared when the offer was made. He had looked away and then turned back, shaking his head from side to side. He had taken a long breath before answering, wiping his hands on the rag hanging from his pocket.

"I like you, Father George. I have since

you built the church and did what you did for this little town. I respect your work." He stepped away from the car. "You have a good heart."

George glanced away.

And then Frank had hesitated before finishing. He shook his head again. "But you can't help my son." He then slid his hand across the back of his neck. "I'm not sure what or who can help him now." And with that, Frank had turned away and walked into the office. George had waited, thinking he might return, but when he didn't, George had simply driven off.

Father George considered that perhaps he should have gone over to Trina's. He didn't need a reason to visit; the young couple knew the priest often stopped by to see parishioners or community members. They both knew he sometimes dropped in on folks without calling ahead. But George had chosen not to meddle, not that time. He told himself he would wait until he gained permission from Trina or Raymond to step in and offer help.

He had decided that the most he could do at the time, the best he had to offer, was to simply say his prayers. And so, there in the meek light of small candles, that's what he did. Father George dropped his face, closed his eyes, and folded his hands. Cloaked in darkness, he prayed.

FIVE

Trina was still hiding in the bathroom, Alexandria asleep, cradled in her arms, when the power went out. She had not heard Raymond for over an hour, but she was afraid to open the door and step out into the hallway.

This outburst had been his worst so far. He had grown more angry and sullen with each passing day since he had been home, but he had never lashed out at her. Not until that evening. She had been surprised by it because she never expected him to become violent toward her; she had never considered that as a possibility. And on that particular day, she thought he was actually better after talking to his father in the afternoon.

Trina, home for lunch, had called Frank because Raymond had found his firearm and was waving the gun all around, claiming he was "taking care of business." She left the garage in hopes that they could enjoy a couple of sandwiches together, and she had even picked up two slices of pie at the diner, enjoying a little time with Francine. Alexandria was with Frieda Roybal, the woman who kept the baby while Trina worked, and since it was slow at the garage, Frank had told her to take more than her usual hour for lunch if she wanted. So that was what she had decided to do.

She knew Frank was happy that she and Raymond had fallen in love. She had felt his support from the very beginning, when they met at Raymond's boot camp graduation in Texas. Trina, pregnant with Alexandria, had been planning to return to her home state, and Frank had given her a ride there. Since meeting him at the graduation, she and Raymond had written each other and talked on the computer for the entire time he had been deployed. They had gotten very close. And through the letters and the emails and the phone calls, Trina and Raymond built a relationship.

Trina trusted Raymond. She trusted that he was honest with her, that he shared from himself deeply and authentically. She had grown to depend on him, even when he was so far away. She waited to hear his thoughts before she made decisions. She couldn't wait to talk to him and share her funny

43

stories about the pregnancy, the birth, the baby, about the garage, about Pie Town. Alexandria had brought new life and love into her life, and Raymond had brought companionship, a deep and abiding friendship, tenderness, support, and a different kind of love than she had ever experienced. And as a result of what she shared with him, she had fallen in love with the young soldier.

And then the explosion happened, and he was sent home, and it soon became clear that he was not the same man she had gotten to know in the last year. Physically, he was mostly healed from the injuries he sustained. He still walked with a limp, his knee having been shattered, and he had lost a lot of strength in his upper body, sometimes shaking badly from the involuntary muscle tremors, but he could walk and use all his limbs. After months of surgeries and physical and occupational therapy, he could pick Alexandria up, cook, and complete tasks around the house. The doctors had fixed all of his physical wounds, but no one had paid attention to or been able to heal the emotional ones.

In the beginning when he came home, he woke up most nights in a cold sweat, screaming and kicking Trina out of the bed. She had quit sleeping with him after the

44

first couple of nights and moved a small cot into the room with the baby. He had not tried to stop her, had even encouraged her to sleep somewhere else, because he knew his actions coming out of sleep were unpredictable. Even though she didn't think he would use it, she had hidden his gun, a small pistol he had bought at a pawnshop when he left the hospital in Albuquerque. That day, the day the power went out, he had found it.

His conversation with Frank seemed to calm him down, and when Trina got home from work around six o'clock, nervous and unsure of what to expect, she actually thought he was better. He had apologized for what had happened, claimed that he had gotten rid of the gun, and said he would go to Albuquerque and make an appointment to talk to someone at the VA about what was going on with him. He admitted that he had been drinking before she came home at lunch and acknowledged that alcohol did make things worse and that he was going to start a twelve-step program soon as well. She believed him, was hopeful for him, and they had even laughed together when she told a joke she had heard from Oris when she stopped at the diner. They had kissed, and he seemed better, more relaxed, more at ease.

She had left him in good spirits, she thought, just like he used to be, when she drove across town to pick up Alexandria. He was watching television, resting on the couch. When she got home she fed the baby, bathed her, and put her down for the night and was boiling a pot of water, planning to cook pasta, his favorite, when she heard Raymond in the other room cursing. He was playing a video game, a form of entertainment that he had discovered during his deployment.

He was angry because the game had stalled, had stopped playing, and then, after Raymond yelled something, Trina had heard a loud crash. When she ran into the den to see what had happened, she discovered that he had thrown a beer bottle into the screen and broken both the screen and the bottle. She had hurried to him, asked him what was wrong, if he was okay, and just like that he seemed to snap.

Trina crouched behind the bathroom door and thought about what had happened next, the things he said, the way he looked at her.

"You think you can tell me what to do?" he yelled. "You think you own me?" He followed her as she headed into the kitchen.

"You don't know me. You don't know what happened to me."

Trina tried to get away, moving first near the sink and then over toward the hallway.

"Come back here," he said, reaching for her, and when she found herself trapped in front of the stove where the water was boiling for spaghetti, he grabbed her by the arms.

"Raymond, stop!" she screamed. "You're hurting me." But her plea had done no good.

She had tried to pull away, and when she did he let go and she fell back into the pot of hot water, knocking it over and spilling the contents onto her back and down her legs. When she tried to run away, he reached for her again and then slipped and fell, hitting his head on the edge of the counter. Trina managed to flee to the rear of the house, grab Alexandria from her crib, and run to the bathroom, knowing it was the only room in the house that had a lock on the door.

She knelt down by the sink, her lower back and legs still burning from the hot water spilled on her. Cradling Alexandria, she listened as he came to the door, trying to unlock it, begging for forgiveness, saying he was sorry.

Trina had stayed in that position for over an hour, maybe two, trying to understand how it was that she had landed in that place, landed in that predicament, how she had missed the signs of impending violence. After a childhood spent living with a heavy-handed father and seeing her mother's scars, her mother's brokenness because of domestic violence, Trina had always guarded herself against abusive men. She had known the signs, the patterns, and had stayed away from any man who resembled her father; she had always avoided the controlling kind of boyfriend. She had been smart and alert and had promised herself that she would never be a victim, that she would never find herself landing in the place where she was. As she felt the burns on her back and her legs, as she sat crouched behind the door, she could not understand how the one thing she had promised herself had come to pass after all.

She glanced down at Alexandria. The baby, having been grabbed from her crib and awakened so frightfully, had finally cried herself to sleep. Being a mother herself now had made her even stronger, even more unwilling to be in an abusive relationship, and even though she didn't think Raymond was like her father, a violent and misogynistic man, she knew she had to take care of her daughter; she had to make sure Alexandria was safe. After this incident, Trina was no longer sure whether it was possible to live in the same house with Raymond.

Trina thought she had heard the back door open and close, then the sound of Raymond's dirt bike pulling out of the driveway not long after he had come to the bathroom door, but she had been too afraid to look out and see. Finally, when the lights went out and there were no sounds for what seemed to her to be a very long time, after she found her courage and recognized her resolve not to be victimized by anyone, she quietly stood up, opened the door, and peeked out into the hallway.

It was dark, and she took a breath and headed out beyond the bathroom. When she made it to the kitchen, she could see that the back door had been left open. She glanced out, Alexandria asleep in her arms, and saw that the dirt bike was gone. She and the baby were alone.

■ ■ ■ ■ ■

PART TWO

■ ■ ■ ■ ■

Six

When the phone rang, Roger couldn't tell what time it was. The light on the alarm clock was blinking, evidence that the power had come on sometime while he and Malene had been sleeping. He rubbed his eyes and reached for the phone. He blinked and could see it was not yet light outside.

"Sheriff Benavidez," he answered.

"Sheriff," came the voice on the other end, "it's Danny." The caller waited for an acknowledgment.

"What's wrong?" Roger asked, glancing at his watch. It was just before seven o'clock in the morning.

"We got a robbery," Danny reported. "Figured it happened sometime last night or early this morning. I'm at the scene."

Roger sat up. Malene stirred.

"Where?" Roger asked.

"Datil, the Silver Spur," came the reply. Roger knew the location. It was a bar where a lot of the folks from the county liked to hang out. He knew the owners, Gilbert and Oscar Diaz. The brothers ran a legitimate business, and there was usually not much trouble at the local watering hole. He had just checked on them earlier the previous day when he drove the federal officers over to Alamo. The bar was on his way back to Pie Town.

"Gilbert called it in," Danny added. "He's pretty hot. Wants you to come down here. He says he knows who did it and he wants you to take care of it."

"Can't you handle it?" he asked, glancing over at his wife and wondering if he should wake her.

"He says he deserves to have the sheriff handling his complaint, doesn't want to deal with me," Danny replied. "He wants you to come down here and then go out and get the guy he says did it."

Roger sighed. "You see any evidence to support his identification of the thief?"

"I haven't seen anything that looks like evidence," Danny answered. "Except I did find a gun in the Dumpster."

"A gun?" Roger asked, sounding surprised. "What kind of gun?"

"Small pistol, Model 10."

Roger paused.

"You wearing gloves?" The sheriff was concerned about compromising the scene.

There was no immediate answer.

"Got 'em on right now," Danny replied sheepishly.

Roger shook his head. He understood what just happened. "How does Gilbert know who did it?" he asked.

"He says there was some trouble here last night, and he's convinced that the trouble-maker came back to steal from him."

Roger dropped his head on the pillow. It was not how he wanted to start his day. "Give me about half an hour and I'll be down there. Try and keep everybody away from the crime scene. Tell Gilbert he's going to have to close today."

"Yeah, I already did that. He wasn't too happy," Danny explained. "Today is pay day, you know."

Roger rubbed his eyes again. He remembered it was the last day of the month, and usually that was a banner day for bar and lottery business.

"Don't you want to know who Gilbert is accusing?" Danny asked.

"Sounds like you're going to tell me." Roger waited. "I'm listening."

Malene rolled over and stretched. She peered at the clock, the numbers blinking, and then at her watch. When she realized the time, she jumped out of the bed. She was going to be late for work.

"Raymond Twinhorse. He and some other guy got in a fight. Gilbert threw them both out, but he says Raymond didn't want to go. He says he had to physically push him out the door, and when he did Raymond promised he would be back, made some lame threats. He also says it was Raymond's gun in the Dumpster, had it with him last night waving it around."

Deputy White stopped, and Roger could hear somebody talking in the background. "I told him," Danny said to whoever was at the scene listening to the conversation. More than likely Gilbert, Roger thought.

Roger rolled out of bed and sat on the edge. This was news he didn't want to hear. He had been concerned about his friend Frank's son ever since Raymond got home from the hospital. He could see the boy was changed by whatever happened to him in battle. Roger had noticed that cold, distant look in Raymond's eyes as soon as he got home, even at the homecoming party. Malene had tried to dismiss it, said Raymond was just medicated for the pain, tired from the weeks in the hospital, but Roger knew it was much more than that.

He recognized what was going on from the look he had seen in the eyes of lots of other veterans over the years. Shrinks and doctors had finally come up with a name for what was causing that look, PTSD, post-traumatic stress disorder, but Roger had seen the violence and despair, the trauma and the consequences, long before there was a name for this mental illness.

He had arrested and driven violent, traumatized men to the VA Hospital in Albuquerque ever since American troops had pulled out of Vietnam in the late 1970s. Since the Afghanistan and Iraq wars, he had seen an escalation of all kinds of problems across New Mexico among the young people who had been discharged from the military, including drugs, domestic violence, and suicide.

Because he had been worried about Raymond as soon as he first laid eyes on him, Roger had warned Trina about the risks of moving in together before giving Raymond a chance to settle back home on his own. Even though he had agreed to let them rent his house, he had not thought it was a good idea for them to live together. He worried about his young friend and her daughter, and he had told her so.

"You still there?" Danny asked.

"Yeah, I'm still here," Roger replied. "Look, I'll be there in a little while. No need trying to find Raymond just yet."

"All right, Sheriff, your call. I'll go ahead and seal the area and try to keep Gilbert from selling beers to the onlookers."

"Thanks, Danny. Oh, and don't go broadcasting this information until I've had a chance to review everything. I don't want every business owner in Catron County thinking we got a thief running loose or somebody making the decision that they ought to go find Raymond on their own. Hearing this kind of information just makes people crazy."

"Got it."

"I mean it, Danny. No calls to your buddies."

"Got it, Sheriff, over and out."

Roger reached over and hung up the phone. He heard Malene in the shower and stood up, grabbing his uniform from the chair next to the bed. He dressed, already resigned to the fact that it was going to be another long day.

SEVEN

Father George awoke early. Glancing at the battery-operated clock on the nightstand, he could see that it was a few minutes after seven in the morning. The sun was just rising. He considered staying in bed a bit longer, thinking he might go back to sleep, but then decided, after counting the hours he had already been sleeping, that he had had enough rest and wanted to begin his day. He had a sermon to write, a premarital counseling session to plan, and a few visits to make before the noon Mass.

He got out of bed and headed to the kitchen to heat the water for his morning tea. As he walked to the stove, he was thinking about breakfast, wondering if there was enough milk for cereal or whether he should just boil an egg, when he glanced out the window that opened onto the parking lot that stretched between the rectory and the Holy Family Church. A truck was parked near the front door of the church, the entryway that opened into the narthex and led into the sanctuary. He immediately recognized it as Trina's vehicle, the truck given to her by Frank when she started working with him at the garage earlier in the year.

It was an old pickup, broken down and worthless to the rancher who had towed it over to the garage, but valuable to the garage owner. Frank had tinkered with it for months, rebuilding the engine, rewiring the whole system, getting it a new paint job, new tires, and he had created a decent-looking vehicle. Father George remembered how pleased Trina had been with the gift. The day Frank surprised her with the truck's title she had driven over to the rectory, insisting that the priest was to be her first passenger. She was very proud of that truck because she had also been involved in getting it to run again. The truck had been her classroom while she learned about auto mechanics. Frank had used the opportunity to rebuild the engine and get it working again to teach his young apprentice everything he knew about cars and trucks.

George glanced around the church parking lot, the area around the rectory, and could see no other vehicles. The church doors were closed, and there were no lights on inside. He couldn't figure out what Trina was doing at the church and where she was at that specific moment since he could see the truck was empty.

Had Trina driven over last night? Had she just parked and then walked home? Had someone stolen her truck and abandoned it in the church parking lot? And what about Alexandria? Who was with the baby if Trina was at the church that early in the morning? All kinds of questions filled his mind, and he started to feel a bit anxious as he found some clothes, dressed, and made his way over to the church.

The congregation had decided as soon as the new Holy Family Church was built that there would be no locks on the doors. Even though the first building had burned down after trespassers broke in, lit some candles, and left them burning, it became a matter of principle, of hospitality, to the people of Pie Town to keep the doors unlocked at all times. They did put visible signs on the front and rear doors reminding visitors to extinguish any candles they might have lit and to turn off the lights before leaving, but they didn't want to restrict the availability of the town's sacred gathering space. They wanted Holy Family Church to be a place of respite and solace and worship at anytime for any-body.

For the first year the open-door policy had been in place, no one had abused the church's hospitality. There had been no more fires and no misuse of the building. George knew that a few people drove or walked from town to use the church for meditation and prayer, and other people came and went as well, all throughout the daylight hours and the evenings. However, no one George knew of had been in the sanctuary overnight or at that hour in the morning. He found himself hurrying across the parking lot as he headed to the church.

He opened the front door and stepped inside. It was dark and quiet, and he hesitated to turn on any lights for fear that he would disturb whoever might be there. He stood at the door and waited until his eyes adjusted to the darkness. Then, as he panned across the sanctuary, he could see the body of someone lying near the altar. The figure was small and appeared to be a woman; apprehensive about her condition, he switched on the overhead lights.

Instantly, he could see it was indeed Trina, and it seemed something was terribly wrong. She struggled to lift herself up.

"My God, what happened?" He hurried

to the young woman's side, and as he came closer to her he glanced over and saw the baby wrapped in blankets, carefully laid on the first pew. He made his way to the young woman, but when he reached out to her she started to pull away from him. She began shaking her head, but didn't explain why she was in the sanctuary and what was wrong.

"What happened?" he repeated, trying to understand what she was doing there. "Are you okay? Is something wrong with Alexandria?" He peered over at the baby, but she seemed to be resting comfortably, unharmed. He turned again to Trina, who had stood up. He couldn't see any physical evidence that anything was wrong.

"She's fine," Trina finally answered. "I didn't know where else to go."

"Did something happen?" he asked.

She waited and then, without explanation, turned away from him and lifted her blouse. Immediately he could see the injuries. The skin across her back and legs was dark and red.

"Trina," he said, staring at the burns, "what on earth . . . ? What happened?" And then, "Let me call an ambulance," he said. "Let me call 911." He started to head to his office.

Trina reached out, grabbing George by the sleeve. "No," she said. "No calls."

Father George was at a loss. He stood, watching Trina, trying to understand what was going on and what he should do. He could see she had been hurt, and it appeared as if something had spilled on her: the hair on the back of her head was damp and matted, and her clothes were stiff. He knew that her injuries needed to be assessed and tended to by a medical professional, but he also knew that she had come to the church for protection and that for whatever reason she did not want to contact the authorities.

"Can you tell me what happened?" he asked. "How long have you been here?"

She didn't answer. And without pressing her any further for information, Father George led her to the front pew, sat down with her, and waited until the morning light began to pour through the windows.

Finally, the priest spoke again. "Trina, I think we need to get you to the hospital. These burns on your back, they may be serious." He pulled away from her, hoping she would let him get a better look. When she didn't, he simply touched her forehead, smoothed down her hair, and held her face in his hands.

"What happened? Did you have an accident?"

And then, as soon as he asked that question, he noticed something about the way she wouldn't look him in the eye, and that led him to have another thought, to ask another question.

"Trina, did somebody hurt you?" he asked, his voice breaking. "You have to tell me so I can help you," he added.

Tears fell down the young woman's cheeks, and she turned aside, making sure the baby was still safe, still unharmed, and then turned again to face Father George. She swallowed and finally spoke with a clarity the priest could hear and understand.

"He didn't mean it" was all she could say.

EIGHT

A lizard, a small one, darted across the top
of Raymond's hand. He stirred, feeling
around where he lay, touching the hard
place beneath him where he had spent the
night. He blinked a few times and then sat
up. Glancing around, he tried to recall what
had happened, and where he was.

He was in the desert, but upon first wak-
ing, he was having a difficult time remembering exactly which desert he was in. Was
he still in Afghanistan? Was he still in battle?
He reached for his gun, which wasn't there,
and peered down to see what he was wearing. He was not dressed in fatigues. He tried
to remember, but his mind was foggy. He
shook his head, hoping to gain some clarity.
He looked around again, gathering clues.

The mountains surrounding him were
familiar. That was Horse Peak to the east,
he thought. Eagle Peak stood to his south.
He recognized them, knew them by name.

A coyote barking in the distance, the hawks flying overhead, juniper bushes, mesquite . . . he counted the things that he knew, that he remembered, and finally concluded he was at home; he was stateside, outside somewhere in Catron County.

His mouth was dry. His head hurt. His back was sore, and his knee, still healing from the surgeries, ached. He felt in his pockets and realized he had no water or pain pills with him. He took a breath and slid over to a large rock near his head and leaned against it. How did I ever get here? he asked himself.

Raymond closed his eyes and thought about the place he had landed. He thought about why he had joined the military in the first place, how proud he had been to go to boot camp, how proud he had been to serve his country. He thought about the boy he once was, the boy who believed the army would make him an even better man.

He thought about Catron County, Pie Town, his home, and how, even though he recognized landmarks, knew their names, knew how to get from place to place, everything felt strange to him now that he was home from the war. Intersections he had sat at a thousand times, dirt roads where he had learned to drive, the church he attended with his grandmother, the school he graduated from, everything seemed foreign. And no matter how he tried to convince himself that this was his family's home, this was *his* home, it felt like a place he had only visited a very long time ago.

Even the people, most of whom he had known since he was a child — teachers, friends, parents of friends, employers, everybody he had grown up around — seemed vaguely like people he once knew, once understood, people who once knew him and understood him. Mostly, however, he thought they just seemed like strangers.

He had only been back a few weeks, but he hated how it felt like everybody watched him. He was uncomfortable with the attention, the party that was thrown in his honor, the way everybody spoke to him as if he were ill or broken or fragile, and it actually seemed to Raymond that the people in Pie Town studied him like he didn't look the same to them either. The sheriff, the new priest that had come to Pie Town just as he was leaving for boot camp, the people at the diner, his father, Trina, everybody had a look of worry or suspicion when they spoke to him.

Raymond thought about Trina, the woman he had come to love, and realized that even she, who made him laugh and wrote him every day while he was away, giving details of life back home, of life with a baby, of life in peace, even she seemed as if she didn't know him at all.

He glanced around at where he had passed out the previous night, recalling that he had slept out in the desert many times. And he knew that he had loved this place once; he was sure of that. He had learned things in the desert, things about the sky and the earth. He had known how to trap rabbits and how to track deer and elk. He had slept under those stars so many nights and walked those hills, ridden horses along the trails. This had been home to him in a way he thought he could never forget. But now even this place had somehow become unfamiliar to him.

Raymond closed his eyes again and tried to remember when his feelings of being lost had started. He wasn't sure if it had been while he was away, while he was facing the things he never imagined he would face, or whether it had occurred since he returned.

When did I lose my home? My place? When did I lose all the memories and connections? he asked himself. When did I become this man?

He leaned his head against the rock behind him and began to think about the night before and what had brought him out into the desert. He thought about the way he hurried away from the house, jumping on his dirt bike, riding so hard. Had there been a fight? he wondered. The way the road curved and dipped, and how he had stopped and watched as the lights flickered and finally went out. Where had he been when that happened?

And then he remembered the bar, the drinks, some man pushing him from behind, calling him a drunk Indian, yelling in his face. He recalled another man telling him to move or get up, being told to leave, and the way he was thrown through the door, like a criminal, an animal, and how he had stumbled out to his bike, the other man behind him, his breath hot on his neck, and then finally walking away.

Raymond felt in his jacket pocket and remembered trying to find his way through the parking lot, finally spotting his bike, but then stopping at the Dumpster. He remembered throwing his pistol away, tired of the weight of the thing, tired of the temptation to use it, tired of the agonizing thought that he should shoot himself. He recalled throwing it in the Dumpster and then just getting on his bike and driving away. To here, he thought. Here, out in the middle of the desert. Alone. Lost.

He started to get up, to look for his bike and head home, to Trina, to this life he didn't understand or fit in, to try again, and then he remembered something else. It was a look on a face. Trina's. He tried to think. What had happened to cause that look? What had been done? And then that memory came back too.

He had hurt her. They were arguing. She was backing away. He had followed her into the kitchen and ended up trapping her against the stove. He reached for her, not to hurt her, just to grab her, get her attention, try to make her listen to him, try to get her to see him, really see him, and she had kept backing away, trying to get away from him, and she had that look, that frightened look. And when he had seen that, her look, that mixture of fear and pain, he had let go with a push, a push that somehow landed her in the pot on the stove, a push that had harmed her, a push that caused the pot to spill and its contents to splash against her.

He recalled how she had screamed and fled, and how, when he had tried to go after her, he slipped and fell. He reached up and touched a tender place on his forehead, recalling the event. When he was able to get up and walk, he had heard Trina slam a door. And by the time he had gotten to the bathroom door, the one she had locked, he was denied access to her and to the baby. He tried to see if she was okay, tried to fix what had happened, tried to apologize, but she wouldn't let him in, wouldn't talk to him, and finally he had given up and left.

Raymond suddenly couldn't breathe. What had he done? He felt the nausea rise and his stomach burn. His mouth began to water, and he turned his head to the side just before throwing up. He wretched and vomited until there was nothing left inside of him.

Raymond suddenly knew he had no choice, not after what had happened. He knew he had to leave Pie Town. He had to leave Trina. He had to leave everybody who loved him because, he realized at that moment, he had become dangerous. The effects of war had touched him deeply, and he had harmed an innocent woman. He had harmed the woman he loved. He was so sick of himself that he knew he could not even return to their home and face what he had done. He knew that he had to get away and stay away from the people who were too close. He could hurt the baby. He could hurt Trina again. He could hurt whoever was in front of him.

Raymond stood up and looked down at himself. He knew he didn't recognize the place he used to call home. He didn't recognize the people who raised him, who taught him, who loved him. He didn't recognize the ones he knew he once had loved. But he also understood something else. Standing there, looking at himself, recalling what he had done to Trina, to his family, he knew the one person he least recognized was himself.

He got on his bike and headed away from what had happened and the place he had once called home and the people he once loved. Raymond got on his bike and headed away from Pie Town.

NINE

Deputy Danny White was leaning against his car when the sheriff pulled into the parking lot beside the Silver Spur Saloon. There was only one other car in the lot and no onlookers that Roger could see. It appeared as if the news of a robbery at the bar hadn't made the county grapevine as of yet. This was good news to the sheriff.

Danny was talking on his cell phone, to Christine Day, Roger guessed. He knew that his deputy was engaged to Malene's co-worker at the nursing home and that the young woman kept postponing the date of the wedding. Originally, it was scheduled for February, a Valentine's Day ceremony, but then it was pushed to March, and now it appeared as if the date was being changed again. The deputy glanced up, eyeing his boss, and quickly took his phone from his ear and placed it in his shirt pocket.

"You got here faster than you said,"

Danny noted.

"Didn't wait for my coffee." Roger paused. "You all right?" he said, facing his deputy. "You look kind of pale."

Danny cleared his throat. "Just been up too long, I guess," he replied.

Roger studied the deputy. "Maybe you need some breakfast," he noted.

Danny nodded. "Yeah, that's probably it."

"Gilbert inside?" Roger asked.

"Still pretty mad. I think he's calling Frank, trying to find Raymond. Wants to take matters into his own hands."

"Well, that's no good." The sheriff shook his head.

Roger knew the one thing he didn't need was Gilbert trying to get to Raymond before he did. He was glad that at least the bartender had called in the robbery. Maybe he'd have the chance to calm Gilbert down, get him to back off of the idea of trying to handle things himself.

"You check the scene for prints?" he asked, glancing around the parking lot.

"There were a few around the cash register, but I doubt they're any good," Danny said. "Gilbert's had his hands all over everything. I dusted already. Didn't find much. And the doors and the windows don't look like any forced entry. Here's the gun," and he pulled out a plastic bag. A small pistol was inside.

"All right." Roger reached for the bag and took a good look at the firearm. It was a revolver, Smith and Wesson Model 10, the anchor of Smith and Wesson products since 1899. Roger had one himself. He preferred the revolver to the semiautomatic pistols that most law enforcement officers had started carrying. He didn't know whose gun it was, but he knew it most likely belonged to someone experienced with firearms. The Model 10 was also known as the Military and Police Model. Roger guessed that, with a gun found on the property, Gilbert would probably want to add additional charges to the robbery. He placed the bag under his arm and cleared his throat. "She give you a date yet?" he asked, changing the subject.

Danny blushed, embarrassed that his boss had seen him on a personal call. "She says fall will be a better time for her family." He glanced away. "They moved down to Florida a couple of years ago, and they don't like to travel in the summer. We're still going to Father George for counseling, though."

"Give her some space, Danny, she'll come around. Just a case of cold feet is all. You still going to your anger management classes?" Roger waited for the answer. He knew that Christine had been concerned about Danny's temper. He also knew that she was right. His deputy did have a problem with his anger. He had agreed that the classes were a good idea.

"Every Tuesday night," he answered.

Roger smiled. "Good. So what did you find out about last night at the Silver Spur? They lose power and shut down?"

"No, they didn't shut down. Gilbert says he was still serving drinks when the lights went out. Claims he can tell the difference between a Miller Lite and a Budweiser just by the feel of the bottles." Deputy White opened his small writing pad where he had been taking notes.

"Well, we are a county of extraordinary people. What else?" Roger asked.

"He says he closed not too long after the power outage. He turned on the generator, but his customers left about ten-thirty. He claims he left the cash in the register since he planned to be back at six this morning to write up his deposit. He got here at dawn and noticed the register was open. No sign of a break-in, but he's sure Raymond Twin-horse is the one who returned to the bar and robbed him."

"Why is he so sure about that? There any witnesses?"

Danny shook his head. "He says he threw Raymond out sometime after the lights went out. Apparently, he had been drinking already and was trying to start a fight with some guy from Las Cruces who was in there. They were arguing pretty loudly, and Gilbert made them both leave. The other guy complied. Raymond refused to go. Told Gilbert he had a right to drink if he wanted. Gilbert practically picked him up and threw him out. He says Raymond was pretty mad about it, yelled something about getting him back."

"And Gilbert thinks he did it by taking the money?" Roger eyed Danny.

"That's what he says," the deputy answered.

"What do you think?" Roger asked.

Danny shrugged. "Just sounds like a guy blowing off steam to me. I figure if he was really that mad, he would have messed up the place, not just sneak in a couple of hours later and take the cash."

Roger smiled, proud of his deputy's assessment skills. "You tell that to Gilbert?"

Danny shook his head. "He's made up his mind already, and you know how he is once he's made up his mind."

"Like a dog with a bone," Roger replied.

"A mean dog," Danny responded.

Roger nodded.

"Hey, did you ever catch any drug dealers yesterday?" Danny asked. "I never read any final report."

"That's because there was no final report. FBI had nothing. Had me drive them over to Alamo, scare a woman to death for nothing. There aren't any drugs over there."

"Well, yeah, everybody knows that," Deputy White noted. "Didn't they ask you that before they went out there?"

Roger shook his head. "The only thing they asked me was whether the road could handle the traffic."

"Didn't you report that house out there near Old Horse Springs to the feds?" Danny asked. He remembered the sheriff's mention of a possible drug operation at the old abandoned ranch house.

"Weren't interested," Roger answered. "Of course, maybe they will be now since they made such a mess at Alamo." He gave the gun back to Danny, pulled out a stick of gum, unwrapped it, and started chewing. "Oh well, that's yesterday's news. Whoever was there has pulled up stakes and left," he noted. "Of course, the FBI agent in charge was mighty pissed that he didn't find anything. I suppose if he has his way, he'll be back trying to find something to justify the bust."

He looked at the bar. "Well, let me go get this over with." He headed past the deputy, stopping to slap him on the shoulder, and moved toward the Silver Spur. "Go get yourself something to eat. I think I can handle it from here. I doubt this is as big a deal as Gilbert is making it sound. Oh, and run a background on the gun, see if it's registered to anyone we know."

"Sure thing. I'll also check on the prints," Deputy White replied. "I'll let you know if I find out anything."

Roger just nodded and raised his hand in agreement. He was walking in the front door of the bar when he heard the squad car pull out of the parking lot and Gilbert start to complain.

TEN

Francine had awakened early and was milling around Bernie's kitchen while he slept. She wanted to fix breakfast for the two of them and was relieved to see that the power was back on. She wouldn't have to turn on the generator to fix coffee and heat the oven. After finding the necessary ingredients, she decided to bake a cinnamon coffee cake, and after figuring out how to turn on Bernie's fancy coffee maker, some brand shipped from Europe, she started the coffee as well.

Francine was impressed with Bernie. He was not at all what she expected in a lifelong bachelor. He had flour and butter, brown sugar, milk, and even a fine spice rack filled with all kinds of spices. His refrigerator was fully stocked, and when she opened the cabinets down beside the oven, she found a new baking dish that she would be able to use for her breakfast special.

"It's almost as if he knew I was coming," Francine said to herself and then paused to think about that.

Even though the two of them were considered a couple by most everyone in Pie Town, the overnight stay at Bernie's had come as a total surprise to her. In the last few months, they had gone to dinner at least once a week, driven down to Las Cruces for a day of shopping, and visited her friend in Phoenix together, and she had cooked more than a few meals for him at her house. They had never slept together, however, never even been all that intimate, enjoying only a short kiss at the saying of good-bye or a bit of hand-holding when they sat alone in the car or in the dark at a movie theater.

When he had invited her the previous night — or more like just reported what was going to happen — she had agreed, and it had been the easiest thing she had done in a lot of years. It was as simple as going home with a family member or talking to a friend like Trina. When they arrived at his house, they had a cup of tea, sharing the piece of pie she had brought home from the diner, and then proceeded to get ready for bed as if it were the most natural thing for the two of them to do.

Francine smiled as she recalled the night.

She was glad they had stopped by her house before driving to the ranch and gotten her gown and robe, her toiletries, and a change of clothes for the next day. Bernie had gone inside the house with her, shining the flashlight wherever she had asked, never pushing her along or showing any signs of impatience. He had been the perfect gentleman, and it had been the same when later, in his bed, in the still of the dark night, they made love for the very first time.

He was kind and gentle, asking her with every movement he made if she was okay, if he was hurting her. In the end, the act itself had not lasted more than fifteen or twenty minutes, but after it was over they had stayed under the covers, wrapped around each other, for more than an hour. It seemed that neither of them wanted to change position, somehow worried that if they moved just the slightest bit they would disturb the beauty of the moment they had just shared.

Francine shook her head and was surprised to discover that there were tears in her eyes. She couldn't believe how light she was, how wonderful she felt. She couldn't believe that after so many years of living alone, so many years of being by herself, having finally accepted her status of old maid, that she could so easily and tenderly open her heart to another. She blew out a breath and slid her hands down the front of her robe, readying herself to get to work. She tightened the belt around her waist and tried to focus on the task of preparing breakfast.

She opened the cabinet next to the refrigerator and found a large mixing bowl. She took it down, found a wooden spoon and measuring cups, and began to mix together the ingredients she knew by heart to make the coffee cake she had been making since she was in her teens.

She kneaded the dough with her hands and was smiling as she listened to the coffee perking. She raised her nose to get a good sniff. Francine loved nothing better than the smell of coffee in the morning. She was just about to grease the baking pan, using a slab of butter and sliding it across the bottom and sides of the pan, when she noticed something move outside the kitchen window.

At first, she thought it was just the limb of the big cottonwood tree that stood at the corner of the house. The wind had been blowing, she thought, causing it to dip and sway, catching her eye. And then she thought it was an animal of some kind, a cow moving out across the pasture, a coyote maybe, but then changed her mind about that. It was bigger than a coyote, and it appeared to walk on two legs. She put down the pan and the butter and leaned into the window, curious now about what or who was moving across the yard toward the back acreage of Bernie's ranch.

It had been a few months since Bernie had taken her for a drive to see his property. It had taken more than an hour to get from one border to the other, and in some places the two of them had to exit the truck and walk. There was a canyon, several washes and arroyos, a small grove of Russian olive trees, and lots of land for grazing. She knew that the King ranch went on for miles beyond what could be seen from the house, territory stretching past McAllister Draw to the north and practically out to Tres Lagunas to the east. She knew there were lots of trails on Bernie's land that hunters used to get up to Techado Mountain and Veteado Mountain and even over to Highway 117 and Fence Lake. Bernie never seemed to mind letting the locals use his land as long as they didn't cut the fences, vandalize the property, or harm the livestock. He was particularly generous to hunters, knowing the elk and turkeys were plentiful on the North Plains.

She blinked, clearing her vision, and saw now that it was a person moving across the pasture. She wondered what hunting season it was and whether or not she was just watching somebody set out to get his family's dinner. She kept looking, the figure close enough to make out but moving away from her line of vision, and as she studied the view out of the window, the person in the distance, Francine thought there was something familiar about the way the trespasser walked, that this was someone she recognized. It was the limp, a leaning to one side, and as soon as she recalled who she had recently seen walking with that gait, Bernie slipped into the kitchen and eased behind her.

He followed her stare, peering out the window, and wrapped his arms around her. He had been so quiet, and she had been so intent studying the man in the distance, that he startled her when he kissed her on the cheek and said, "I wonder what Raymond Twinhorse is doing out here at this time of the morning."

Eleven

"Make sure you don't overcook the bacon this time," Oris yelled in the direction of the kitchen. He was the second customer at the diner the day after the storm. Frank Twinhorse was sitting at the counter when Oris made his way inside. They greeted each other with a nod.

"You know I like my pork chewy," he added. He had taken his place at a table next to the door and ordered his usual: two eggs, three slices of bacon, side order of skillet potatoes, tortillas, and chopped green chile, coffee with sugar and cream.

"You'll get it the way I cook it," Fred yelled back. He was used to the old man's complaints. "Drive over to Magdalena if you don't like our breakfast."

"I am not driving all the way down there because you haven't learned how to fry bacon. Just cook the strips like you do for everybody else except take them off the heat

87

when you get ready to flip them over the fourth time."

Bea poured him a cup of coffee, and he reached across the table and grabbed a couple of packs of sugar. "Ain't rocket science."

Fred shook his head and went back to work. He was fixing Oris's breakfast on the large grill in the center of the kitchen.

Frank laughed.

"What's so funny to you?" Oris asked.

"Just how nothing ever changes around here, Oris." Frank took a bite of his breakfast.

"Well, that's a good thing, right?" the older man asked. "Living in a place where you count on folks being the same week to week."

"Not when they're assholes," Bea said with a wink. She was cleaning up the area around the coffee maker and was already making another pot.

Oris waved her off. "Ya'll lose anything in your coolers last night?" he asked, deciding not to respond to her comment. He stirred the sugar in his coffee and reached over for the creamer.

"No, I don't think the power was off that long. Everything seemed okay when we got here this morning," she replied.

"You mean you don't know if your meat is spoiled?" Oris asked, sounding concerned.

"Nope, you're the guinea pig, Oris. Frank only ordered a sopaipilla with honey. So we're glad you're here so early. If you fall over dead before you finish eating, we'll know we need to throw out the pork and the cream."

Oris still held the creamer in his hand. He thought about it and then set it down without pouring any in his cup.

Bea grinned.

"Francine quit working mornings?" he asked.

"She stays pretty busy baking all afternoon and evening," Bea answered. "She must have been here late last night because she didn't put her pies away. And the lights were on in the kitchen when we got here this morning."

"Must have been here when the power went out, and she didn't know which lights she left on," Oris noted. He shook his head. "Same thing happened to me. I went to bed in the dark and then about eleven o'clock, the television started blaring and every light in the house came on. Scared the devil out of me."

Bea brought over some silverware for him.

"Well, wouldn't that be a great day?" she asked.

Oris seemed confused.

"You getting the devil scared out of you," she responded. "Why, that'd be worth going to church on a weekday, wouldn't you agree, Frank?" She glanced over at her other customer.

"Yep, I think that might even get me through the doors," he replied.

Bea turned to Oris. "There's nothing wrong with the cream," she said, eyeing his cup. She knew how he liked his coffee.

"I think I'm going black from now on," he said, taking a sip and then frowning.

"Order up," Fred announced. "Eggs, browns, tortillas, and green chile on the side." He paused. "With three slices of bacon, extra crispy," he added, grinning.

Oris rubbed his hands together and made room for the plate of food Bea brought over. He picked up a strip of bacon and broke it. He just shook his head. "You're right, Frank, nothing changes." Oris started to eat.

"Guess there was a lot of excitement over in Magdalena yesterday." Fred headed out of the kitchen and was making his way around the counter to sit down and read the paper.

"You mean the bust that was a bust?" Oris

asked while he chewed. He wiped his mouth. "Roger said it took him all morning having to deal with the feds from Albuquerque."

"I saw it on the news last night," Bea said. She had picked up Frank's plate and was setting it in the dishpan underneath the counter.

"What did I miss?" Frank asked. He drank the last of his coffee.

Bea pulled out the pot and walked over to him.

"The FBI thought there was a drug operation over near Alamo," Fred announced. He folded the paper to show the headline to Frank. It read, "Major Drug Sting in Catron County."

"I knew sooner or later your people were going to get in trouble for your desert weed smoking." Oris had another mouthful of food.

"My people are not from Alamo," Frank responded. "Those are the Puertocito. We've not associated with them for over a hundred years. And peyote is not a weed, it's a cactus, and you eat it, you don't smoke it."

"Still Navajo, ain't they?" Oris asked.

"Tsa Dei'alth," Frank replied.

He paused while the three others looked at him to translate.

91

"Stone chewers," he said. "They'd get so mad when they fought in battles, they chewed rocks."

"Well, they could have just asked Fred to cook 'em some bacon." Oris grinned, taking the last strip of bacon and breaking it into pieces to make his point.

"Your people are from Ramah, right, Frank?" Bea asked. She had walked over and poured Oris another cup of coffee before returning the pot to the maker behind the counter.

"Home of KTDZ-FM," Oris announced. "I used to listen to that radio station every evening I got off the ranch," he added. "I liked to hear who was stuck at the bus station in Gallup." He reached for the creamer and poured some cream in his coffee. He looked up to see if Bea was watching.

She was. "I remember that station too," she said.

"Yeah, we're from Ramah, and we were so spread out around there, that station was the only way our folks could communicate with each other," Frank responded.

"What? No smoke signals?" Oris drank a sip of his coffee.

Frank shook his head. "No, Oris, no smoke signals for my people, just desert weed smoking ceremonies."

Fred laughed. He was still reading the paper. "Looks like your son-in-law got a line in the story." He read, "Catron County Sheriff Roger Benavidez reported that even though there had been no arrests made in this sting, there had been some suspicious activity in the county in the last few weeks."

"That was just his way of trying to make nice with the FBI," Oris said as he continued to eat every bite of his breakfast. He chewed and swallowed. "He told me last night that they were forty miles from where he suspected the drug runners were, but that the feds refused to listen to him. They drove up Highway 169 blaring at full blast, making such a racket that the Puertocito" — he turned to Frank — "as you like to call them, thought Kit Carson had come back to life and was taking them back to Fort Sumner."

Fred nodded. "Yeah, there's a mention here that the sixty-four-year-old school principal had to be taken by ambulance to the hospital over in Socorro. It appears as if they scared her so bad, she went into cardiac arrest." He turned the page of the newspaper and started giving out the base-ball scores.

It was Bea who first noticed Father George when the station wagon pulled into the parking lot. She was standing behind the counter, facing the door. However, Frank immediately noticed her staring out the window and turned to look in that direction.

"Well, he sure seems troubled for it to be so early in the morning." Bea reached down to get a cup and set it at the counter for the priest to join them for breakfast.

Fred and Oris turned to see him just as he walked in.

Father George glanced at Oris, nodded, and then turned immediately in Frank's direction. His tone was soft but severe. "I need to see you, Frank," was all he said and then headed back out the door.

TWELVE

Gilbert had fixed a pot of coffee and was sitting at the end of the bar, glancing over receipts, when Roger made his way into the Silver Spur. He watched as the sheriff walked over in his direction. "Took you long enough to get here," he commented.

Roger smiled. He headed toward the bartender. "You got enough of that to share?" He was eyeing the coffee.

"Help yourself," Gilbert replied. "Mugs are on the left side."

Roger reached behind the counter and pulled out a coffee cup, then walked over to where Gilbert was sitting, poured himself some coffee, and sat down on the stool beside him. "Feels like it's going to be a hot one," he noted.

"You come to talk the weather?" Gilbert asked. " 'Cause I ain't interested in talking about the heat."

"No, I guess you aren't," Roger responded. He took a sip of his coffee. "So why don't you fill me in on why I'm here."

"I already told your deputy, Barney Fife out there. Raymond Twinhorse threatened me, and then he robbed me, stole my money, and let me just say, when I find him I'm going to get back every nickel he took and a little more for the trouble he's caused." Gilbert had stacked the receipts beside him.

"Well, let's just hold up on that idea," Roger said. "Why don't you tell me exactly how you know for sure this was a robbery and that Raymond Twinhorse is involved."

"First of all, it's a robbery because my cash is gone." Gilbert glanced over at the cash register. The drawer was open, apparently left that way to show the sheriff. "There was a couple hundred dollars in there when I left last night. Now, if you're paying attention, you can see there's nothing in there. Where I come from, when you had money and then you don't and you didn't take it out yourself, then it's a robbery."

Roger nodded. He had known Gilbert most of his life. He knew it was his nature to be ornery. "And you're sure you didn't take the money and move it somewhere, put it in the cash bag last night?"

Gilbert blew out a breath. "The power was out, if you recall, and I turned off the generator when everybody left. After I did that and then got back to the counter, I couldn't open the cash drawer because it can't open without electricity. Never should have bought this new computer. The old one took money just as good." He reached in his shirt pocket for his pack of cigarettes. "Instead of turning the generator on again, I just decided to leave it."

Roger thought about his answer. "Then how would Raymond or the alleged robber have opened the drawer later?"

"Hell if I know. Maybe he waited until the power came back on." He held out the pack to Roger, who shook his head, refusing the offer. "Oh, that's right, you're still on the wagon." He knew the sheriff had quit smoking.

Roger nodded.

Gilbert took out a cigarette and lit it, and then he stood up and poured himself another cup of coffee. He held out the pot to offer Roger some more.

Roger shook his head and took another sip from his cup. "Where's Oscar?" he asked, referring to Gilbert's brother, the co-owner of the Silver Spur.

"Left this morning for a camping trip up

north, going with an old army buddy from Houston."

"He didn't work last night?" Roger wondered if Oscar might have something to add to the mystery of the missing money.

"He worked the day shift. Left about five, when I got here. Said he was going to Socorro to gas up. I haven't talked to him since. Can't reach him while he's camping." He took another draw on his cigarette.

Roger thought for a bit, lifting his face to breathe in the smoke. He still loved the smell of cigarettes.

Gilbert continued. "But I can tell you right now that I don't need to talk to Oscar. I don't need to talk to anybody. Raymond Twinhorse snuck in here sometime this morning and stole from me. He was mad that I threw him out, mad that I didn't let him finish his beer, flashed that stupid gun of his around, and he threatened me. And I know that he made good on his threat. And when I catch that little. . . ."

"I know," Roger interrupted. "You've made it clear you intend to make him pay you back."

"Worthless, lazy son of a bitch." Gilbert spat the words out. "I want him charged with armed robbery, not just burglary." He flicked a few ashes in the ashtray near his arm.

Roger shook his head. "It doesn't really qualify as an armed robbery if there was nobody here."

"There's a gun, right? He waved it around. I'd call that armed. Worthless, lazy. . . ."

Roger broke in. "Let's just hold up a minute, Gilbert, because I'll be truthful with you, I don't believe any of this about Raymond Twinhorse. He's a good kid, never in any trouble with the law, always had a job when he was in school, helped Frank at the garage. He was an exemplary young man. Then he served his country as a soldier in Afghanistan. Let's not forget what he faced over there."

"Listen, I don't have no beef with Frank. He's a good mechanic, honest, hardworking, always has been. But his boy is messed up. Everybody in town knows that. He ain't been right since he got back. You've seen him loitering around here, around the diner. He don't talk to anybody, drinks too much. I didn't know him when he was a boy, but I know him now, and he's trouble, I tell you. I figure he's doing drugs, probably wanted the money to buy some more." Gilbert put down his cigarette and drank some of his coffee. "Why else would he need a gun?"

"I thought you said the motive for the robbery was just revenge," Roger noted.

"Started that way maybe, but you know those druggies got to have their fix." Gilbert paused. "Maybe he's dealing too." He picked his cigarette up again, held it to his lips.

"Gilbert, that's a long stretch to make from robbing you out of spite to becoming a drug dealer. And I have to tell you, I think you're wrong about all of this." Roger shook his head. "Raymond Twinhorse isn't a thief, and he isn't dealing drugs. There is no evidence that he's the one who did this. And besides, we both know that it's still legal in New Mexico to carry a firearm."

"I ain't got no problem carrying a gun, unless you're a criminal or crazy. But you know it seems like to me somebody's dealing something to bring the FBI out here. Maybe they were actually searching for Raymond." He inhaled from the cigarette and then crushed it in the ashtray.

"Maybe I'll call them and tell them about his robbing me, about him being armed last night. Maybe they had some of their story right when they headed over to Alamo. Maybe they just went after the wrong Indian."

Roger put down his coffee mug and peered

straight at the bartender. "You can do what you want, Gilbert, but since you made a report with my office, this is presently a matter for the county. Besides, I don't think the FBI is going to be interested in your little bar and a missing couple hundred dollars."

He stood up. "You do what you want," he said as he wiped his mouth with the back of his hand, "but if I find out you're harassing either Frank or Raymond, accusing them of this crime and making trouble for either of them, I'll have you arrested for obstructing justice." He studied Gilbert. "Now you let me handle this the right way." He paused. "Am I clear?"

"Oh, you're clear all right," Gilbert answered. "But you can't stop me from telling who I want to tell about this." He grinned.

"Just don't do anything stupid," Roger warned.

"You just find the boy, and I expect to be given a report when you arrest Raymond Twinhorse. I expect justice for my trouble and all the money he took."

Roger turned to face the door. "Thanks for the coffee, Gilbert," he said.

There was no reply, and Roger walked out of the bar and headed to his car out in the parking lot. This was one of those cases he wouldn't consider a real emergency, but he knew he had better find Raymond before Gilbert sent out his own posse.

He got in the car, started the engine, and began to pull out of the lot. He was just about to ease onto Highway 60, driving over to Alamo, when he heard a loud horn blow. He had not seen the eighteen-wheeler truck barreling in his direction. As he slammed on the brakes, he suddenly felt the steering wheel in his chest.

He was taking in a deep breath when he turned to check out the rear end of the vehicle that almost hit him. It was a car carrier, loaded with about ten SUVs, all black, all new, and the driver seemed to be in a hurry. Roger glanced at the license plate and almost thought about flipping on his sirens and lights, chasing the guy down and giving him a ticket for speeding, but then thought better of it. He had enough on his plate at the moment.

"Crazy Texans" was all he said as he carefully pulled out onto the highway.

THIRTEEN

Frank followed Father George in his truck to the garage. He parked behind the office and walked around to pull down the doors of the bay, which he had left open while he went to the diner. He checked all the locks, put out the CLOSED sign on the front door, and got into the station wagon driven by the priest. He closed the passenger door as he slid in, and Father George took off in the direction of the church.

"She didn't want me to call anybody, but I got Malene to get off work and go check her. She's with her now," George explained. "I left to find you before she got there, but I just called, and she said she was bandaging Trina's back and had given her a couple of anti-inflammatory drugs, but that there isn't much else she can do." He was glad when he found Frank at the diner. He had gone out to Frank's trailer, then to the garage, and finally decided to look around town. "She only wanted you," he added.

Frank didn't respond. He stared out the window as they drove away from town and out into the country to the Holy Family Church. This news about Trina had clearly upset him.

"She won't go to the hospital, but the burns look bad, Frank." George felt as if he was rambling. He had hoped Frank would say something, maybe tell him about the fight that went on between Raymond and Trina, how the event could have happened. "Malene says the same thing. I thought you could get her to go to the emergency room if you say that she could tell the doctors that she got burned from a radiator or something."

There was no reply.

"I thought, since she works in the garage, they might believe that was what happened." George glanced over at Frank, who was facing the window. "I mean, it's weird to say that when the burns are on her back, but she could just say she turned around and the top blew off." He waited.

"Can't a person get burned from opening a radiator when it's too hot?" George asked. "I don't know if they're the same as the wounds from boiling water spilling on you, but maybe Malene knows. Maybe nobody would be able to tell."

Still no answer.

"She doesn't want to press charges, Frank. She says it was an accident. She thinks he probably won't even remember what happened. He apparently tried to get to her after he did it, tried to apologize and check on her, but she wouldn't let him in the room. She was too scared." Father George blew out a breath. "She's worried that he got in some accident last night." He turned to his passenger. "She said he was pretty drunk when he took off."

Frank watched the scenery beyond the window. It was the landscape he had known his entire life. Sage and snake weed, rabbit brush, broom trees — there wasn't a plant he didn't recognize, not a one that he couldn't tell you, just from a leaf or a twig, what it was and what could be done with it, whether it should be ground or boiled, dried or rolled up in something else, and whether you ate it for nutrition or drank it for healing properties.

The big cats, prairie dogs, jackrabbits, coyotes — he knew every track, could tell the slide of lizards, the trail of snakes. He read storms, knew formations of clouds, knew within the hour when the rain was approaching. He had always had an eye for things in nature.

Of course, he never let on about those kinds of things to the people in Pie Town. Instead, he pretended he had given up his Navajo ways when he left the reservation, his family, in Ramah. He quit wearing the traditional bun and had long ago started wearing his long black hair in a braid. He rarely attended ceremonies, did not speak the language in public, and acted as if he knew nothing more of the desert and the world in which he lived than any of the other settlers who had decided to make Catron County home.

But Frank Twinhorse knew a lot. He had learned much about the natural and supernatural world from his grandparents, his neighbors, his mother. Everyone said that he could have stayed in Ramah and become a leader. Great achievements were expected of him at the house, and maybe even with the entire Navajo nation, even if most of the off-reservation groups had rarely excelled in that arena. His family had had high hopes for him. And then, he had finished school, gone off to the military, and fallen in love with a white woman who gave him a son and then left him. He had never gone back to Ramah.

He had been angry with how his family

treated his wife and son, angry that they had never fully accepted her, and he blamed them for his wife's departure. He had believed that they were the reason she was unhappy and abandoned her child. So he had rejected his past and all of its traditions and learned the auto mechanic trade, while living in a small trailer off the reservation and near Pie Town.

He wondered as the priest drove them along the dirt road across the desert how it was that he could know so much about nature — plants, animals, weather — and yet know nothing about his son. He wondered how he could pinpoint the arrival of a storm just by the way the grasses swayed, the clouds danced, and the air smelled, but had not noticed the tempest brewing in his only child's mind. He wondered how he could be so proficient at listening to the idle of an engine and knowing whether there was a loose belt or a faulty wire, but had sat in a room with his son probably a hundred times since he returned from the war and had not heard or seen the pulling away of the threads in his mind.

"You saw Raymond yesterday, right?" George was still trying to engage his passenger. "How did he seem?" he asked. "Didn't you say you had been with him in the afternoon? Didn't you say you had been with him yesterday?"

Frank wasn't listening to the priest. He was not interested in having a conversation with him. Instead, he was watching the world outside the car window and wondering if he was the ultimate cause of the demons his son wrestled. He had, after all, kept Raymond away from the only family he really had; in distancing himself from the boy's grandparents and extended family, he had left Raymond in a kind of no-man's-land.

He had not allowed his son to participate in the ceremonies and rituals as other Navajo boys and girls did, and he had seen that being one of the few Navajo children in the white schools of Catron County had been difficult for him. All of Raymond's life, Frank now realized, had been spent walking a fine line between two worlds, two cultures. Raymond was never completely accepted in the white world and never allowed into the Navajo one.

Frank wondered if he had created the landscape that led to Raymond's breakdown when he returned from the war. Frank worried that, by keeping his son away from the Navajo ways and forcing him into the white settlers' world, he had pushed him into deciding on military service and ultimately into harm's way. And he wondered now, as he and the priest drove along the empty road, heading to the church where his son's girlfriend had taken refuge after a violent episode with him, whether it was too late to do anything about the choices they both had made.

"Frank, did you see Raymond last night?" Father George asked.

Frank finally answered a question, with a shake of his head.

The church was just ahead of them in the distance, and Frank worried about what he would see. He was afraid that the burns were even worse than George was saying and that Trina might be left scarred for life.

He worried about his son, wondered where Raymond could be, whether he was in a ditch on the side of some road, drunk, hurt, dead. Frank could only imagine what had happened after he left Raymond, after Trina had called him at work the previous afternoon worried that Raymond was going to shoot himself. Frank had talked to him for a couple of hours, and in the end Raymond claimed he was fine. He was sorry for getting Trina upset and said he was getting rid of the gun. He gave his father the box of bullets and promised he would contact the

VA Hospital for some help. He wasn't going to have anything else to drink, he had said. And Frank, desperately wanting to believe his son, had chosen to do so.

When Frank had left Raymond the day before, he had known that things were still not great, but he had assumed the crisis was over. He had been hopeful that the army would take care of his son and everything would soon be okay; now he realized that the crisis had not been over, that things were not better, and that the army might never have the chance to try to fix Raymond. He had missed the signs, ignoring what the landscape clearly showed him. He had never fully grasped the nature of his only child.

Frank closed his eyes as they pulled into the church parking lot and wondered what exactly had happened the previous night when the lightning flashed and darkness swept across the county. He wondered what had happened while he was walking north of town, out beyond his trailer, following a pack of coyotes as they chased a pair of rabbits, after he had caught the image of someone hiking up Techado Mountain. He wondered what had caused his son's brain to fracture and finally snap, what would

110

have led him to injure the girl he claimed to love.

He opened his eyes as the car came to a stop. Malene was standing at the front door of the church.

FOURTEEN

"I found it by the northwest corner of the pasture. Out of gas, leaning against the fence post." When Bernie finally returned to the house to tell Francine what he had discovered, he had been gone for more than an hour. There was a small motorcycle in the back of his truck. He got out, walked around the truck, opened the tailgate, and jumped up in the bed. "I'm pretty sure it's Raymond's. I guess he left it out there and started walking north. That must have been when we saw him."

"Well, don't you think he'll be looking for it?" Francine asked. She had gone outside as soon as she saw Bernie driving up the driveway. She had changed out of her robe and pajamas and was dressed for the day. He had promised her he wouldn't be long, that he just wanted to make sure there was enough feed for his cows. Once he took care of that task, he planned to drive her to her house so that she could get to work by the afternoon.

"He's going to need gas anyway, so I just thought I'd load it on the truck and bring it here. Save him from having to push it the whole way." Bernie stood in the truck bed next to the motorcycle. "I figure he'll know I have it here."

"I guess he'd walk it down to the house for gas, right?" Francine asked.

"Nobody else around these parts to give him help," Bernie replied. He stood over the bike. "I always liked Raymond Twinhorse. He worked out here on the farm almost every summer after school from the time he was twelve until he was eighteen." He paused. "Had I told you that?" he asked.

Francine nodded. They had spoken about the young man's work for Bernie before.

She watched as Bernie picked up the motor bike and set it down by the side of the truck. "There ain't much to these things," he said.

"Looks heavy to me," Francine noted. She smiled at Bernie. She figured he was showing off how strong he was. She was impressed.

"This is really nothing more than an old dirt motor bike, not really built for road travel. I remember when he got this thing."

Standing next to the truck, Bernie wiped his face with his handkerchief. "He was only fourteen or fifteen. Frank bought it at some auction he went to."

He stuffed the handkerchief in his pants pocket and grabbed the bike by the handlebars to push it. "I'm surprised it still runs. He had to work on it all the time when it was new." He rolled it forward a few paces. "I'll just take it over to the barn and put it inside for him."

"Here," Francine said as she stepped off the porch and walked over to Bernie. "I'll go with you."

Bernie smiled. He faced Francine. "You look beautiful today," he said. "Have I told you that already?"

Francine blushed. "About four times," she answered. "But I don't mind hearing it again."

The two of them headed to the barn behind the house. Bernie was pushing the bike, Francine beside him.

"Good thing I went out to that part of the pasture to check. The water was real low in the trough by the rear fence. It would have been empty by the afternoon for sure."

Francine smiled. She loved hearing Bernie talk about his work on the ranch.

"I don't know what Raymond could be

hunting for this time of year," Bernie said. "It's too early for quail, and I know he wouldn't be able to carry anything else on this bike bigger than a bird." He stopped, glancing across the pasture in the direction where they had seen the young man earlier, the same area near where Bernie had found the bike.

"Maybe he's not hunting," Francine said. "Maybe he just wanted to get out of town, get away by himself for a little while."

Bernie nodded. They had both visited the young man when he was in the hospital in Albuquerque. They had taken him magazines and a couple of books, at Trina's suggestion, and Francine had baked him a brown sugar pie. They knew he had been having a difficult time since he returned from the war.

The two of them stood a while, just staring across the horizon.

"Shame about that boy," Bernie finally spoke. "We think we're so smart as a country, think we've gotten so advanced with our weapons and our military." He shook his head, turned to Francine. "War is still hell, and it's always our young people who suffer."

Francine knew how Bernie felt about war. He was a true patriot, but he didn't always think war was the answer. He had suffered his own losses earlier when several men in his family died fighting in World War II. He was drafted as well, to go to Vietnam, but released from duty since he was the only child of his parents. It was argued that he was needed to run the family farm.

"Well, at least he's home now. At least he's out of that godforsaken place and here at home. And he doesn't have to go back. That's a blessing." Francine slipped her arm inside Bernie's.

He glanced down and smiled. Being with Francine had become so easy for him, so natural. "I just hope there wasn't too much damage already done," he said, and then kept walking with Francine holding on to him. "He hasn't seemed himself since he got back. Remember the party?" he asked.

Francine nodded. They had talked about how uncomfortable Raymond had seemed at his homecoming party. He had stayed outside for most of it. Trina and Frank had to keep going out and bringing him in. He didn't seem pleased that an event had been held in his honor. He hardly said three words to anyone. And it just seemed he had gotten worse since then.

When they got to the barn, Bernie held out the dirt bike to Francine, who took the handlebars while he went ahead and opened the door. "Still, I'm surprised Raymond went out there without talking to me. He's always been real polite about asking before he went hunting on the property. He never drove up there before without asking my permission." He moved back to the bike. "Just isn't like him."

"Maybe he thinks now that he's older he doesn't have to ask anymore," Francine guessed. She followed Bernie into the barn, glancing around as he pushed the bike inside and leaned it against the far wall. "I never knew you had a Cadillac."

An old black car was hidden inside the barn. It appeared to be in good shape, clean, waxed. Francine thought it was from the 1960s. She remembered the model from when she had been younger and seen the ads, but she had never actually seen a real one.

"It was my folks'," Bernie replied. "My dad only drove it when he took my mother out for something special." He smiled, running his hand along the top of the car. "My mother always said he loved this automobile more than he loved her. Called it his mistress. He called her Mattie." Bernie laughed.

"I don't know — when they died, I just couldn't get rid of it. I've kept it in here all these years." He opened the driver's door. "Still runs, though. I drive it out of the barn on occasion, just over to the house and back, maybe down the road a little ways is all."

Francine opened the passenger's side. "How come you never drove it to town?" she asked, sliding in and sitting in the front seat. She slid her hand along the side of the seat, then up along the dashboard.

Bernie took her lead and got in behind the wheel beside her. "Oh, I don't know. Didn't want folks thinking I was high and mighty, I guess."

"It's a great car, Bernie," Francine commented. "Puts Oris's Buicks to shame, that's for sure." She grinned.

"Frank's come over a couple of times and tuned her up for me. He's nice enough to work on it here instead of making me drive it to the garage." Bernie gripped the wheel. "He asked me a while back if I would sell it to him. I think he was going to give it to Raymond when he returned from his tour of duty." He put his arm across the back of the seat. "But I don't know. Just sentimental, I guess. Told him I'd think about it." He reached up and adjusted the rearview mirror.

The two of them sat in silence a while.

"You should, Bernie," Francine said, surprising herself that she would offer any advice to Bernie. "You should let Frank buy it and give it to Raymond. Maybe it would help if he had something of his own, something that could really take him out of town, give him some freedom, something he could drive other than that silly old bike. Maybe that's just what he needs to be able to let go of what happened to him over there. Maybe if he has a new car, he'll feel better about being home."

Bernie didn't answer. He thought about the suggestion. He shrugged. "I never drive it anyway."

Francine smiled. She leaned against the seat. She thought it was a great idea.

"Maybe it's time to let the past go. Maybe it's time to live in the present, stop trying to hold on to the way things used to be." He hit the steering wheel with his fist. "I think I'm going to do it. That boy deserves something special. As far as I'm concerned, he is this town's hero, and I want to honor him. So, by golly, I'm going to do it. I'm going to sell ole Mattie to Frank so that he can give it to Raymond." He turned to Francine. "You know, your kindness is only part of the reason I love you."

Francine blushed. It was the first time he

119

had used those words. She leaned over, and they kissed.

"Of course, maybe before I let ole Mattie go, we should give her a run for her money," Bernie said.

"You mean rev up the engine and take her for a spin?" Francine asked. "I'd love to take a ride in Mattie with you."

"No, that's not what I mean," Bernie noted.

Francine appeared confused. She waited.

"I mean rev up *your* engine and take *you* for a spin," he replied, the grin widening across his face.

"Bernie King," she commented, her face reddening.

"Well . . ." was all he said.

"Aren't we kind of old to be making out in the backseat of your parents' car?" she asked.

"Why should we let the young people have all the fun?" he asked, with a wink. He reached over and placed his hand on Francine's knee.

Francine laughed, and then together they opened up their doors, got out, and crawled into the backseat.

FIFTEEN

"You got any pie?" The trucker flashed a smile. He was of medium height and build, wore his hair sort of long, had on a T-shirt and jeans and a pair of Tony Lama boots.

"Desserts are written up on the board," Bea replied, turning and pointing toward the chalkboard near the counter where they kept a list of the daily specials and the types of desserts offered that day.

"I'm glad because I drove way out of my way to come for pie," he responded.

Bea nodded. She had heard that sentiment before. The diner got a lot of tourist traffic. Seems everybody liked having pie in Pie Town. She didn't complain, of course, since it was good for business. She was glad that Francine had started baking. It had always been disappointing before when she had to explain to tourists that they only had brownies.

"You driving that load of cars?" It was

Oris who asked. He was still drinking coffee and chatting with Fred and Bea a couple of hours after having finished his breakfast.

"Yep, just got a new shipment from Denver, driving them over to Phoenix, then to Tucson. They'll use them down at the border." He studied the list of pies. "How's the lemon?" he asked.

"Tart," Oris answered for Bea. "Take the blueberry. It's a couple of days old, but it's sweet."

The trucker chewed on the inside of his lips. "I don't know. I like tart." He grinned. "I'll try the lemon."

"Suit yourself, stranger," Oris said. "Just don't complain when you can't get your mouth unpuckered."

The truck driver nodded. "I'll keep that in mind."

Bea headed behind the counter to get a slice of pie.

Oris watched the driver. "You from Colorado?" he asked.

The driver shook his head. "Texas," he answered. "Abilene."

Oris nodded. "And you drove way off Highway 25 just for a slice of pie?"

"It is Pie Town," the trucker replied. "You've gotten kind of popular since you started that big pie festival in the fall. I read about your town in a trucker's magazine I get. Plus they closed Highway 40 at Gallup yesterday. Wildfires," he added.

Oris nodded. He had heard about the road closures.

"So I've been planning to drive over here for about a year anyway, figured I'd just take the back roads, miss the fires, and have some dessert even if it is still morning."

"You were planning to drive way over here for Francine's pie?" Oris asked.

The man stretched his legs under the table where he was sitting. "You saying it's a waste of my time?"

"It is for the lemon," Oris answered. "Chocolate maybe, blueberry, okay, but she doesn't even use real lemon in that recipe. Gets the pudding from a box."

"Oris Whitsett," Bea called out as she brought the slice of pie to the customer. "The man drove all the way from Abilene to have pie, leave him be."

Oris shrugged. "I'm just saying he could get that lemon pie at any truck stop in the country. If he drove all the way out here, he should have at least gotten the blueberry."

Bea shook her head as she placed the dessert on the table in front of the trucker. "Don't pay him any mind. We try to keep him out, but nowadays you got to serve everybody."

The trucker smiled. "It's fine. I meet all kinds of folks on the road," he said, lifting his fork. "Anyway, I'm glad to be here. And, mister, since you seem to know a lot about things here, maybe you can help me out."

Oris waited.

"I need a part for the truck, a new headlight. Bulb blew last night. I figure that since I'm sidetracked, stopping for pie, I'll still be driving at dark. Is there a garage or auto parts store around here?" He glanced up at Oris, who was watching him. He took a bite and smiled. He didn't want to say so, but the old man had been right: it was tart. "Mmmmm," he said, still smiling.

Oris grinned. He could see the pucker coming. "You'll need to go to Frank's," he noted. "He has a place on your way out of town. I expect he'll have what you need."

The trucker nodded. He still hadn't swallowed.

"Those government cars?" Oris asked. He had turned again to face the window and was peering at the truck loaded with cars parked outside in the lot.

The man nodded. He smacked his lips together and raised his eyebrows. Then he reached over and took a sip from his water. "Border patrol vehicles," he answered.

"What a waste," Oris commented. "New SUVs like that driving across the desert. Seems to me they'd do better just using old army jeeps from the war."

"*You're* talking about the waste of buying new cars?" Fred called out from the kitchen. He had stuck his head through the window. "Well, if that ain't the skillet calling the kettle black, I don't know what is."

Oris jerked his head around to face Fred. "I pay cash for every vehicle I buy, return it to the dealership after fifty thousand miles, and get a nice trade-in. I keep my cars clean and running well and maintain a low mileage. Tell me a government agency that has bought its own vehicles and paid cash and I'll wash dishes for a year." He stopped. "In fact, now that I think about it, all the taxes I've mailed in over the years, I probably paid for one of them fancy cars on his carrier. I should just back one off the trailer and drive it home."

"You pay taxes?" Bea asked. She was refilling the water in the trucker's glass.

"Federal and state," Oris answered, with a grin. "I write a check for at least ten dollars every April 15."

"Well, one of those vehicles costs a little more than ten dollars," the trucker noted.

"Guess you'll have to wait a couple of years."

Oris nodded. "I 'spect so. And I'm a little partial to the Buick."

It was quiet in the diner for a few minutes. Bea had gone to the kitchen, and Fred joined her. Oris was watching the traffic outside, and the trucker finished his dessert. He glanced down at his watch and started making his way out of the booth where he was sitting.

"Well, I guess I better get to the highway," the trucker announced as he made his way to the cash register. He turned to Oris. "Where's that garage you mentioned?" He fished out a few bills from his wallet.

Bea came out and took the man's money. "It's just a mile or so up the road. Frank Twinhorse runs it," she answered for Oris.

" 'Cept the priest come and got him a little while ago, he might not be over there," Oris chimed in. "But maybe Trina's working," he added.

The trucker returned his wallet and had just stuck a toothpick in his mouth. He pulled it out and turned to the man at his right. "Trina?" he asked, repeating the name he had just heard Oris call out.

Oris laughed. "I know it's odd that a girl would want to be a mechanic. I never imagined that it would work out either. But she actually knows her way around an engine pretty good."

"She's been with Frank about a year. Trina Lockhart's her name," Bea noted.

Oris studied the trucker, sensing an interest. " 'Course, I only let Frank touch my Buick." He stopped, still noticing the response of the trucker. "What? You know her?" he asked.

The man stared at Oris for a minute and then shook his head. "No," he replied. "I doubt I'd know a girl in Pie Town."

"Oh, Trina ain't from Pie Town," Oris said. "She's from your home state." He grinned. "Maybe ya'll have met."

The trucker shook his head. "I wouldn't think so," he said. "Texas is a big place." He took the coins Bea handed him and placed them in his front pocket, the expression on his face suddenly changed.

"I guess that's right," Bea responded. "And besides, I think Trina is from Amarillo, not Abilene." She smiled.

"I think you're right, Bea," Oris noted.

They both watched the trucker, who had turned his head and was staring out the window.

"I sure hope you'll come again," Bea said.

And the man didn't respond as he headed

out the door.

Bea and Oris watched as the trucker climbed up in the cab, started the engine, and drove away in the opposite direction from where they had given directions to Frank's garage.

"Well, that seemed an odd way of taking his leave after having been so talkative while he was eating," Bea noted.

They watched as the dust kicked up behind the truck as he drove away.

"Told you that pie was too tart" was the only thing Oris had to say.

Sixteen

"Oh, it's already twelve o'clock." Father George sighed. "How did that happen?" he asked, not expecting an answer. "Just give me a minute and I'll take care of this." He stood up and noticed what he was wearing. He tucked his shirt into his pants and then tried to smooth out the wrinkles with his hands.

Malene and Frank glanced out the window where the priest was watching and saw the two cars that had pulled into the parking lot. Trina sat up to see what was going on and immediately noticed the squad car stopping in front of the church. She turned to Malene and started to get up from the sofa where she had been resting. "What's he . . ." she started to ask.

"It's just a premarital session," Father George answered, realizing that Trina thought that the three of them had finally discounted her request and called law enforcement. "It's Danny and Christine."

Trina didn't respond.

"I have an appointment to meet with them at twelve," George added. He walked around the sofa and placed his hand on Trina's shoulder. "It's a standing appointment," he explained. "Just lay low," he said, trying to reassure her. "I'll make something up and reschedule." He hurried out the front door of the rectory before anybody could respond.

The three inside the pastor's house watched as he greeted the couple and began a conversation. They couldn't hear what he was saying, but he was smiling and seemed apologetic, shaking his head and apparently offering some explanation about why he couldn't meet with them at the arranged time.

Christine seemed disappointed or frustrated, it was hard to tell. She kept checking her watch while folding and unfolding her arms across her chest. She shifted her weight from side to side as if she were bored.

Frank noticed the deputy glancing around the church while George talked, probably making a mental note of Trina's and Malene's vehicles parked in the lot. He peered over the priest's head, stopping his gaze in the direction of the rectory. Frank pulled Malene away from the window and over to the sofa to sit next to Trina.

Father George was back in just a few minutes, and not long after his return they watched Danny and Christine drive off.

"Well, I guess I better come up with the reason I needed to leave work and come to church," Malene noted. She knew both Danny and Christine could recognize her car.

"I took care of that," George responded.

Malene waited.

"I told them that an emergency had come up, that a woman and her children had been dropped off here by a family member, that she needed assistance, and that I had called you and Trina to help me find them some groceries and clothes. And then later I plan to drive them down to Socorro to the shelter."

Trina studied George. She seemed better since Malene had washed the wounds and she had taken some nourishment. She was sipping water through a straw, trying to stay hydrated. "I thought priests didn't lie," she said, attempting to smile. She shifted her position gingerly. It was easy to see that she was still in some pain.

George rolled his eyes. "Creative situational management," he said. "It's not really a lie. That actually did happen."

The three in the room waited for an explanation.

"Last week," he said. He scratched his head.

The others kept staring.

"Of course, I didn't call you or Trina." He turned to Malene. "And it wasn't a woman and her children." He drew in his bottom lip, biting it.

"Wasn't really even a person." He cleared his throat. "It was a dog."

He hesitated. "Okay, I lied."

Malene laughed. "I think creative situational management is called upon from time to time."

Trina reached over to try to punch the priest, who had sat down beside her. She missed and spilled some of her water, flinching a bit because of the pain her movement caused.

"I'm a klutz," Trina acknowledged as Malene rushed over and cleaned up the spill. She glanced up and noticed Frank, who was still watching out the window. "Don't look so serious. It's going to be okay," she said to him. "Frank," she called out, trying to get his attention.

He kept staring out the window and shook his head. "I'm so sorry about this," he said.

Father George sighed. He had already spent more than a couple of hours trying to reassure Frank that he wasn't responsible for his son's actions.

"Would you please stop beating yourself up?" Trina said. "You came when George asked you to come," she noted. "You got Alexandria over to Frieda's without spilling the beans to her. You went to the house and got me some clothes. You gave me that really awful tea that seems to have helped my pain a lot."

She reached her hand out to him, but he didn't come over to her. "Quit doing this to yourself. I wouldn't have asked you here if I'd known you were going to be like this."

Frank still had not faced anyone in the room.

"Frank, I'm okay. I'm sure Raymond is okay or we'd have heard something from somebody." She had finally started to relax about her boyfriend, finally started to believe that he was fine or that they would have been contacted if he had been in a wreck or gotten hurt. "We're going to find Raymond and get him some help from the VA."

Malene stood up and walked over to her friend. "She's right, Frank. That was Danny, and he was on duty last night. If something

133

had happened he would know, and he would have reported it, and Roger would have called us."

She could see that nothing was getting through to her friend. "Frank, we can't be held responsible for our children's choices." She rubbed her eyes. "Lord knows, I've had to learn that lesson more times than I care to say."

Frank finally turned to Malene. He knew she was talking about her daughter Angel, who had struggled with a drug addiction for many years. He had thought the young woman was finally clean, that she had gotten help when her son died, but he understood that you never know with addicts and drunks. "One day at a time" was not just a bumper sticker they put on their cars. It was a way of life for them and everybody who loved them.

He nodded. "I know" was all he said.

Trina leaned against the pillow that had been placed behind her and set her drink on the table next to the sofa.

"I still think we should get a doctor to take a look at you." George was watching her. He was concerned about her burns.

"I'll be okay," she replied. "I don't feel so hot anymore, and I'll keep taking the pills Malene gave me."

"The tea," Frank responded. "Keep drinking the tea," he instructed.

Trina blew out a breath. "There's more?" she asked.

Frank nodded. "A cup every two hours. George, you'll make sure she takes it?"

Father George agreed. "You'll stay here for the rest of the day," he said to Trina. "I'll take you to pick up Alexandria this evening when you'd normally be getting off work."

"Where's everybody else going?" Trina asked, understanding that it was starting to sound like a mass exit.

"I need to get back to Carebridge," Malene answered. "If I clock in by twelve-thirty, I can still get my morning rounds in."

"I'm sorry I had to call you out of work." It was Father George apologizing this time. "I just didn't know who else to call."

"Not a problem," Malene responded. She glanced over at Trina. "I'll stop by your house tomorrow and check your burns, make sure there's no infection, but I think you should still go over to the clinic in Socorro and get proper care."

Trina nodded. "I will. And you won't say anything to Roger?" she asked.

Malene didn't respond at first. She turned

to Frank and George, who were waiting for her answer as well. "I don't usually keep secrets from my husband," she replied. She sighed. "But if he doesn't ask specific questions about what I did with my day today, then I have no reason to give him any information about what happened here or what happened at his house last night."

"Creative situational management," Trina said, winking at George.

Malene smiled. She hesitated. "It's not my story to tell, Trina. But I do think you may need to tell it to the authorities. For Raymond's sake," she added.

Trina nodded, keeping her head down.

"And I'm going too," Frank said. "If it's okay to borrow your truck?" he asked Trina. He didn't have his own transportation since Father George had driven him over to the rectory.

She looked up at him. "Of course, you can borrow the truck, especially since it sounds like Father George will take me to pick up Alexandria this evening."

"I'll take you home," Father George responded.

Frank nodded.

Trina pulled the keys from her pocket and held them out to Frank.

He walked over to take them, and she

reached for his hand. "Just tell him to come home," she said, understanding that he was going out to search for Raymond. "Just tell him I'm okay and that I want him to come home."

Frank nodded. He squeezed her fingers tightly.

After they said their good-byes, Father George walked Frank and Malene out the front door, smiling nervously as they got into their vehicles and drove away.

SEVENTEEN

Roger thought it was odd when Malene's supervisor explained that she had gotten an emergency call from the priest and had been gone for most of the morning. He had called her at work to see if she wanted him to bring her lunch. He drove into town after seeing Gilbert and then after stopping over in Alamo to check on things there. He wondered if he should stop by the church or head over to Carebridge to see if she had returned. He wondered what kind of emergency the priest was involved in and whether or not he should have been called as well.

He knew Father George and Malene were close. She was the good Catholic in the family. She always had been. Even though her mother was Zuni and "Pueblo Catholic," which he considered to be a religion all its own, and Oris, her father, was agnostic and never too fond of institutions, their daughter had become very involved in her faith, and very involved in Holy Family Church.

Roger believed in God, didn't mind attending worship services with his family, prayed over meals, and still lit candles and talked to his grandson as if he were now a saint, but he wasn't religious, not like his wife.

Malene counted on God, sought guidance from God, prayed for favors from God. Roger counted on himself, sought guidance from experience and science, and did not believe in asking for favors from anyone. He figured God had created the world and everybody in it and that the act of creation, truly a generous and unselfish thing to do, was the only display of God's miracles he needed. God created and then God let it be. It was the only way Roger could explain evil and suffering and the way God usually didn't rise to the occasion and do anything about it.

No matter how many times he and Malene talked about it or how many books Father George suggested, God and the mess in this world were two things Roger could not reconcile. So, while others were praying for sick family members or world peace to descend once and for all, Roger thanked God for the warmth of the morning sun and the cool in the evening. He thanked God for surprising spring rains and desert flowers. If he wasn't simply having a conversation with his grandson Alex, who had been dead a year, his prayers were only litanies of thanksgiving because he figured it was better just to focus on what he could accept from God, a beautiful and miraculously created world, rather than on what he knew God did not control. He could think of God as creator, but that was as far as his theology took him. He figured that organizing and managing and running the world had been left to what or who had been created. God, Roger suspected, was out making other worlds somewhere else and maybe having better luck with the other creations.

Pulling into Pie Town, he decided not to go to the nursing home to see if Malene had returned to work, and he decided not to go to Holy Family Church either. He didn't want to bust into whatever Father George had pulled his wife into and figured it was probably some young woman who needed the wisdom or care of a mother. Father George, as he had done in the past, had probably just called the most faithful woman in the church to assist.

Roger drove past the diner. Noticing Danny's squad car in the lot, he wondered if he had already finished with his counseling appointment. He knew his deputy had clocked out after leaving the Silver Spur, having worked more than a couple of hours' overtime. He remembered that Danny was meeting Christine for a session with Father George and considered stopping in to ask him if he had seen Malene at the church, but then he chose to keep driving past. He didn't want to appear to be checking up on his employee or his wife.

He turned toward his house, the one he was renting to Trina and Raymond. He decided it was time to locate Raymond and find out what really happened at the Silver Spur the previous night. He pulled into the driveway and wondered if the young man would be forthright and tell the truth, and then he worried that the truth might mean Raymond would be spending time behind bars.

"I hope Frank can afford a good lawyer," Roger said out loud as he stopped the car and put it in park. "Maybe they can even use the PTSD as a line of defense." He knew a good attorney would look into getting that diagnosis for a recently discharged and wounded soldier. Maybe with that diagnosis there wouldn't even be a sentence, he thought.

He knew he would be able to get rid of

any charges having to do with the gun. That was easy. However, if Gilbert was right, and Roger didn't know that for sure, if Raymond had stolen the money there was going to be a charge of burglary and breaking and entering. Jail time would probably be required even with a mental illness diagnosis. But maybe, he thought, the young veteran would just get some time on the sixth floor and then be sent home.

The sixth floor was the behavioral health unit at the university hospital in Albuquerque where he usually transported mental patients, and that was usually what he and the other officers called a transport operation of that kind: "time on the sixth floor."

Roger sat behind the wheel, thinking about the best way to handle the interview. He glanced around and saw that both Trina's truck and the little motorcycle Raymond rode were gone. He knew he was likely to see Trina at the garage at that time of the day, but he wasn't sure where he would find Raymond, since he hadn't gotten work yet. And he especially wasn't sure where he'd find Raymond the day after he might have robbed a bar. Roger suddenly considered that locating Raymond Twinhorse might not be as simple or as easy as he had first thought.

He was just about to exit the car when his cell phone rang. He sat down again to answer it. "Sheriff Benavidez."

"Sheriff, it's Agent Williams."

Roger had to think who Agent Williams was. He suddenly recalled the unsuccessful drug bust from the previous day. He was the agent in charge. He was the one Roger never liked.

"Yes, Agent Williams," he responded, trying to mask any negative emotions. Only a day later, the memories of the Alamo bust were very fresh.

"We understand you had a robbery last night," the federal officer announced. He waited for a response.

Roger cleared his throat. "There was a small amount of money reported missing in Datil this morning," he answered. "I haven't yet ruled it as a burglary." He didn't want to give any information out to the bureau until he had full reports, and he especially did not want to give anything to Agent Williams.

"Silver Spur."

Roger wondered how the identification of the crime scene had been disseminated so quickly. He wondered if Gilbert had reported it or if it was somebody from the county, his office, who had made a call. And he wondered why the FBI was suddenly interested in something as small as the robbery of a bar.

"I'm calling just to let you know that we'll be investigating this crime. It's no longer a case just for Catron County. Without revealing too many details, let me just say that this involves the FBI and the DEA. We'd like you to pass on any evidence you collected this morning as well as any that you have discovered since leaving the scene."

Roger didn't know what to say. He wondered how much the agent really knew. He wondered if the FBI agent had already spoken to Gilbert.

"Sheriff, you still there?" the agent asked.

"I am still here," he answered. "As far as evidence goes, that was bagged and taken to the lab this morning. Deputy Danny White was the first responding officer. Prints were taken from the scene."

"Yes, we have all that," the agent responded. He sounded smug. "We know there was a gun found."

"Which we don't know is related to the alleged crime." Roger could feel the tightness in his throat.

"I imagine we'll discover there is some tie-in. There usually is in these kinds of cases," Agent Williams responded.

"What kind of cases are we talking about?" Roger asked.

"Drugs," the agent replied.

"I hardly see a missing two hundred dollars and a loudmouth bartender who likes to jump to conclusions as evidence that any drugs are involved." He was angry. "I don't think this is something you need to waste your time on."

"Yes, well, that will be for us to decide. We'll gather that information ourselves." The agent was brusque.

There was a pause in the conversation, and Roger wondered if the agent had hung up. He heard a cough and knew he was still there.

"Then I can't think of what else you need from me," Roger said.

"Just to give us anything you find out and otherwise stay out of our way," Agent Williams replied.

Roger could feel his face flush. "I plan to finish up my investigation as I see fit," he announced. "As I complete my investigation, I am happy to work with the bureau any way I can."

The agent didn't respond.

"Pleasure speaking to you, officer." Roger knew how the agents hated to be called "officer," but he was mad. He clicked off his phone without hearing any more from Agent Williams.

The sheriff knew that he really needed to speak to Raymond as soon as possible. He wanted to hear his story and find out what happened at the Silver Spur before the FBI found him. He was worried what it might do to the young man if FBI agents showed up and made an arrest. He worried that if Raymond was in a fragile state of some kind, getting picked up and questioned by strangers, accused of a crime by the FBI, could really set him off.

Roger glanced around the driveway and the backyard. He returned his phone to the holder on his belt and got out of the car. He walked to the rear door of the house and knocked. He peeked inside and could see into the kitchen. Nothing seemed out of the ordinary. There was a pot and a few dishes in the drain. Alexandria had left a couple of toys on the table. It was about what he expected. Trina was at work, Alexandria was at Frieda's, and Raymond? Well, that was the big mystery, wasn't it? he thought. He knocked again, but it seemed clear that no one was home. He felt for the keys in his pocket and considered using his house key to enter.

He waited and then, thinking maybe an

unlawful entry without a warrant was not the best way to go, turned and walked away. It would be inappropriate for him to go in, even if he was the landlord and legally had the right to enter his property. Roger walked around the house, looked up at the garage apartment in the back, and climbed back into his squad car. He thought again about Raymond, wondering what the FBI and Agent Williams knew about the previous night and whether they were already searching for his suspect.

Eighteen

Frank noticed the sheriff's car as it headed down the highway into town. He had just come from Raymond and Trina's house, having stopped by there to see if his son had returned home. He found it exactly as it was when he had gone by earlier to retrieve some clothes for Trina and a few things for the baby: nobody was home. He watched Roger as he drove past the diner, moving in the direction of the house he rented to the young couple. Frank didn't think that the sheriff was going to see Raymond or Trina, but he was glad that he had cleaned up most of the mess in the kitchen.

Frank had picked up the pot still lying on the floor, washed it and the other dishes in the sink, scrubbed the stove and counter, and mopped the floor. He wasn't sure whether it was shame or duty that made him put the keys down on the table as soon as he walked in and start cleaning the scene of

148

his son's violence. He did it as quickly as possible, knowing Trina was waiting on him, knowing he had to stop by his trailer as well and pick up the herbs for the tea he knew she needed, but he did it. He didn't want Trina or Raymond to return home and be given another reminder of the terrible thing that had taken place.

Frank planned to go by the garage and pick up his truck, leaving Trina's there. He was then going to start driving everywhere he knew Raymond liked to go. There was a pool hall in Magdalena, a bowling alley in Socorro, the bar in Datil; he planned to check every place his son frequented until he found him. Then he was going to bring him home, sit him down, and demand that he go into Albuquerque to the VA Hospital and get some help. His days of being the quiet, laid-back father were over. Raymond needed help, and Frank was determined that he was going to get it.

The burns on Trina's back and legs would heal, and whatever scars they left on her body would disappear over time. But what worried Frank was that she was now afraid of his son and might never recover from that. And worse was what Raymond would say or do when he saw what he had done, when he was face-to-face with the violence he would now understand he was capable of doing.

Frank knew that his son was damaged by whatever had happened in Afghanistan, changed in some profound way. He knew that Raymond was deeply affected by the roadside bomb that blew up his company, his group of friends, but he also knew that in many ways Raymond was still the same boy he had always been. He was still sensitive and impressionable, and he was going to be horrified at what he had done to Trina.

More than being concerned about Trina, Frank worried most about how Raymond was going to handle seeing the consequences of his outburst. He knew that it could very likely be the agent of change for his son, the event that would move things in some concrete direction. The problem was trying to figure out whether that change would be toward healing and wholeness or toward self-destruction and a complete downward spiral — whether he would go in the direction of life or the direction of death.

Frank shook his head, knowing his son was in for the fight of his life, and drove around to the rear of the garage. He could see through the bay windows that a truck had parked on the other side, in the front, and that somebody was standing outside

the office door, looking like they were trying to get in. He parked Trina's truck at the
rear door and got out. He unlocked the
door and walked to the office, where he
could see through the window that it was
Bernie King standing there, knocking on
the glass. He sighed, not wanting to deal
with townspeople at that particular time,
but knowing he had now been seen. He
unlocked the door and opened it.

"Frank. . . ." Bernie smiled. "Everything
all right?" He glanced around. "I never
knew you to close the garage on a weekday."
He walked in. "You okay?"

Frank masked his emotions. "Fine. I just
have something I need to deal with today."
He hoped Bernie wasn't stopping by for a
social call.

Bernie nodded, casually moving inside the
office. "Trina off too?" he asked, glancing
around the office and then behind Frank
and inside the garage.

"She's not feeling well," Frank replied,
closing the door and moving next to the
rancher.

"Oh. I hope she's not coming down with
something."

Frank shrugged.

Bernie paused. He cleared his throat to
make his announcement. "Well, I just

wanted you to know that I made a decision." He stepped all the way in and took a seat in one of the chairs beside the desk where Frank wrote bills and talked on the phone.

Frank slowly moved behind the desk. He didn't sit down. He waited for Bernie to explain.

"I'm going to sell you Mattie," Bernie said proudly.

Frank was confused. He didn't know who Mattie was, but he certainly wasn't intending to buy her.

"Mattie," Bernie repeated, appearing a bit disappointed that Frank didn't understand the gist of his grand announcement. "The Cadillac?" He waited. "My father's black 1962 Cadillac."

Frank finally understood. He recalled working on the old car in Bernie's barn because Bernie had not wanted to drive it into town for some reason. It was in excellent condition, V-8 engine, plush interior, not a scratch on the body anywhere, the Cadillac signature flared fins. "I didn't know she had a name," he said.

"Mattie," Bernie said again. "And you wanted to buy her last summer," he reminded Frank.

Frank nodded. Now it was making sense

to him. He had asked Bernie if he wanted to sell it when he drove over to give it a tune-up the previous year. By that time, Raymond had been deployed for several months and was writing his father and Trina that he didn't want to stay in the service past his initial four-year commitment. Frank had thought the Cadillac would be a nice car for him when he returned home. It was an impulsive idea; he hadn't even thought about it again, but apparently Bernie had remembered the conversation well.

"I don't think now is the time to talk about buying your car," Frank said, hoping the rancher would leave so that he could get on with the business at hand, the business of trying to find his son. "Raymond isn't really fit to be driving yet, and I think he might want a smaller car anyway."

Bernie nodded. He hadn't thought about Raymond preferring another car, probably a newer model. He remembered that, as a boy, Frank's son had not been all that interested in cars. He had not acquired his father's passion for engines and automobiles. He recalled that Raymond had seen the Cadillac in the barn every summer he worked there and had only made a few comments about it to Bernie. He wasn't as taken with Mattie as Frank had been.

Suddenly, Bernie began to consider that this wasn't as great a gift as he had first imagined when he and Francine discussed it. "You're probably right," he finally said. His voice had softened. "I guess I got to thinking about our conversation last summer and just thought Mattie might be a good thing for Raymond to have now. But I suppose kids today don't care about old cars. They want sleek bodies, fast engines, and big speakers."

Frank tried to smile. He really wanted Bernie to leave. He really needed to find his son.

There was an awkward pause between the two men.

"Well, I guess I'll be going," Bernie said. It was easy for him to see that Frank was in a hurry. He got up from his seat.

"If you change your mind, just let me know," he said, sounding a bit disappointed. "Francine and I thought it would be a nice thing to let Raymond have the Cadillac. We thought he might like something special for him and his girl to drive around town." He headed toward the door, grabbed the handle, and then turned again to Frank. The garage owner was only a step behind him, reaching around to make sure the door was locked.

154

Bernie was startled at how quickly his friend had moved from the desk to the door. "Oh . . . ," he said, pausing and studying Frank. He was about to ask again if he was okay, but then decided to let it pass. Frank wouldn't tell him anyway — Bernie knew that.

"I just remembered: in case Raymond misses me at the ranch and he walks here, tell him I rolled his bike into the barn. He can get some gas from the tank out back." Bernie opened the door to leave.

"Wait," Frank stopped him. "What?" he asked.

"Raymond rode his bike out to the ranch this morning. I saw him walking up toward Adams Diggings. I figure he was heading up Techado to do some hunting, although I didn't see him carrying a rifle." Bernie hesitated, trying to recall if Raymond was carrying anything when he saw him.

"This morning?" Frank asked.

"Yeah, about six. His bike must have run out of gas, and he left it at the fence at the far north border. Kept walking in that direction." Bernie noticed Frank's piqued interest. "North," he added. "I suspect when he's done he'll go to the house and look for his bike. He knows his way around there pretty good. I just thought I'd put it in the barn for safekeeping. That's where he used to keep it when he worked there." Bernie studied his friend. "That's all right, isn't it?" he asked.

Frank thought about his son driving way out to Bernie King's ranch sometime before dawn. He wondered where the boy had been all night, what he was doing, where he was going, and what he was planning. He peered up at the clock above the door and started to think about where he would find his son at that time, more than six or seven hours after he was seen at the bottom of the trail.

From Bernie's place, Raymond could have headed west and gone up Techado or over to Veteado Mountain, or he could have taken the path to the east and walked over to the North Plains. He could already be back down and picking up his bike from the ranch. Still, the good news was that Bernie had spotted Raymond and he was okay. Frank was sure his son was somewhere north of town, a familiar area to them both. He was safe, Frank thought, just walking the land he had hiked and hunted since he was a child.

"Frank?" Bernie didn't know what to do. "Is Raymond all right?" he asked. "Should I go take the bike to the fence, over where he left it?"

Frank shook his head, turning to Bernie. "No, you were right. He'd know you had taken the bike to the barn. He knows you would have found it and taken it back for him. I'll, um . . . ," he searched for the words. "I'll let him know if I see him."

Frank paused. "Or maybe I'll drive up there and look for him, give him a ride home, or down to your place. Yeah, that's what I'll do. I'll drive up 603 out past your place to Techado and give him a ride back." He nodded, having made up his mind. "If that's okay to go on your property?" he asked.

"Of course it's okay," Bernie answered and then just watched Frank for a minute. He could tell something was wrong, but it was clear that it wasn't his place to ask questions. He turned and opened the door. "All right, that's fine." And he walked out of the office and got into his truck. He started the engine and watched as Frank locked the door and moved quickly toward the rear of the garage.

Frank hurried out of the office and jumped in his truck. He wouldn't have to drive around the county after all, just maybe walk a few miles out to his favorite hunting spot. He wasn't exactly sure where to find his son, but at least he knew now where Raymond had gone.

NINETEEN

Malene met Frank as he turned onto the road leading to the church and wondered if he was returning to check on Trina or if he had found Raymond in town and was driving over to let the girl know he was okay. She lifted her hand to wave at him, but it was as if he didn't even see her. She stopped her car and watched as he kept moving in the opposite direction, the dust swirling behind his truck. She figured that whatever he was doing heading back up the road to the church, he was doing it in a hurry.

She pulled out onto the highway and drove toward Pie Town, returning to work at Carebridge. She had been gone for almost the entire morning, and even though she had told everyone where she was going, she knew her supervisor would be likely to expect a more detailed explanation.

Carebridge Nursing Center had recently hired a new executive director, a woman from Gallup who had worked in rehabilitation centers and retirement facilities for many years. Malene liked Dorothy Griegos, who understood the population they cared for and knew how to run a business. She was also a former nurse, and Malene had always preferred the nurses who served as executive director more than the MBA types. She guessed that in the thirty years she had worked at Carebridge there had been at least twelve directors, and each one was different.

She drove into the lot next to the facility, parked, and walked in through the rear door, stopping to punch in her time card. Dorothy was rounding the corner when she looked up.

"Malene," she said with a smile, checking the clock on the wall above the door. "You help the priest?" she asked.

Malene had gotten the director's approval before leaving. She had received permission from her shift supervisor, but she knew it was always best to let everybody in charge know what she was doing.

"Yes, ma'am," she answered, being respectful even though Dorothy was actually a few years younger than herself. "It was a woman who had been. . . ." She hesitated. She wasn't sure how much she should say.

160

"A woman in trouble," she continued. "Father George thought she'd rather talk to another woman than to him," she said, smiling, pleased with her explanation.

"He's wise to think that," the director responded. "Most priests think they can handle anything." She winked with a knowing look.

Malene wasn't sure what the wink meant. She hadn't talked religion with her boss. She didn't know Dorothy's history or preferences.

Dorothy explained: "I've been a Catholic a long time. In fact, I was a nun for twenty years."

Malene didn't respond.

"You didn't know that, did you?" Dorothy asked.

Malene shook her head.

"Finally thought I'd rather try things on my own. I got tired of having to achieve consensus among a group of thirty women, then having to get the permission of a priest for every decision we finally made, whether it was buying new measuring cups for the kitchen or changing the color of the paint in the chapel." She sighed.

Malene didn't know what to say, so she just smiled.

"Anyway," the director continued, "you

didn't miss much this morning, and since you worked overtime yesterday, you can just clock out when the shift is over." Her phone buzzed, and she reached for it in her pocket. "No worries," she added, glancing down at her phone and walking away.

Malene, breathing a sigh of relief, was glad her boss was so understanding. Then she began to wonder about Dorothy's past as a nun. She wondered which order she had joined and the real reason she had left. Malene didn't think about Dorothy's life as a nun for too long, however, because she realized that she had many more pressing things to consider. She shook the thoughts from her mind and headed toward her station. She was relieved that Dorothy had not been upset and that she hadn't asked too many questions. She was pleased that Dorothy was an executive director who made her feel at ease in her job. Walking to her work area, Malene recalled that it hadn't always been that way.

When she first started at the nursing home, the executive director at that time, Mr. Lee, would dock the pay of anybody who left their job early and fire a person for taking more than the allotted sick days. There had been years of emotional distress, and she was constantly afraid of losing her position. She was glad things were better at Carebridge and hoped the ex-nun would stay longer than the other directors she had liked in the past.

Malene rounded the corner to the wing where she had been assigned, knowing she had a lot to do to catch up. Mornings were always the busiest shifts. There were medicines to dispense, orders from doctors to fill, baths to give, beds to change. It was very fast-paced. She hoped that everything was fine with her patients and that there had been no emergencies. Emergencies slowed everything down for nursing assistants.

"Where you been?" It was Christine. "I saw your car at the church. You helping Father George with that woman all this time?" she asked.

Malene moved into the station and began picking up charts. "Did everybody get their morning meds?" she asked, glancing over the reports. "I left before finishing," she explained.

"I took care of it," Christine replied. "I just didn't give baths," she added.

Malene turned to her.

"I mean, I love you and all, but still. . . ." Christine grinned. "I have my own baths to do." She walked over to stand across the counter from Malene.

"Father George seemed rattled," she said, hoping to have a conversation with her friend. "Everybody's eating lunch, so it's okay." She knew Malene was going to try to make up for every minute she had been gone. "Did you get lunch?" she asked. "Angela made tortilla soup. It's in the break room. Danny and I went to the diner since the appointment at church was canceled."

Malene studied the charts. Christine had given the meds and was thorough enough to have written it in the patients' charts. She was glad her coworker was so meticulous.

"So?" Christine asked. "What about this woman?"

Malene didn't answer. She was confused. "What woman?" she asked.

"The woman at the church?" She leaned across the counter, getting very close to Malene. "Was she beat up?"

Malene shook her head. "I can't go into it, Christine," she replied. "He asked me to talk to her because he thought she could relate better to another woman than to him." She decided that since the explanation had worked with her boss, it ought to work with her coworker too.

Christine thought about it. "What about

Trina?" she asked.

Malene seemed surprised by the question. She studied her colleague. "What about Trina?" she repeated.

Christine shrugged. "Why did he need two women?"

Malene cleared her throat, thinking how to proceed. She noticed the nurse supervisor coming down the hall. She knew she needed to get busy. "Trina was going to run some errands for him, buy some things for the woman." She recalled what George had told the couple earlier and thought this was a good answer. She watched as the supervisor stopped in a room down the hall.

"How many sessions do you have left?" she asked Christine, referring to the premarital counseling she and Danny were doing with Father George and hoping to change the subject. "And how is Danny's temper?"

Christine blew out a long, exaggerated breath. She held out her hand and studied her engagement ring. "He seems better. But I don't know. He won't talk much about it. He hasn't been really mad for a while, so I guess that's good, right?"

Malene nodded.

Christine continued. "And as far as the sessions, we're on number six. I think there's ten." She rolled her eyes. "Father George said he would like us to go on a retreat with some other young couples in Albuquerque. I guess he knows some counselor there or something." She dropped her hand. "But I don't know. I'm sort of tired of talking about me and Danny to somebody else," she explained. "I just want to be sure that Danny isn't crazy or anything. What do you think?"

Malene thought about the question. "I think you're right to slow things down. If it's meant to be, it won't matter putting off the wedding for a while. And a man with a temper. . . ." She stopped. She was thinking about Raymond and his violent outburst. "A man with a temper can be dangerous."

"You thinking about that woman at the church?" Christine asked.

Malene nodded without offering any further explanation. She changed the subject. "Did we get a new patient in room 322?" She wondered why the nursing supervisor was visiting someone on their hall. Malene knew the supervisor usually only dealt with patients after they had first arrived or if there was trouble of some kind.

Christine glanced behind her. She had not seen the supervisor. She shrugged and turned back. "Not today," she answered.

"Far as I know, Mrs. Baca and Janie are still there."

Malene made a kind of humming noise, wondering if something had happened to one of the patients on her hall.

"Janie thinks somebody's stealing her candy," Christine noted. "I wrote it up for her."

Malene nodded. The nursing supervisor's visit suddenly made sense: she was following up on the report. There was a strong commitment to safety at Carebridge, and that included property as well as personal safety. Theft was taken very seriously at the nursing center, even though there were a lot of patients who were known to pick up things from other rooms that weren't theirs. And there were a lot of patients who reported missing property that had never been there in the first place. It was just a part of life at a nursing home.

"Well, Linda just went in the room," Malene announced, knowing Christine would want to know her boss was only a few feet away.

The young nursing assistant had been reprimanded a number of times because she was often found talking to coworkers or playing computer games instead of doing her job. Usually, it was Linda Lujan, the first-shift nursing supervisor, who gave the reprimands, wrote up the personnel reports, and placed them in her file. Malene knew that Christine did not get along with Linda Lujan.

The young woman was glad for the heads-up from Malene. Turning to go down the hall to pick up meal trays and get out of her supervisor's line of sight, she quickly turned back again. "Oh, my God, I can't believe I forgot to mention it, although maybe you already know." She paused.

Malene had a few charts in her hands and was getting ready to leave the station and check on her patients as well. "Already know what?" she asked.

"About the robbery," Christine answered. Her eyes were wide with excitement. She suddenly seemed to forget about her supervisor down the hall.

"What robbery?" Malene asked, thinking Christine was still talking about an incident at the nursing home. She returned one of the charts to the shelves, remembering that Mr. Ortez had been taken to the hospital for an X-ray. He was leaving by ambulance just as Malene had arrived for work. He wouldn't need a bath or a meal tray.

"At the Silver Spur last night," Christine continued.

Malene stopped, realizing that Christine wasn't talking about something stolen at the nursing home. She shook her head. She hadn't talked to Roger since he left early that morning, but that must have been the call that woke them both up. She guessed that he would phone her soon and tell her the news, although he wasn't one to talk about his cases. Danny, on the other hand, seemed to love sharing information about his work.

"Gilbert said there was about two hundred dollars missing," Christine explained. "He left the money in the cash register last night and planned on picking it up this morning," she added. "Danny was the first officer on the scene." She smiled proudly. "But . . . ," she said, peering around, though Malene wasn't sure if she was just being dramatic or checking for Linda's whereabouts, "what's really jacked up is who Gilbert said was in the bar last night causing all kinds of trouble, making threats, and waving around a gun."

Malene waited. She wasn't really concerned about the incident, but now Christine had piqued her interest.

Christine glanced around again. She whispered, "It was Raymond Twinhorse, and Gilbert thinks he stole the money and may have done even more than that."

Malene suddenly felt the breath catch in her chest and the blood drain from her face. She didn't even realize it when the charts slipped through her fingers and Christine called out her name.

Papers were falling out and drifting all across the nurses' station when the young nursing assistant quickly departed the area and the supervisor left the room down the hall, briskly walking in Malene's direction.

■ ■ ■ ■

PART THREE

■ ■ ■ ■

TWENTY

"I think they're CAE." Oris made the comment as everyone was staring out the window at the diner.

"CIA," Bea corrected him. She was the one closest to the door, and she was the one who had announced the arrival of a dark sedan, two men in suits seated in the car, both talking on cell phones. They had been in the parking lot for almost twenty minutes.

"CAE," Oris repeated.

"What are you talking about, Oris? CAE? Do you mean the DEA?" Fred had come out to take a look for himself and was watching from behind the counter. "The Drug Enforcement Administration?"

"CAE," Oris announced again. " 'Certainly Ain't Eating' here." He grinned. "But I guess that's really CAEH."

Fred rolled his eyes. "Bea, get away from that window. They're likely to come in here and arrest you for spying." He walked back into the kitchen.

"I heard there were some meth labs over in Red Hill." Fedora Snow had asked Oris to drive her into town that morning. She was meeting someone from Quemado who was driving down to Socorro. They were planning to visit a friend in the hospital. She thought it would be nice to have breakfast before leaving.

"What do you know about meth labs, woman?" Oris asked. "Your yard boy was growing marijuana in your greenhouse for years and you thought they were miniature palm trees."

Fedora waved away her neighbor's comment. The two of them had fussed this way for years, and even though a bond had formed between them, some strange friendship since they both participated in building the new church, everyone knew that Oris's teasing of the older woman would never change.

"I read in the *Glenwood Gazette* that a family of gypsies from Arizona had camped out in a trailer near Forest Road 19 and were making that meth and selling it to school bus drivers in Catron County." Fedora sat up in her seat in the booth and took a sip of coffee.

"*Arizona* gypsies?" Oris asked. He was sit-

174

ting at the table next to her. "You're telling me we got *Arizona* gypsies on our forest roads?" He pretended to be deeply concerned.

"Well, I'm going right out there to that car and get those boys to drive me out 19, and I am personally going to hog-tie and whip 'em all. Nothing I can't stand worse than an *Arizona* gypsy." He started to get up from his seat.

Fedora could now see what her neighbor was doing. She just shook her head and turned away from him. "You keep making fun of me, Oris Whitsett, and one day when you need my help you're going to come over to my house and I am going to see who it is and shut my door right in your face."

"Fedora," Oris said, leaning in her direction, "if I ever come across the street claiming I need your help, then you have my permission to do more than just shut the door in my face. You can shoot me in the head, because if I have come to that, if I have come to the place where I need your help, you can be pretty sure that I am on my way to glory and you might as well shorten the trip."

Fedora hissed at her neighbor. "Oris Whitsett, you are an old coot," she said. She watched out the front window. A car was pulling in from the highway. "Here comes my friend to take me to Socorro. Thank God I don't have to sit here and listen to you mouth off anymore." She opened up her pocketbook and pulled out her wallet. She fished out a few bills to cover her breakfast and the tip and stepped out of the booth. "You are an old coot," she repeated as she walked past Oris.

When she was beside him, he reached out and pinched her on the behind, causing her to jump. "Make sure you stop off and tell those officers about the gypsies," he called out as she headed to the door.

She threw up her third finger and walked outside. Fred and Bea laughed.

"Why do you pick on her so much?" Fred asked Oris. He had come out of the kitchen again and taken a seat at the counter. "Fedora isn't a bad person." He had a cup of hot tea with him. "I mean, she's ornery and nosy, but I doubt she deserves all you give her."

"Oris has to pick on somebody." Francine was sitting in the back booth. Up to that moment, she had not joined the conversation; however, like everyone else in the diner, she was also interested in the men waiting in the parking lot. She was eating breakfast and reading a recipe book. "It's just his nature."

"My nature?" Oris asked. "Well, ain't that a fancy way of saying something nobody can figure out." He had a toothpick in his mouth, and he pulled it out and took a sip of coffee. He glanced over at Bea, who was cleaning up the area around the cash register. She wasn't paying any attention to the two of them. Fred had started reading the paper.

Francine shrugged. "I think anybody who has known you more than a day can figure out what I'm talking about," she said as she jotted down the ingredients she had found for a new recipe.

"He's an old coot," Fred chimed in.

"Bea, help me out here. They've gone and ganged up on me," Oris called out to the other woman in the diner.

"You're on your own." She pulled out a new pack of napkins and started sliding dispensers from across the counter to fill them. "But if you ask me, I'd agree. You got an old coot nature, always have."

Fred smiled.

Oris didn't respond. He stuck the toothpick back in his mouth and stretched out his legs in front of him.

Bea had turned again to glance out the window at the men still sitting in the car in the lot. One of them had stopped talking on his cell phone and seemed to be looking into the diner. "What do you really think they're doing here?" she asked.

Fred glanced up from the paper and turned to see what was going on in the parking lot. He shrugged. "Could just be two businessmen driving down from Phoenix." He knew Highway 60 was a popular route from Albuquerque to towns west and across the border. The diner got a lot of those travelers.

"Don't look like tourists," Bea noted. She kept studying the men as she filled the dispensers. "Look like cops."

Francine glanced up. "Or insurance salesmen."

Oris could see out of the window too. "I suspect they're here about Raymond Twinhorse," he said.

The other three turned to him.

"Why would insurance salesmen want to talk to Raymond Twinhorse?" It was Fred who asked.

Oris chewed on the toothpick. "Well, first of all, they ain't insurance salesmen. We all know that." He studied the car in the parking lot and the men inside. "They're feds all right, and Raymond Twinhorse is now officially wanted by the law."

Francine waited to hear more of what Oris had to say. She knew he was crazy, but she also knew that he was the sheriff's father-in-law. Francine respected Roger and knew he didn't have a loose tongue, but she had heard that everybody was talking about Raymond and what had happened the night the power went out across the county. If Oris did know something from the inside, she wanted to hear it. After all, even though she guessed that no one really knew it yet, she and Bernie were probably the last folks to see Raymond before he ran off.

"Roger said they have a sudden interest in the Silver Spur robbery." Oris took a sip of coffee. The others were waiting, and he was enjoying having all the attention. "Claims the FBI wants to talk to Raymond. Them and the Drug Enforcement Administration." He put down his cup. "Hell, it sounds like everybody with some letters after their name is trying to find Frank and the boy."

"Why are they trying to find Frank?" Fred asked.

"He took off a couple of days ago, searching for Raymond. Nobody's seen him either." Oris turned to face Francine. "Roger said that Bernie told him he stopped by the garage day before yesterday and told him he saw Frank just before he took off." He waited to see if Francine was going to add anything.

She didn't respond.

"Did Bernie know where Frank was heading?" Bea asked. She considered Frank a good friend and had not heard that he was missing for two days. The news unsettled her.

Oris kept eyeing Francine.

She dropped her head and pretended to be reading her cookbook. She clearly had nothing she wanted to add.

"Nah," Oris answered. "Roger said that Bernie didn't have any idea. He just claimed Frank seemed to be in an awful hurry. Garage's been closed three days in a row now."

Francine could feel Oris watching her. She didn't look up.

"Trina missing too?" Bea asked.

Oris shook her head. "She had some accident with radiator steam. Burned herself pretty bad," he added. He hadn't seen her, but he had heard Malene explaining to Roger about the proper medical care for radiator burns when he had been over at their house eating dinner earlier in the week. For some reason that Oris didn't know, Malene had been called out to help Trina when it happened.

"Well, I still don't understand why the feds would be interested in a bar missing cash in Catron County. Sounded to me like it was just a case of Gilbert forgetting where he put his money." Fred folded the paper and was about to start reading the sports section. "I hate it for Raymond," he continued. "But I would think he could find a good lawyer and give an alibi for himself the night of the robbery."

"You sound like you know what you're talking about, Fred," Oris commented. "You been accused of stealing or you watching those Andy Griffith lawyer reruns again?"

Fred turned to Oris and grinned. "I have a history," he replied. "And I also have satellite TV."

Oris laughed.

"Well, it appears like you were wrong about them not coming in to eat," Bea said to Oris. She finished with the napkins and placed the dispensers back on the counter. "They're either hoping to get breakfast or they're coming here thinking we know more than just how to fry an egg."

The other three turned to see the two men stepping out of the car in the parking lot and heading in their direction.

TWENTY-ONE

"Are you sure it's all right for you to be working again?" Father George had stopped by the garage after Trina called to tell him that the part for his car had been delivered. She wasn't sure, however, when Frank could work on the station wagon; she hadn't seen her employer since the morning she was at the church.

"I'm taking antibiotics to decrease the chance of infection. I've got some really good pain meds if I start hurting. Besides, I don't plan to work on engines yet." She sat up a bit. It was still a bit uncomfortable for her to sit upright and lean against the back part of the chair. "Malene was right; that doctor at the clinic in Socorro was real nice, didn't ask a lot of questions."

"Still, are you supposed to return to work so soon?" George asked again.

"I just figured I could check on the bills and do some paperwork. I thought Frank might want me to hang around at least for folks when they show up."

"Have you seen or heard from him?" the priest asked. He was sitting in the office across from Trina, who had taken a seat behind the desk.

"No," she replied. "I thought maybe you had." She had hoped that was the reason Father George was stopping by.

He shook his head and glanced around the office. He knew that the longer the garage owner was out, the worse it was going to be for him when he got back. He had heard that the FBI agents weren't making any bones about the fact that they were searching for Raymond and his father, that they had now concocted a story that the father and son were involved in some drug ring. He thought it was ludicrous and had told the agents so when he encountered them at the diner the previous day. "No, not since I drove him out to the church to see you." He sighed. "I don't even know if he's heard what kind of trouble Raymond is in."

Trina had heard the news about the robbery in Datil from Malene, who had come by the house when she got off work the day after the power outage, the day Trina was hiding in the church. Malene had told her that she heard the report from Christine and expected that Roger would be looking for Raymond.

Malene had said that Trina should expect a call from the sheriff, but she had promised that she wouldn't tell her husband what happened between the young woman and Raymond. She had already explained to Roger, she told Trina, that she had treated her for some injuries she thought she got at work. She had even volunteered to stay with Trina that first night, but Trina had said she would rather be alone. Trina hadn't explained to Malene why she didn't want company, but she thought Raymond wouldn't come in the house if he knew someone else was there. Even though she wasn't sure that she was going to let him stay, she had still been hopeful that he would return, even after she heard about what happened in Datil.

Malene, of course, had been right about the sheriff. She hadn't been gone fifteen minutes before he pulled up in the driveway, claiming that he was stopping by to check on her. Trina had realized that his story was partly true — he did care about her, and she knew it — but she also knew he was hoping to find Raymond. When she asked him why he wanted to see her boyfriend, pretending not to know about the robbery in Datil, he had given her the same report Malene gave her. Even to hear a second time that Raymond was a person of interest in a breaking-and-entering case, and with the information coming this time from the sheriff, Trina still didn't want to believe that the story was true. She knew that the crime behind these accusations would have been completely out of character for Raymond.

"I called Frank every hour after Roger left. He never went home that night," Trina said, recalling how she had tried to contact Frank after she heard about the trouble from Malene and then Roger.

"I think he must have found him," Father George guessed. "I think Frank found Raymond, and he's trying to talk him into coming home." He was worried about his friend. To be gone for a couple of days, close the garage, and not explain even to Trina where he was or when he'd return, George knew this wasn't like Frank.

"Yeah, maybe," Trina responded softly. "But it sure is taking a long time to talk him into it."

George could see that the young woman wasn't convinced by his idea. He could see she was thinking something else. "What?" he asked her.

185

Trina moved up and then back into the office chair. She seemed uncomfortable. Considering that she might be in pain, George was about to suggest that she go home. He would even drive her if she needed him to — drive her home and go pick up the baby for her.

"I'm worried that Frank found Raymond and that Raymond is still like. . . ." She hesitated. ". . . Like he was when he left." She slid her feet back and forth under her. "That maybe Frank found him and Raymond hurt Frank too."

Father George had not thought of this. It was possible she was right. And yet, he just didn't think that Raymond could harm his own father. He looked up at Trina to say as much, but then, remembering her wounds, realized that he had also thought the boy would never have hurt her either.

"Do you think Frank knows about the robbery? That he knew before he went out to find Raymond?"

Trina shook her head. "I don't know," she answered. "How would he have found out?"

Father George shrugged. "Doesn't he have a police scanner in his truck?" he asked, recalling that he had seen one when he had ridden with the garage owner before.

"Yeah, he keeps it so he'll know if there's

a wreck or so he can get the report if a vehicle breaks down. Sometimes he tows for the county," she explained.

"I thought that's what he told me before" came the reply.

"So you think he found out and he's trying to keep Raymond hidden?" Trina asked.

George thought about the possibilities. Either Frank didn't know about the robbery — and was trying to talk his son into coming back and getting help for what he thought was just the one violent episode that had happened with Trina — or he did know about what happened at Datil. George didn't have any idea what Frank would do once he learned about that. Would he try to hide his son or try to talk him into returning and facing the situation? He didn't know.

"Or maybe," Trina said, "Raymond's told Frank about getting thrown out of the Silver Spur and . . . the robbery." Like George, Trina wasn't sure what was happening between the father and son.

George didn't respond. He really didn't know what Frank would do if he knew about Raymond being kicked out of the bar and the threats he made to Gilbert. He didn't know what Frank would do if he found Raymond with the money he was accused of stealing. He thought the man would want his son to do the right thing and return to answer the questions of the authorities and deal with the consequences, but he also knew that Frank had some serious issues with the government and what it had done to his people, the Navajo, as well as with what he thought the military had done to his son. Maybe he would prefer for Raymond to stay hidden. Maybe the father didn't want his son to face any charges, any time in jail. These thoughts ran through George's mind, but he didn't think he should share them with Trina.

"I'm just worried for them both," Trina said, leaning forward. "You know how close they are."

Father George nodded. "He was really concerned about Raymond after the explosion. He practically moved into his hospital room in Albuquerque. And then, since Raymond's been home, he's been like a mother hen." He rested his head against the wall behind him. "Remember how he acted with Raymond at the party?"

"I remember," Trina noted. "He kept going back and forth to the table, bringing Raymond whatever he wanted, trying to get him to eat. Then when he went outside for so long, Frank kept trying to get him to come in."

"If I recall correctly, Raymond wasn't too keen on the idea of the party," Father George commented. "I think Frank felt guilty for agreeing to it before he had checked it out with his son."

"Frank just thought it might lift his spirits; we all did. He thought he needed something after the hospital stay. And besides, Raymond used to like parties. I mean, he was never interested in being the center of attention, but he used to enjoy being around folks, from what I've heard from the people in town."

"I heard the same thing," Father George responded. He slid his fingers through his hair. "He used to be active at church when he was a little boy too. Sang in the children's choir, was an acolyte. He was even quite popular in high school, from what his teachers say." He shook his head. "From all the stories the church folks tell me, Raymond doesn't even seem like the same person."

Trina turned away. "I'm worried about him. I'm worried about both of them out there together."

"Do you want me to go try and find them?" Father George asked. He dropped his hands in his lap and considered the idea. He had no clue where to start searching.

He didn't know where Frank had gone looking for his son, and even though he had been in Catron County for more than a couple of years, there were still areas around Pie Town that he had never visited.

Trina shook her head. "No, I don't think you need to be running around the county trying to find Frank and Raymond. They both know this land like the back of their hands, so they could be anywhere." She reached for her water bottle and took a swallow.

"How's Alexandria?" George asked, deciding to change the subject. He realized that he hadn't heard how Trina's baby was doing since the accident. The child had seemed unaffected by what had happened between her mother and Raymond after the night of the storm, but George was not sure since he had not seen the little girl in a couple of days. He knew that the caregiver had kept her for the first night after the incident.

"Fine," Trina answered. "I picked her up yesterday from Frieda's. She seems fine. I mean, she misses Raymond, keeps looking around for him at the house, but she doesn't seem to know anything's wrong."

George nodded. "You okay taking care of her?" he asked. He wasn't sure how the wounds on her back and legs might have hindered her from the work she had to do as a mother.

"Yeah. I really only have one place that got burned bad. It's on my butt, and it's healing pretty good. Malene said that I should wear the bandages just to make sure the burns don't get infected, but they're really a lot better now." She stood up and turned around. "You want to see?" she asked.

George blushed. "No, no . . . ," he stammered. "I trust you."

Trina turned around and saw his red face. "You're so easy to embarrass," she said.

George cleared his throat and didn't respond. He thought about the young woman and how much he had come to care for her. They had first met when Trina hitched a ride with him just as he was starting his new job in Catron County, and it had seemed to him during his first few months that she was nothing but trouble for him. He recalled the fire at Holy Family: after the church burned down, he had not stood up for her by telling the townspeople she had been with him that night. He had let her take the blame for arson even though he knew she had not been responsible.

He was still ashamed of his actions toward Trina, and it meant a great deal to him that the young woman had never held his silent betrayal against him. She had, in fact, taught him more about kindness and generosity of spirit than anyone he had ever met.

He just watched as she gingerly sat back down at the desk and returned to her work on the computer. Even with her teasing, it was easy to see that she was upset about Raymond, and now Frank, but he also knew she was a person who did not let anything keep her down. He remembered her pregnancy and the last few weeks when she had to stay on bed rest. She never seemed anxious or afraid. Trina was young, but strong.

The phone rang, and Trina answered. "Frank's Garage," she said. And there was a pause. "Hello? Hello?" She waited a few seconds and then hung up. She shrugged at George. "Wrong number I guess, or maybe it's somebody trying to see if Frank answers." She stared at the phone.

"Maybe it's your old boyfriend." George was trying to tease her.

"Is that meant to be a joke?" she asked. "Is the priest trying to make a joke?"

He blushed again.

There was a pause.

"I'm going to tell Roger what happened. I'm going to call him when I get home this afternoon and tell him." She shrugged again. "I feel like he should know the truth."

Father George nodded and then noticed the dark sedan as it slowly drove past the garage. He knew that the FBI agents had been in town every day since the incident at the bar in Datil. As the car passed, George noted the two men inside the car staring into the garage bays and into the office where he and Trina were sitting.

"What would you do?" she asked George.

The priest faced away from the window and looked over at Trina. "What do you mean?" he asked. He folded his hands in his lap. "Would I tell Roger?" he asked, thinking about what she had just said.

Trina shook her head. "No. I mean, would you try to talk your son into coming home and possibly spending time in jail, or would you help him run?" Trina had a pencil in her hand and was lightly tapping the desk with it.

George sat back and started biting his bottom lip, a nervous habit he had developed. "I guess I would try and talk him into turning himself in," he finally replied. "To come and face the charges, clear his name."

Trina nodded. "Yeah, that's what I think Frank will do too," she said.

"What about Raymond?" he asked.

She waited for more. She wasn't following him.

"Will Raymond choose to come home and deal with the situation, or will he run?" George knew that Trina knew Frank's son probably better than anyone else in town.

"He'd come home," she answered right away. "If he's, you know. . . ." She paused. "If he's right in his mind." She shook her head. "But I don't know. He's so different than who he used to be."

She placed the pencil in the cup on the edge of the desk. "You know, when he first got to Pie Town, after the hospital stay, I thought he'd be okay. But now he just seems so angry, so not like himself." She glanced down. "I'm worried about Alexandria being around him. I'm worried that he might hurt her. . . ." She snapped up her face, realizing what she had said. "Oh, but not intentionally," she noted, hoping George wouldn't think worse of her boyfriend. "I don't think he meant or means to harm anyone intentionally. I just think he's not . . . I just don't know what he'd do now."

"I know," Father George responded.

"And it worries me that the FBI might be the ones who find him, because I'm not sure how he'll react to them and I'm worried that they might hurt him. I'm worried that this thing could really blow up."

George glanced away.

"I wish Roger would find him first and bring him in. That would make things a lot better, don't you think?" Trina asked.

"I do," George replied.

There was a pause in the conversation.

"Well, we just have to hope for the best, and we also have to remember that we don't know the whole story," Father George noted. "All we're hearing is bits and pieces, and some of it isn't even true."

He recalled hearing one of the church members explaining to someone else that Raymond had robbed the bar at gunpoint, stealing from Gilbert while holding the customers hostage. Somebody else talked about hearing that Raymond had been dealing drugs with a soldier he met in Afghanistan, that he was involved with some military drug ring out of Albuquerque. There were already lots of versions of what happened at the Silver Spur and a lot of versions of what had happened to Raymond, and he knew most of them weren't based on fact.

"He may not have been the one to steal the money. We don't know if what Gilbert is telling Roger is the real truth." Father George took a breath. "We can't know what really happened until we hear Raymond's side of the story."

"Hear Raymond's side of what story?"

Father George and Trina had been so involved in their conversation that neither one of them had even heard the truck pull into the rear of the garage. They didn't know Frank had walked into the office until he asked the question.

TWENTY-TWO

"I'm only saying that you should have told me the truth to start with." Roger sounded angry.

"It wasn't my truth to tell," Malene responded.

She had been sitting on the front porch when he drove up. Roger was just returning from Trina's after she had called the sheriff from work explaining that she wanted to talk. He had just discovered the real reason she had needed medical attention, the real reason Father George had called Malene to come to the church. She had finally come clean to him about the last time she had seen Raymond Twinhorse and what had happened between them. She had also informed him that Frank was home, and after he talked to Malene, confronted her about what he now knew, Roger planned to head over to the garage and talk to him.

"What does that mean?" he asked. "If it's

the truth, then everybody ought to tell it."

"That's not the way I see it," she said. She folded the newspaper she had been reading when Roger pulled up and placed it in her lap.

He leaned against the porch railing in front of her. "Why is it not the way you see it?" He glanced up, trying to decide if he was going to sit beside her or just remain standing there on the steps. "The truth is the truth no matter who tells it."

Malene leaned over and cleaned off the rocking chair next to hers, making a space for her husband to sit. "I don't think it was my place to tell what Trina asked me not to." She threw the magazines and blanket down beside her.

Roger waited. "It was domestic abuse," he said.

Malene looked up at him. "She said it was an accident, and I believe her."

"An accident?" Roger sounded surprised as he remained standing on the steps. "Malene, you saw those wounds. He pushed her into a stove. She has blisters on her back from the pot of water." He shook his head. "You're a medical professional. You're supposed to report those kinds of injuries."

Malene faced her husband. "I have known Raymond Twinhorse since he was a baby."

198

10/13/2020

LEYDEN CAITLIN ROSE

Item Number 31901051859314

Contra Costa County Libraries are open for front door pick up of holds. Masks and social distancing are required. For faster service, book an appointment at: https://ccclib.org/front-door-service/ Book drops are open. Pinole Library and Ygnacio Valley Library remain temporarily unavailable.

Hold Shelf Slip

10/13/2020

LEYDEN CAITLIN ROSE

Item Number: 31901051859314

Contra Costa County Libraries are open for front door pick up of holds. Masks and social distancing are required. For faster service, book an appointment at: https://ccclib.org/front-door-service/ Book drops are open. Pinole Library and Ygnacio Valley Library remain temporarily unavailable.

Hold Shelf Slip

She patted the seat of the chair next to hers, inviting him to sit down. When he did, she continued. "And so have you, Roger Benavidez. He was Angel's best friend when they were children. He was like a son to us both. And you know as well as I that Raymond couldn't hurt a fly." She took a breath and started rocking.

"He's a good boy, Roger. Something bad happened to him over there in that war, and Trina and Frank are committed to getting him help. They're going to make sure he goes for counseling. That's what they both told me and Father George, and that's what I believe to be the truth." She stopped rocking and peered at her husband.

Roger didn't move in his chair. He studied his wife. She was right, he realized. Raymond was like a son to him. He had helped Frank raise the boy. And he wasn't a violent person. At least he wasn't before he joined the military. But still, he thought, Malene should have told him about Trina's injuries.

"This incident is important to the other case, to the robbery in Datil," he explained. "It gives us information that Raymond was in a disturbed state of mind when he got thrown out of the bar. It's helpful information."

"Helpful to whom?" Malene asked.

Roger turned away.

"Helpful to the prosecution, right?" She folded her arms across her chest and kept rocking. "Helpful for you to gain evidence to arrest him so you can close your case? Helpful to try and calm Gilbert down?"

"It could also be helpful to a defense. If it's determined that he was mentally incapacitated, had a kind of psychotic break, a good lawyer could prove that Raymond wasn't in his right mind when he got upset at the bar and also when he returned the next morning to steal from Gilbert. Somebody with any sense would say he suffers from PTSD and needs help." He thought his argument sounded convincing.

"It was not my truth to tell," Malene repeated. "Besides, you don't know what happened at the Silver Spur. You need to talk to Raymond before you start making up your mind about that boy. What's happened to you? You never used to jump to conclusions like you've jumped to this one. You always used to wait before you decided who committed the crime. Don't you need to at least hear from Raymond before you make up your mind? He doesn't steal. He's not a petty thief or a vengeful person. You know that. These accusations are crazy. And if you ask me, Gilbert is making this all up to cause trouble."

Roger put his arms behind his head, interlocking his fingers. "I would love to talk to Raymond, but it seems that he is making it hard for me to locate him at the present time."

"Have you heard from Frank?" Malene asked.

Roger rocked, starting to relax. "Trina said he was back, that he showed up at the garage just before she left. She said that he's sticking to a story that he went to visit family in Ramah."

"Maybe he did," Malene responded. "Maybe he went to see his mother. Maybe he thought he needed to tell his family what was happening with his son, ask for their help."

"We both know there's more to Frank's story than him just taking a couple of days, closing the garage, and driving up to visit his family. He was searching for Raymond, and I think he found him." Roger stretched up his arms and then brought them down to rest on the sides of the chair.

Malene closed her eyes. "I thought the FBI took the investigation away from you anyway."

Roger didn't respond.

Malene glanced over at her husband, waiting for him to reply.

"I informed Agent Williams that I intend to complete my work, and when I am finished I am happy to give them a copy of my report."

"Is that why you're in such a hurry to name Raymond the thief, to finish the investigation before the FBI can take credit for an arrest?" She immediately could see that Roger was hurt by the accusation. She reached over and touched him on the arm.

"I'm sorry. I know that's not true. I know you're not competing with the FBI to close the case. I know you'd rather be the one to speak to Raymond before they do. I know that's why you want to find him." She studied Roger, hoping for forgiveness. "I'm sorry. I was out of line."

He nodded without making a response.

"What I don't understand is why the FBI is so concerned about this case anyway," Malene said. "Why is the robbery of a bar of any interest to them?"

Roger shook his head. "I can't figure that one out, but I suppose it may have something to do with the bust they bungled in Alamo. Gilbert's running his mouth all over the county, telling anybody who will listen that Raymond had a gun and that he acted like he was on drugs. Maybe the feds think he's the guy they're after." He reached over and took his wife's hand still resting by his arm. "But of course, as usual, I don't know any of this for sure because nobody's telling me anything."

Malene had heard about the FBI from Oris. He had been at the diner when the two agents came in. One of them gave Fred his business card and asked him to call if he saw Frank or Raymond Twinhorse. It had been the agent Roger had spoken of before, Agent Lewis Williams. She knew he was the same man her husband had worked with previously. She knew Roger didn't like the man from Albuquerque.

"Do you think they're searching for Raymond?" she asked.

Roger sighed. "I think they'd love to find him, and I think they're convinced that Raymond is somehow connected in this drug business."

"Well, that's just crazy," Malene responded. "Raymond's not selling drugs."

"You know that, and I know that. But the federal agents don't know that. They've probably already made up their minds that Raymond is a dealer, and the longer he stays away the worse it gets for him." He glanced up just as a truck passed the house. It was one of the ranchers who lived up the street.

Roger threw up his hand.

"That's why having the news about what happened to Trina might have helped," he explained. "If I had known that Raymond had already made a violent attack on his girlfriend, what happened at the Silver Spur would have appeared less like the premeditated action of some drug dealer and more like a guy who was just messed up." He wiped his forehead with the back of his hand. "Maybe if I had known this in the beginning, I could have told Agent Williams and he would have left the case alone."

Malene turned, watching her husband. "You don't really believe that, do you?" she asked. "You're just angry because you didn't know the truth, and you're angry because I did and didn't tell you."

Roger glanced away. "Yes," he replied. He faced Malene, pulling away his hand. "I'm angry that no one trusted me enough to tell me the truth. I'm angry that you and Trina would decide that you couldn't confide in me. That the priest, my best friend, my wife, and a young woman whose child is my goddaughter would take matters into their own hands, choose not to report a case of domestic abuse, and then lie to me about what really happened." He exhaled. "Yes, Malene, I am angry."

Malene reached over and took her husband's hand again. She looked at him. "I didn't know what else to do," she confessed. "None of us knew the right thing to do," she added. "Trina asked us not to tell, convinced us that she would get Raymond some help and that she would not be alone again with him until he did." She blew out a breath. "After I heard about the robbery at Silver Spur, I didn't know what to think, and Trina promised that she would tell you." She shrugged. "I'm sorry," she said. "I'm sorry I didn't tell you the truth."

Roger softened. He knew she had been put in a very unsettling position and that she had acted as she had only because she had thought it was the right thing to do. She loved Trina and Raymond and didn't want to do anything to harm either of them. He knew that if he had been called, if he had been told what she had been told, he would probably have done the same thing. He really couldn't blame his wife and his friends for not reporting the event. And he knew he was mostly angry and upset because, with the feds involved, Raymond Twinhorse was going to be in a lot more trouble than if Roger had been able to just handle the situation himself.

He was about to tell Malene that he

understood what she had done and forgave her when his cell phone notified him of a text. He dropped her hand and reached down to his belt and removed the phone to read it.

"Damn" was all he said.

"What is it?" Malene asked.

"Frank Twinhorse has been arrested."

TWENTY-THREE

Father George promised Frank that he would let Roger know about the arrest and that he would go to Albuquerque to visit him as soon as the authorities granted him permission. He tried to go with Frank when the FBI agents came for him at the garage, but they had not permitted the priest to get involved.

The two men in the dark sedan that he had seen driving past the garage earlier in the afternoon drove by again, this time stopping and coming in, flashing badges and ordering instructions to both George and Frank. It was after five o'clock, and Roger was at least relieved that Trina, who had to pick up Alexandria, had already departed. The two friends were talking when the FBI arrived. George had gotten some snacks from the vending machine, Frank made a pot of coffee, and they were discussing Raymond and the fight at the Silver Spur when the agents walked in and arrested Frank. George had yelled and screamed about there being no charges to lodge against his friend, but it had all fallen on deaf ears. They made some claim about national security, another claim about drugs and illegal activity, and insisted that Frank knew more than he was saying. George could do nothing to stop them.

George texted Roger as soon as the agents arrived at the garage, as soon as he knew who they were and what they were doing. After the arrest, unsure of what to do or where to go next, he simply drove back to the rectory. He did not call Trina. He did not go to Roger's house. He did not call or visit anyone else. He was trying to figure out everything that had happened and everything that was still taking place.

It turned out that Frank had not known about the robbery, but he was sure that Raymond had not been involved. He explained to Trina and George that after a day of searching and a night of camping, he had found his son the next morning, and that the two had been together, talking, until he left. He then asked them not to tell anyone where he had been, as he planned to say he was visiting Ramah. Trina and George agreed.

"Never," George remembered Frank had said, "never did Raymond mention any problems in Datil. He said that after he left Trina's he went to the bar, that he drank too much and drove his bike when he probably shouldn't have, but that he stopped out near Old Horse Springs, south of town, and spent the night in the desert. He even said he threw his gun away." It was clear to Frank that his son had been upset about what he had done to Trina, but he never spoke to his father of anything else that had occurred later that night.

Frank was certain, George recalled the conversation, that his son had not stolen from anyone. He was sure that Raymond would have told him if he had. Frank relayed to George that all Raymond remembered about what occurred the night the power went out in Catron County was what had happened to Trina. There was no conversation about any bar fight or any confrontation with Gilbert. All that Raymond told Frank about that night was that he had the fight with Trina, drove away on his dirt bike to Datil for a couple of drinks, and then left there, heading south on Highway 12, and camped for the night in the desert.

Frank had not told Trina or George where Raymond was hiding. He had not mentioned any specific locations except for the one where Raymond had camped that first night, off Highway 12 near Apache Creek, about forty miles south of Pie Town. Based on that little bit of information, George thought the boy must still be near there. It was, however, a big area, and George wasn't sure that he would ever have a chance of finding Raymond if he went searching for him.

When Trina had asked if Raymond was coming home — *when* he was coming home — Frank confessed that he did not know for sure. He had explained that he left Raymond after he asked his father for just a week to get his head on straight, to be alone, to think about things, and then, Frank thought, he would probably come home, face Trina, and go to the VA Hospital for help.

The FBI agents had walked into the garage and questioned Frank before George could find out any details of where Raymond was when Frank left him. They had then arrested Frank for failing to give them information about Raymond's whereabouts. Both Frank and George had claimed the arrest was bogus. They both said the charges of obstruction of justice and aiding and abetting a fugitive would never stand. And yet, there seemed nothing they could do. The agents had handcuffed Frank and taken him away, and now, as he stood in the rectory, pacing back and forth, worried about Frank, worried about Raymond, George had no idea how he could help.

"Roger will work this out," he told himself. He assumed that the sheriff would have access to Frank, could talk to him and figure out the best way to handle things. He hoped that Roger would find Raymond before the FBI did so that he could talk to the boy and prepare him for the charges that had been filed against him, as well as the questioning the FBI intended to carry out about drugs and Raymond's involvement. He hoped that Raymond would be treated for the PTSD and not as a common criminal. Trying to convince himself there was nothing for him to do but pray, George paced and prayed until he was interrupted by a knock at the door.

He was surprised when he opened it, expecting to find Malene or Trina or even Roger; instead, he discovered Francine Mueller standing on the porch.

"Hello, Father," she said.

George glanced around her. Hers was the only car in the church parking lot, and she seemed to be alone.

"Francine," he called out, the surprise showing in his voice. "Please, come in." And he moved aside while the woman walked in past him.

"I'm sorry," she immediately said. "I know it's late and I should have called."

George smiled. "It's fine. Please," he motioned her into the living area, "have a seat."

Francine nervously walked over to the sofa and stood there, waiting for the priest to join her. She seemed very uncomfortable, and George had no idea why he was receiving this visitor.

Francine had made it very clear when the priest first arrived that she was Protestant. And even though she, like everyone else in the community, had helped build the new Holy Family Church, Francine had only attended church sporadically. She went to weddings and funerals, the high church days, Christmas and Easter, but she mostly stayed away on Sundays.

"Are you all right?" he asked, quite aware of his guest's discomfort. He motioned for her to sit down.

Francine nodded and sat on the sofa. She clutched her purse in her lap and moved up in her seat. "No," she replied. "I'm not all right."

George sat down on the coffee table across from her, appearing very concerned. "What is it?" he asked.

She didn't answer right away.

"Is it Bernie?" Unlike Francine, Bernie was a devout Catholic. He came to church almost every week.

She shook her head. "Bernie's fine," she answered. "Well, no, he's not fine either. We're both torn up about this, and I just didn't know what else to do. So he's gone to Silver City to buy some farm equipment, something he does when he's stressed or needs to think, and I decided I wanted to talk to you."

George waited. He considered offering her a cup of tea, but he could see she was eager to talk, even if it seemed to be taking her a long time to begin.

"We know where Raymond Twinhorse is," she blurted out. Then she shook her head. "Well, not exactly we don't. We saw him walking out by Bernie's ranch a few days ago, the day after the storm, the morning really." She swallowed hard. "I stayed the night with Bernie." She paused and waited for a reaction from the priest.

There was none.

"And we were up fixing breakfast at about dawn, and we saw him walking. Bernie went

213

out and found his motorcycle and brought it to the house because it was out of gas and he thought he'd save Raymond the trouble of having to push it. We put it in the barn because we weren't sure how long he was going to be gone and Bernie thought it would be safer there. We thought he was hunting or maybe just getting out in nature. And then, later, Bernie told Frank about finding his bike, and he could tell Frank was real upset about something. He said that as soon as he mentioned the bike, Frank was all in a hurry for Bernie to leave so he could lock up the garage. And then Frank was gone for two days, and then we heard about the robbery, and then the FBI was searching for Raymond because of drugs, and then Frank. . . ." She finally stopped and took a breath. "We didn't know what to do." She faced George.

George pulled away from Francine. He had just heard a lot of information from her, and he was trying to process it all. Based on what Frank had told him, he thought Raymond was still south of town, but now Francine was saying she had seen the young man north of Pie Town, up around Bernie's ranch, which was nowhere near Apache Creek.

Francine started to get up. "I'm sorry, this

214

was a mistake. I shouldn't have come. You don't know anything about this, and I shouldn't have bothered you."

"No, no." George reached out and took her by the arm. "No, this is fine. It's fine that you've talked to me."

She sat down again, appearing somewhat relieved. She reached in her purse and took out a tissue. She blotted it beneath her eyes. "We didn't put the bike in the barn to hide it from anybody," she said, sounding as if she was trying to convince herself. "We just put it there for safekeeping. We didn't know Raymond was in trouble."

After using the tissue to wipe her top lip, she slipped it into the sleeve of her blouse, then folded her hands in her lap.

George tried to think of the right response but didn't come up with anything, so he just waited for his guest to keep talking. She didn't disappoint him.

"I thought we should go right away and tell Roger about seeing Raymond and having his bike, but Bernie didn't think it was any of our business. He told me not to tell." She blew out a long breath. "Now I'm just afraid we waited too long. Now I'm worried we'll be in trouble for hindering the prosecution or whatever it is we can be arrested for." She pulled out the tissue and blotted her face again. She looked at the priest in desperation. She paused. "There's nothing you can say?"

George cleared his throat. "I don't know what to say," he admitted. "I think. . . ." He hesitated. "I guess you should tell somebody what you saw, but I don't know. . . ." He was at a loss for words.

Francine leaned back in her seat. She suddenly seemed a bit less anxious than when she had arrived, even if the priest had not offered any helpful response to her admission. She had at least gotten the story off of her chest.

"He's obviously somewhere up on Techado or maybe all the way to Veteado Mountain by now." She thought about the area north of Bernie's ranch. "Although I suppose he could have gone east over the plains and is out there on the Malpais." She shook her head, thinking of the places near Pie Town. She had considered everywhere the boy could have gone in a few days. "And if he got a ride or walked all the way out 117 to the Narrows, well, they'll never find him out there." She paused.

George was thinking of all the places Francine was naming. He had taken the back road from Pie Town to Grants with Oris Whitsett the previous summer. The old man wanted to show the priest the lava beds, formed from a volcanic eruption from Mount Taylor years and years ago. He had explained how the beds were full of fissures and ravines and how lots of hikers and wanderers had fallen to their deaths climbing in the area.

"El Malpais has to be thirty or forty miles north of Bernie's place. Raymond couldn't have gotten that far, could he?" George wasn't sure why he was asking.

Francine thought about the question. "Well, no, but if Frank found him, he could have driven him out there, or they could have hiked over to Fence Lake." She shook her head again. "There are miles of trails between here and Interstate 40. He could be anywhere out there," she surmised.

George thought. "I don't know what to tell you, Francine." He studied his visitor. "You're going to have to make up your own mind about whether to tell the authorities or not. You and Bernie have to make up your minds together." He paused, thinking of how best to counsel this community member. He was trying to think of the right thing to say.

She waited.

"I suppose knowing where Raymond was a couple of days ago might be helpful in

217

finding him," said the priest, "but you could also take the stance that it was a few days ago and, just as you said, he could be anywhere now. Besides, now that Frank is arrested. . . ."

"Arrested?" Francine interrupted the priest. "Wait. They arrested Frank?" she asked. The news was certainly distressing.

George nodded. "This evening, about twenty minutes ago, in fact."

"Frank returned to Pie Town and got arrested?"

George reached out, holding Francine's arms. "I'm sure they'll let him out soon. They don't really have a reason to detain him."

"They think he knows where Raymond is," she said, the nervousness having returned to her voice, her appearance. "And they could arrest me and Bernie if they find out we're hiding his bike," she added.

She pulled her right hand away from Father George and held it up to her chest. Her breathing became shallow. "I could be a felon," she said. "Bernie and I could be arrested by the FBI. This is not good, not good at all."

As George watched Francine spiraling downward, he realized that he had probably made things worse for her. He wanted to assure his visitor that it wasn't likely that she and Bernie would be arrested for not reporting what they had seen, but he also knew that he wasn't sure about anything involving Raymond and his apparent flight into the wilderness. He couldn't tell what the FBI was doing. He certainly had never expected them to arrest Frank. He was at a complete loss for something else to say. "Maybe we can tell Roger what you saw," he suggested.

Francine thought about that. "But wouldn't Roger have to report it to the FBI?"

George wasn't sure. He shrugged.

"And I don't want to put the sheriff in the middle of this," she said. "He's a good man, and I don't want him to have to worry about us. Besides, he needs to focus on getting Frank out of jail, don't you think?"

George nodded. He guessed that Roger would do the right thing and make the report to the FBI, and he knew that the sheriff would not be happy to put Francine and Bernie in a position similar to Frank's. He also knew that Frank needed Roger's full attention at that moment. He remained silent; he couldn't think of another idea.

"I could just make an anonymous call," Francine said.

"They'd figure out who it was," he replied.

The two sat in silence, wondering about the situation, trying to think of the best plan to make, the best action to take.

Finally, George thought of something. It was risky and perhaps not ethical, but it was something. He reached up and again took Francine by the hands. "Maybe you and Bernie should take a little trip somewhere," he suggested.

Francine quickly turned to the priest. His advice surprised her.

"Nowhere far," he continued, shaking his head.

"Just get away for a couple of days?" she asked, sounding sheepish, but also as if she liked the idea.

George shrugged.

There was a pause.

"I'm sorry," the priest apologized. "I don't mean to lead you down a slippery slope."

Francine shook her head, still considering the idea. "It doesn't seem so slippery," she replied.

Father George waited.

Francine cleared her throat. "My oldest friend lives in Phoenix," she said. "Bernie likes Phoenix, and he likes my friend. We've visited her before, just a few weeks ago, in fact. It was a fine visit. We picked oranges."

She pulled her hands away, dropped the tissue in her lap, and touched the sides of her hair. She sat up straight, grasping the handle of her purse. "You know, I think a little trip would do us both good."

"I'm sure in a few days, when you get back, things will be clearer for everyone." George nodded, a slight approval.

Francine smiled. The relief spread across her face.

"Yes, Father, I think this is a good idea," she agreed, taking a deep breath. She put the tissue in her purse and stood up from the sofa. George stood up as well, moving aside as Francine started walking to the door. Her voice had become calm. She suddenly seemed much more at ease.

"It's going to be a lovely moon tonight, wouldn't you say?" she asked, opening the door and facing the night.

George nodded.

She exhaled a big breath of air. "Yes, I think taking a mini-vacation to Arizona sounds like a fabulous idea. I think Bernie will like it too," and turning once more to George for a final good-bye, she reached out her hand and said, "I'm sure this will all blow over in a couple of days. I think this is for the best. Thank you, Father."

He took her hand and squeezed it and

then let it go. He watched her as she walked out the door, down the porch steps, and out to her car, and kept watching as she drove away.

Francine had been relieved of her burden by telling the priest about the possible whereabouts of Raymond. But in giving him a clearer idea of where Raymond was, as he thought about whether or not to go and find him, she had only added to Father George's.

TWENTY-FOUR

Agents Lewis Williams and Kevin Cochran had taken a seat in the back booth of the diner. They ordered their meals and listened to the conversation happening over at the counter. Agent Cochran was smiling. Williams didn't see the humor in anything Oris Whitsett said, but the old man knew how to make Cochran laugh. "This is the same pie you had last week." Oris had eaten his lunch and was ready for dessert. "What happened to your pie baker?"

"Francine and Bernie went to Phoenix for a few days," Bea answered. "This pie is fine, and it isn't the same as last week. We had Pio-O-Neer Pecan Oak Pie last week, this is chocolate pecan. Francine made this one before she left."

"Looks the same as the pie last week," Oris said, just before taking a sip of coffee. He was sitting at the counter.

Bea just walked away, rolling her eyes.

"Weren't they just in Phoenix last month?" Oris asked, wiping his fork on his napkin.

"What if they were in Phoenix last month? Francine's got a good friend in Arizona," Bea replied. "Last time I heard, there's no law against going to Phoenix every month."

"Maybe Francine and Bernie have something to do with Fedora's meth-making gypsies camped out on the forest road." Oris grinned.

"I'm sure that's why they ran off to Arizona, Oris," Bea responded. "Bernie and Francine are running the big Catron County drug ring everybody's talking about."

"Well, you just never know; you might want to run it by those guys." Oris motioned over in the direction of the FBI agents. "It seems like they could use a real lead."

Bea just shook her head.

"Is there coconut in this?" Oris asked as he picked at the pie with his fork. "You know I don't like coconut."

"There's no coconut in chocolate pecan pie, Oris." Fred had decided to join the conversation. "There's chocolate, and there are pecans. If coconut was an ingredient, it would be a chocolate pecan coconut pie." He hit the bell in the window and yelled, "Order up."

"There's sugar in it, isn't there?" Oris

asked, taking a bite. "It ain't called chocolate pecan sugar pie," he noted. "And butter? There's butter too." He chewed. "That was a stupid argument you just made. Just because there's an ingredient in the recipe doesn't mean it's in the name of the dish."

Bea walked over to the window where Fred had placed the plates of food and picked up the two lunch specials. She headed over to the booth where the two FBI agents were sitting and put the plates in front of her customers. "You want extra chile?" she asked the younger agent, the one who had taken to ordering extra chile when he came in for lunch.

Agent Cochran smiled at Bea. "That would be great," he replied. "The hot one," he added. "And some more tea, if you don't mind."

"You need anything else?" she asked the other agent.

He just shook his head.

Bea wiped her hands on her apron and headed to the kitchen. She returned to the table with a bowl of hot chile sauce.

Agent Williams watched his partner pour the red sauce on top of his chicken enchilada. He turned up his nose. "That can't be good for your digestive system," he said. "I'm surprised you don't have holes all the way down your esophagus."

Cochran shook his head as he took a big bite. "Nah, that's the thing, red chile is good for the system. The heat keeps everything moving." He was tall and skinny, wore his dark hair in a crew cut, and preferred brightly colored, narrow ties.

"Yeah, that's what bothers me," Agent Williams responded as he took a bite of his turkey sandwich. "It moves with heat when it comes into your system, and it moves out with heat when it leaves it." He chewed his bite of lunch. "I'll stick to my American food, thank you very much." Williams was stocky and short. He was carrying more weight than he should have been as an FBI agent, but even heavy, he always managed to pass his annual physicals.

Agent Cochran shrugged and kept eating.

The two were back in Pie Town after having been gone a couple of days. Frank Twinhorse was still being held at the Albuquerque Detention Center, and even Roger had been denied visitation. They were claiming that his arrest was still being processed and the detainee couldn't meet with anyone other than the federal agents until the process had been completed.

They had brought other agents into town with them this time. There were a couple of young guys at the garage with orders to get another statement from the fugitive's girlfriend. Two new recruits were parked outside Frank's trailer in a stakeout, and a vanload of others had driven up with horses and were out combing Catron County on horseback.

The FBI had questioned everybody in town about the suspect Raymond Twinhorse and about where he might be, but it appeared as if the people of Pie Town had collectively decided to seal their lips and say nothing to the federal agents about the boy who had grown up in the area and now was considered their local hero. The only one who seemed interested in helping them was the bar owner, Gilbert Diaz, and he was starting to rub them the wrong way with his accusations and threats. If anyone listened to him, they'd think Raymond Twinhorse was not only the biggest drug dealer in the state but was probably fighting on the side of the Taliban when he was in Afghanistan.

The bartender in Datil might have agreed to help the agents locate Raymond Twinhorse, but in Pie Town they were getting no help at all. The FBI heard lots of statements like, "You should leave this to the sheriff," and, "That boy ain't done nothing to concern the federal government." They had been given more than a few testimonials to how courageous the suspect was, how much he had done for the country, and how it was wrong of the FBI to be involved in a local saloon robbery.

Agent Williams could feel the town's resentment, but unlike the younger Agent Cochran, who thought they'd have an easier time of it with the townspeople if they were a little more congenial and not so pushy, Williams seemed to thrive on being disliked. He thought the disdain actually helped the interviews, and he was not put off in the least by the things he heard. He seemed to enjoy the role of "bad cop."

Agent Cochran had also tried to convince his partner to release the father of the fugitive. It was obvious to them both that Frank Twinhorse wasn't going to tell them anything about Raymond's whereabouts, and Cochran believed that keeping him locked up just made the people of Pie Town even more uncooperative. He also knew that they really didn't have cause to detain the man. There were no drug-related charges lodged against him — or his son, for that matter. There was only speculation, and that came from the bar owner in Datil, the one Agent Cochran was beginning to believe was just a loudmouth who wanted revenge.

On the other hand, Williams thought he was making an important statement by keeping Twinhorse in jail. He thought it added credence to the investigation and represented a necessary show of power to anyone who might be connected to the drug ring he was convinced was being run somewhere in the county. He refused to change his mind or his plan of action, even though Cochran argued that he was only making things difficult for everyone.

"You boys check out my tip about Fedora Snow hiding the Twinhorse boy?" Oris had already eaten his pie. He was drinking his coffee to wash it down.

Agent Williams put down his sandwich and turned to the older man sitting at the counter. "It's against the law to make a false statement to a federal officer," he answered.

Oris had made a call to the FBI office in Albuquerque to report that he had seen a boy matching Raymond Twinhorse's description behind Fedora Snow's house late on the evening after Frank had been arrested.

The agents surrounded Fedora's house when someone else called in the same report. After more than a couple of days, Fedora Snow was still filing complaints about the raid, making phone calls to everyone in the FBI, and demanding that the broken door on her greenhouse be fixed and the medical bills she had been given by her gardener be paid.

Stan Ortez had been tending to Fedora's early tomato plants when he was ambushed, knocked to the floor, handcuffed, and read his rights before the agents realized he wasn't Raymond Twinhorse. He was later taken to the urgent care center in Socorro and treated for bruised ribs. No one admitted to making the second phone call to the FBI, but everyone had seen Oris and Mary Romero grinning at each other every time they were together for the next few days.

"It wasn't a false statement," Oris responded. "There was a young, nondescript brown man in Fedora's backyard. How was I to know it wasn't Raymond?" he asked. He winked at Bea.

"If you make another call like that again," said Agent Williams, turning in his seat and glowering at the old man, "I will personally drive up here and arrest you myself. I like nothing better than to put troublemakers behind bars." He wasn't as amused with Oris as his partner was.

"Yeah, we all know how you like putting people in jail and just how good you are at making arrests. Bad thing is, you just keep making the wrong ones." Oris put down his coffee cup. "I figure that's the real reason why you're so interested in Raymond Twinhorse anyway. You're trying to find some way to clean up the mess you made last week." He paused.

"Hey, if you boys are still in town," Oris continued, "you'll enjoy the Alamo Elementary School Summer Program." He stood up and reached for his wallet to pay for his pie. "Oh no, wait, I forgot. That was called off because the principal is still recovering from one of your personal arrests."

He took out a few bills and placed them on the table and then took a toothpick from his front pocket. "Bruised ribs, heart attacks . . . makes me wonder what other ailments you've caused for innocent folks. Makes me wonder exactly what you're doing to Frank Twinhorse." He stuck the toothpick in his mouth.

Agent Williams turned back in the booth to face his plate of food. "Well, maybe it should make you wonder," he sneered and glanced up at his partner. He didn't see Oris until the older man was right beside him.

Oris was leaning down, talking right into his ear. "You're wrong to come around here stirring up trouble with the locals, accusing people of things they ain't done. Raymond

Twinhorse fought for this country, and he deserves better. He didn't steal no money from Gilbert Diaz, and he sure as hell isn't involved in dealing drugs. And as far as his dad goes, there's not a finer man in this whole state." He inched a little closer.

"And let me just say this, you lay one hand on Frank Twinhorse and I guarantee you that you'll have more than one crazy old woman bugging the hell out of you and your bosses. I may be old," he said, his face right up next to the agent's, "but I'm mean." He turned to walk away.

"I could have you arrested for threatening a federal agent. I certainly have enough witnesses here."

As Agent Williams glanced around the diner, everyone there who had been watching the exchange quickly turned away. No one would make eye contact with the federal agent. No one would look at him at all.

"You ain't got shit," Oris said, walking away. He nodded his farewell to Fred and Bea and headed out the door.

TWENTY-FIVE

Father George was returning to Pie Town after having spent the afternoon in Albuquerque. The sun was setting, and he was heading southwest, chasing the last bit of light. He had visited Millie Watson, back in the hospital after another fall and injury to her hip, and then he had stopped by the detention center hoping to visit Frank Twinhorse again.

Like the sheriff, he had been denied visitation on two previous attempts, but that afternoon Agent Cochran had been at the center and had let the priest in to see his friend. Maybe it was because he was wearing his collar and looked more official, or maybe Agent Cochran was Catholic and believed the priest had a right to visit the detainee. George didn't know.

Before he had left that day, he had seen the young agent in Pie Town with his partner — Williams, George thought was his name

— at the diner for lunch. He had observed earlier that Cochran was less pushy than the older agent, seemed more like he was trying to get along with the citizens in Pie Town, and that day he had seemed as congenial as usual. George had mentioned to a few folks in the diner that he was going to Albuquerque, and he wondered if the agent had overheard his plans and assumed he would try again to visit Frank. He wondered if Agent Cochran had made a point of being in Albuquerque at the detention center and allowing the priest to visit. George didn't know how it all worked out; he was just glad it did.

From what George could see, Frank was fine. He was not hurt, he had been eating, and he had been allowed to go outside his cell once a day. Father George hadn't really expected to see evidence of torture or physical trauma, but after learning that even Roger hadn't been allowed access to Frank, he had begun to worry about how his friend was being treated and what they were doing to him without legal representation or even what appeared to be due process of the law.

Frank didn't talk much. A guard stood close by, obviously able to overhear the conversation, and it felt to George as if they were being watched during the visit. He could tell that Frank was uncomfortable; he fidgeted and glanced around a lot. Between his fingers he had been twirling a string of leather that reminded the priest of rosary beads, but it was just leather and Frank wasn't Catholic.

Father George headed down the interstate, making the turn at Socorro for Highway 60, watching the fading sunlight, and thought more about his visit.

Without giving out too much information, he had tried to explain to Frank that, for the previous two days, he had been searching for Raymond. He mentioned that he had seen Francine and had a lovely chat with her about Bernie and the big ranch he owned, hoping that Frank would figure out that George knew about Raymond's bike being there and that he knew that Francine had seen the boy near Bernie's place the day after the power went out. He told Frank about the camping trip he had taken that started out past the King ranch and continued in the area beyond Highway 603.

He casually called out names of specific places like Tres Lagunas and the Sawtooth Mountains and talked about the falcon he saw flying over the North Plains. He told Frank that he had driven over to the Malpais, gone to the visitors' center there, walked along the lava beds, and enjoyed a morning of exploration around the La Ventana Natural Arch and the Cebolla Canyon. He must have talked for twenty minutes about every square inch he had hiked and walked, hoping for some sign of recognition, some signal from Frank that would let the priest know where he had been with Raymond so that George could go and find him.

Father George sighed. Why hadn't Frank told him somehow where Raymond was? he wondered. Did he think the priest was just going to turn him in? George knew he wasn't trying to find Raymond to turn him in; he was trying to find Raymond to bring him to Roger, to keep him from walking into Pie Town and right into the custody of the FBI. He had wanted to convey that to Frank, but Frank had seemed more concerned that others were listening to their conversation.

George had spent two days searching for Raymond, two days searching everywhere he knew to search north of Bernie King's ranch, but in those two days he had never figured out what he planned to tell the young man when he found him. Even after seeing Frank, he still didn't know what he would say to Raymond if he managed to locate him. He just knew that he needed to get to him before the FBI agents did. He needed to talk to Raymond, make sure that he was safe and that he knew what was waiting for him before he returned to Pie Town.

George drove along, watching the shadows of the late summer evening dance around him. He took in a deep breath and exhaled. It had taken a while, but he had come to love this part of the country. Even after making a mess of things after he first arrived, he had started to think of Catron County and Pie Town as home. It had taken a lot of months, and there were still some folks who were suspicious of the priest from Ohio, but most of the people had come to accept George as one of their own. He had made a place for himself in Pie Town, and they had let him do so.

He loved the desert. It surprised him to think that upon his arrival he had seen the landscape as nothing but brown and barren. Now, he saw wonderful things across this part of the Southwest. He noticed things. Small purple flowers blooming, sagebrush tumbleweeds rolling across paths, thin clouds, and streaks of sunlight falling on canyon walls. He had his breath taken away more than once by what he encountered in the desert.

He drove along and recalled the sights he had seen during his most recent outing. He had walked over the sandstone cliffs and across the plains, up on the Malpais, and through the Narrows, and even though he was supposed to be searching for Raymond, he had found himself lost in wonder in such a magnificent place. He had walked a lot of miles, worn through a good pair of hiking boots, missed a couple of church committee meetings, gotten sunburned and fallen a few times, become chilled to the bone while camping at night, suffered with sore muscles and a painful blister on his heel — but he had never experienced such beauty in his life.

A vehicle sped past George, and he realized that he had dropped below the speed limit and drifted a bit across the yellow lines. He wasn't paying close enough attention to his driving. He shifted in his seat and tried to clear his mind of the thoughts of the past few days and instead focus on where he was; still, George couldn't help but remember all the times in the past couple of years Frank had tried to get him to go out in the desert with him.

Recalling the few times he had agreed to go, he remembered that Frank had tried to show him small details of the desert: the way desert flowers bloomed, the fossils and rocks strewn across the earth, the angle of the sun as a way to tell the time. George had always tried to appreciate what his friend was sharing, but he had never fully understood any of it until these last two days. And he had wanted to tell Frank, explain it to him. As he drove back to Pie Town, he realized, however, that in his excitement about wanting to share what had happened for him in the desert and his anxiety about trying to get Frank to give him details of Raymond's whereabouts, he hadn't been very reassuring or comforting to Frank during his visit.

George noticed that the flatbed truck that had just passed him had pulled over to the side of the road. As he drove by, he could see there was a man behind the wheel, and he seemed to be making a phone call. The license plate was from Texas, and the black truck was a newer model, one of the larger ones. The man watched the priest as he passed. George kept heading west, but he suddenly slowed down, wondering if he should stop and turn around to see if the driver needed assistance. Highway 60, he knew, was long and desolate. He soon sped back up, however, after deciding that the driver of the truck had probably just pulled over to make a call and wasn't in any need of help.

As he continued driving, he recalled the few things Frank had said to him during the visit. Frank had given only one-word answers to George's questions to acknowledge that he was listening as George rambled on about the places he had hiked and camped. He remembered the one question Frank asked, just before George was leaving, and how it had surprised him.

"Did you bring your Bible?" Frank had asked. George had not answered at first. He had patted the front of his jacket, checking the breast pocket, thinking it might hold the small edition of the New Testament that he sometimes took with him to the hospital. Maybe he had placed it in his jacket before leaving Pie Town, he thought, and since forgotten about it. After all, he did go visit Millie Watson; without thinking, he might have left it in his pocket for this visit. But as it turned out, he didn't have the little volume. He had not brought it with him to the hospital or the jail cell. Millie Watson had not asked for scripture, so he hadn't thought of it until Frank made his request.

Shaking his head in response, George had wondered why Frank asked that question. "Was there something you wanted to hear?"

he had asked, knowing that Frank claimed not to read the Bible, claimed not to be a Christian. And Frank had simply stood up from the table where they were sitting across from each other.

"Jeremiah has always been a favorite of mine," Frank had said. "I especially appreciate the prophet's words regarding the joyful return of the exiles. I like that they go back to where they started." And with that he had smiled and nodded. Frank had then glanced over to the guard and that had ended their time together.

George thought about these parting words. He thought about Frank's silence for most of the visit and then his surprising question and final remarks. Had it been a clue? George wondered. Had Frank told him something that would help him find Raymond? Was Frank giving him permission to locate his son — and hinting at the direction to take?

George switched on his headlights as the sun set and tried to think about what he knew about the book and the Old Testament prophet Jeremiah. He recalled from his seminary studies that the book of Jeremiah had a wealth of detail concerning various trials faced by the prophet, as well as a series of laments, words of struggle between a man and God. George remembered that the book included a collection of oracles against Judah and the people of Jerusalem as well as a hopeful scroll, the book of consolation, which prophesied what would come when the people of Israel were allowed to return home after being exiled. This was the part, George suddenly realized, that Frank had mentioned.

He drove along, trying to remember the passage, and finally, realizing that he couldn't recall exactly what was in that section, he pulled off at a roadside rest area, stopped the car, and opened the glove compartment to pull out the Bible that was always in his car. He flipped it open to the book of Jeremiah and searched the pages until he finally found the thirtieth chapter, the beginning of the oracles of hope. He read through that and into the next until his eyes fell upon the fifteenth verse of the thirty-first chapter. Suddenly, Frank's request for the Bible and his final words made sense. He had indeed given George a clue to Raymond's whereabouts:

Thus says the Lord: A voice is heard in Ramah, lamentation and bitter weeping, Rachel is weeping for her children; she refuses to be comforted for her children, because they are no more.

George closed the book and realized that Raymond was likely to be hiding on the Navajo Reservation, north of Pie Town and west of the lava beds, the area where Frank was from and where his family still lived, the area Frank claimed to have recently visited, explaining his absence. By using the Old Testament passage, Father George realized, Frank had let the priest know that Raymond had gone to Ramah, an area in New Mexico with the same name as the place in Jeremiah 31. Even though they were pronounced differently, the two place names were spelled exactly the same, and George was sure it was a clue.

Father George slapped the steering wheel, excited about solving the puzzle. He returned the Bible to the glove compartment and sat back in his seat, pleased with himself for figuring things out. Already planning his trip to Ramah, he laughed and put the car in gear.

He still didn't know what he would do if he found Raymond, whether he would try to talk him into turning himself in or just explain what was going on in Pie Town. He didn't have a script and didn't know what words of assurance or encouragement or comfort he could bring to the young man. But at least he understood that Frank had trusted him with the information on where his son was. That in itself, George thought, was a lot.

He pulled back onto the highway without noticing the dark sedan parked behind him, the one he had seen at the diner earlier that day, the one that had also been in the parking lot at the detention center in Albuquerque, the one driven by FBI agents, the one that had been following him all the way home on Highway 60.

TWENTY-SIX

Trina had had enough. The FBI agents had been sitting in their car outside the garage for two days, they had parked across from her house the entire previous night, and they had even followed her as she drove to Frieda's house to pick up Alexandria and to Socorro to get groceries. After forty-eight hours of surveillance, she had had enough. She knew there was no reason for her to be watched this way. She knew they had no cause to intimidate her with their vigilance, and she was going to put a stop to it.

After she checked and locked all the outside doors at five o'clock, she stomped out of the office, made a beeline to the car parked in the vacant lot across the street from the garage, and walked right up to the driver's side of the car. Her back was still tender, and she moved more slowly than she had before the accident, but she could still get to where she wanted to go without too much difficulty.

The man inside rolled down the window.

"Is there something you want?" she asked.

The driver smiled. The encounter seemed to amuse him. "I beg your pardon," he said.

There was a woman on the passenger side, and Trina stuck her head in the window to get a good look at both of them. She noticed that they were young, maybe thirty, and that they both were wearing dark blue suits, white shirts, and a short hairstyle. The woman appeared more masculine than the man who was driving.

"Is there some reason you're watching me?" Trina asked, pulling her head out of the window now that she had seen both of the agents. "You follow me to work. You follow me home. You follow me to my daughter's caregiver's house. I'm beginning to think you might have a crush on me."

The driver laughed. "Which one of us?" he asked.

"Well, now that I've seen you both up close, I'd have to say I'm not sure about that."

The man punched the woman next to him and laughed. He turned to Trina. "I'd say it was her."

The passenger punched him back.

Trina rolled her eyes. She had expected a

more mature response than the one she had been given. "Look, I don't know where Raymond is. I haven't seen him in almost a week. He's taken off somewhere, and nobody knows where he is. I don't know. His father doesn't know. And you're never going to find out by sitting out here where everybody can see you stalking me." She placed both of her hands on the driver's door.

"Well, we're just going to stay right here to make sure he doesn't need a hug and come home," the driver responded. He grinned at Trina. "Why are you walking so slowly?" he asked. "You hurt or something?"

"Why are you sitting in a car? You fat or something?" she replied.

The passenger laughed.

"Why do you have Frank Twinhorse locked up?" Trina asked.

The driver stared straight ahead and didn't answer. That last question had apparently angered him.

"Because he is a known associate of the fugitive," the passenger replied. "And we have reason to believe that he knows the whereabouts of his son and is refusing to give us proper information. We also have suspicions that Frank Twinhorse may be running a drug operation out of his garage."

Trina laughed. "That's the craziest thing I ever heard. If you have those suspicions, why don't you come into the garage and see for yourself? Come and inspect the place where Frank spends most of his time. Come on, I'll gladly give you a tour."

There was no response.

"Well, I've got some proper information for you." Trina walked slowly to the other side. She tapped on the window, and the female agent watched as the driver rolled down the other window. She leaned inside.

"Raymond Twinhorse is not a drug dealer. He did not steal from Gilbert Diaz. He doesn't even know about the incident at the Silver Spur. He left Datil, and somebody else stole the money you seem so concerned about. And Frank Twinhorse doesn't sell or do drugs. So why don't you save the taxpayers some money and go search for somebody else?"

The female agent glared at Trina. "How do you know what Raymond knows and doesn't know?" she asked. "Have you had contact with your boyfriend?"

Trina grinned. "Well, you ought to know the answer to that since you've been glued to those binoculars following every move I've made in the last two days. Did you see me having any contact with my boyfriend?"

The woman shrugged. "Not lately, but you just never know when lover boy might show up," she said with a sneer.

"Oh, so that's it," Trina said, still leaning into the window. "Miss Secret Agent, you can't find your own boyfriend, so you took this job to watch and learn from other girls who do have a love life."

She stood up.

" 'Course, now that I have seen you in that attractive uniform, wearing that butch haircut, and discovered your winning personality, I'm not sure that even getting a good look at how it's done is really going to help you out that much."

The driver cleared his throat.

"You just watch yourself, Ms. Thing," the female agent warned.

"I don't think I have to do that since it clearly appears as if you're doing that for me," Trina replied. She kicked the car and stormed back to the office.

She had said everything she could think to say, and it was clear that nothing was going to change the agents' plan to watch her. Pulling her keys from her pocket, she decided to get ready to leave for the day.

Confronting the agents hadn't changed anything. They were there to stay. But then she had another thought.

249

She didn't have to pick up Alexandria until after dinner since she had told Frieda that she had to go over to Malene's. She glanced in the direction of the agents. She figured that since she was feeling better and had a little extra time, and since the agents had been so condescending toward her, she might as well have some fun.

She got into her truck gingerly, careful not to irritate her back, and started the engine. She pulled around the garage and stopped in front of the FBI agents' car. She rolled down her window and stuck out her head. "Okay, I know you want to follow me, so here we go. Don't lag behind now," she said with a smile. "Oh, and you might want to buckle up. This little drive may be a bit tricky."

With that, she rolled up her window, revved her engine, and spun her tires as she pulled off. She watched in the rearview mirror as the car hurried to catch up.

She started up Highway 60, heading east out of town, trying to figure out the best road to take. When she got to the intersection, she knew exactly what to do. She waited to make sure the agents were following, then pulled onto the worst dirt road in the vicinity, Forest Road 56, south behind Alegres Mountain.

She didn't know what kind of engine the agents had in the four-door sedan they were driving, but she was sure their shocks weren't like the ones in her truck. The heavy-duty shocks that she and Frank had installed were well suited for the unpaved roads in Catron County. She had also made sure she had four-wheel-drive capability to handle the off-road terrain, and she had bought oversized tires to raise the body of the truck. She was well prepared for this drive.

Trina watched the car behind her as it tried to keep up and laughed when she realized that government agents might know how to handle city streets, but they sure didn't have the skills or equipment to drive the forest roads in New Mexico during monsoon season. She knew what everyone in Catron County knew but most outsiders didn't: the mud in the summer was worse than the snow and ice in the winter.

She kept driving south, watching the agents' car in her mirror, laughing every time she led them over a rough patch, through the deep mud, across the switchbacks. She was enjoying herself. She had always liked four-wheeling anyway. And this spot east of town happened to be an area she knew and liked especially well.

The road returning to town was easy to miss, and anyone who missed it could end up driving around lost for days. She figured that if the agents kept dropping back, she'd be able to lose them by the time she hit the fork at Nester Draw. Then they would be stuck out there until somebody came to get them — if they could contact anyone. The cell signals in Catron County weren't all that reliable.

Trina noticed the car swerve and slide and suddenly felt a twinge of guilt. She thought about Roger and what he would think, about Frank and how unhappy he would be that she had made a tow truck driver have to go out there. On the verge of changing her mind, she hit her brakes and stopped. Maybe it wasn't very nice to drive the city folks out there and leave them stranded. However, her resolve to do the right thing didn't last long. Trina recalled how rude the two agents had been when she confronted them, how arrogant they had both been, and she couldn't help herself — she sped up. She didn't really care what Roger or Frank would say about her actions. She decided for herself that a lesson in humility might be just the thing the FBI agents needed.

She laughed and hit the accelerator, making a quick right while the agents in the car behind her spun and slid, finally landing in a spot where the mud was more than a foot deep. Trina kept driving west on 56 and then headed north on 95 at Mangas. When she returned to Highway 60, just south of Omega, she turned east and drove into town.

"Good luck getting out of there!" She yelled to no one in particular, rolling down the window and laughing.

She slowed down as she made her way into Pie Town and headed toward her house, not wanting to call attention to herself in case other agents in town were watching or had gotten a call from the ones who were now stuck. Passing her house on her way to Malene's, she immediately noticed the black truck sitting in her driveway. At first she wasn't sure if she had company or not, but then she figured it was more likely that the relief agents had already arrived to take over for the two she had just lost.

Trina was going to just drive by and let them try to find their colleagues on their own, but when she got to the corner she turned around, once again feeling a little guilty for what she had done. She decided that, at the very least, she would tell the new pair where the other agents' car had stalled.

Trina returned to her house. She pulled into the driveway and got out of her truck and walked up to the other vehicle. She was grinning as she sidled up to the driver's side. She tapped on the window without looking inside.

"I hate to be the one to tell you, but you boys may need some chains to help pull your buddies out of the mud." She stopped talking as she peered into the lowered window. When the driver showed his face, she fell back a few steps. She could hardly believe her eyes.

"Hello, Trina," the man said with a grin. "Been a while since Tucson."

"It's you" was all she could think to say.

TWENTY-SEVEN

Francine was watching the scenery out of the passenger's window. It was the desert, a lot like Catron County, but it was not Pie Town. Where she was used to seeing empty spaces, cattle ranges, and forest roads, there were apartment buildings and strip malls. This was the big city, Phoenix, Arizona, and after being away for four days, Francine was starting to get homesick.

"You want to eat at that little Mexican place we went to the first night?" Bernie asked. They were driving back to her friend Pam's house after visiting the museum downtown. "Pam was going to church tonight, right?" he asked.

Francine nodded. "Yes, I told her not to worry about our dinner tonight." She shook her head. "I hate how she thinks she has to fix all of our meals while we're here."

"She's just being a good host," Bernie responded.

Francine smiled. She turned to Bernie. She was so glad they were together, so grateful for the relationship. She reached over and squeezed him on the arm. "Thank you," she said.

"For what?" he asked.

"For bringing me here," she replied. "For being with me."

Bernie shrugged. "I didn't do anything special."

"Yes, you did," she said. "You supported my decision. You left everything and came out here with me."

Bernie looked over at Francine. He could see she was bothered by something. "You okay?" he asked.

She shook her head. "I'm just worried about things at home," she replied.

Francine had wanted to call Fred and Bea every day since she left town just to find out the latest on Raymond and what was going on in the investigation, but every time she reached for the phone she stopped herself. After talking to the priest and making a quick exit, she had chosen not to contact anyone. She was afraid that the FBI might be searching for Bernie and her and figured the less she knew the better off they would be. She didn't want to have to make another choice about what to say or tell someone what she knew. She didn't know what to think. She had been miserable back in Pie Town, and she had remained miserable ever since she left.

Bernie turned back to the road and kept driving. "It's lovely here, don't you think?" he commented. "The lemon trees are nice, and I like Pam's little neighborhood."

Francine glanced over at Bernie. She knew he was bored to death being away from home this long. "Bernie, you don't have to lie to me."

"No," he responded, shaking his head, trying to sound convincing. "Really, it's nice to be in Phoenix. So many things to see and do. It's been a delightful trip." He smiled. "I enjoyed the museum today and the movie yesterday. It's been good to get away with you for a few days." He winked at Francine. "And what about you?" he asked.

She seemed confused. "What?"

"Do you like it here or do you prefer the country?"

"Oh, I could never live in a big city like Phoenix," she responded. "You should know that by now. Don't you hate this traffic and the smog?"

Bernie nodded. "It is different than what we're used to, that's for sure. But I was just starting to think you might get used to having a shopping center within walking distance, all these fancy restaurants we've been to. I was thinking you might start liking the city life."

"I doubt that would happen," she noted. "But I have enjoyed all the places we've eaten at since being here. There's lots of choices, that's for sure. We've had some great meals."

"I don't know. I haven't had anything to eat that's better than your pecan pies, and I have to say, I miss Fred's enchiladas."

Francine turned to him. "See, I was right, you are getting homesick."

"Just missing the good life."

Francine sighed. "I know you've got stuff you need to do," she said.

"No need for you to worry about that. It'll all be there when we get back," he responded. He made a turn into the shopping mall where the restaurant was.

"I know," she said. "And we should probably think about heading out. I just don't want to go home too soon. I'm still worried that we're in trouble."

There was a pause in the conversation as Bernie found a parking place. He eased into the space and turned off the engine.

"I don't really think we're in any trouble, Francie." He turned toward her. "I figure

258

by now the whole thing's been cleared up. Raymond didn't steal any money. Frank hasn't done anything wrong. We're really just hiding out for no reason."

Francine nodded. "I felt like it was the right thing to leave when we did, but now I just feel guilty."

Bernie studied her. He waited for more of an explanation.

"I guess I wonder if maybe we should have stayed, stood up for Raymond. Instead, I made this choice for us to sneak away in the dead of night like we're some kind of cowards. That doesn't seem like either one of us." She dropped her face, shaking her head.

"Well, first of all," said Bernie, reaching over and squeezing Francine on the arm, "it wasn't the dead of night. It was lunchtime. And second, it didn't sound to me like the FBI was too interested in what folks said about Raymond. So I don't feel bad about any of this," he commented.

"Yes, but it seems like we actually think he's guilty too, since we ran out." Francine reached into her purse for a tissue. "For us just to take off like that because he left his bike at your fence, it just seems like we think he's done wrong." She glanced at Bernie. She hesitated. "Do you think he's done

259

something wrong?"

"Like what?" Bernie responded.

Francine shrugged. "Stealing the money at the Silver Spur?"

Bernie looked away. "No," he answered.

Francine was surprised by such a short response. "Do you think he's capable of dealing drugs?"

"I don't know. Probably not dealing," he answered.

"What?" she asked. "You think Raymond could be involved in drugs?"

Bernie shook his head. "I don't know," he repeated. He shrugged. "I hear all these stories about soldiers getting into stuff when they're fighting overseas. And then they get home and have all these demons to face. I'm just saying, it makes sense."

"What makes sense?" Francine wanted to know. "That soldiers do drugs or that Raymond is addicted?"

Bernie blew out a breath. He had not really wanted to talk about his thoughts on the matter. "He's been acting strange. You have to agree with that, right?"

Francine didn't respond.

"I mean, at first I didn't want to believe he could be doing anything illegal, but since we've been away, I've been thinking about it a lot. Maybe it is drugs that are making him act this way." He reached up, turned the engine back on, rolled down the windows, and turned the engine off. It was late in the evening, and there was a nice breeze.

Francine considered what Bernie was suggesting, but then shook her head. "I don't think it's drugs," she finally responded. "I think it's that post-traumatic stress disorder, just like we watched on television. These young people get sent over there and see all kinds of terrible things, have all kinds of terrible experiences. How can that not change you, make you turn into somebody else?"

"I know you're right," Bernie responded. "Of course Raymond isn't involved with drugs. I know him. I know he's not an addict. I don't know why I said that."

Francine studied Bernie. There was a long pause.

"I know why," she replied.

Bernie turned to her, waiting.

"You said what you did because none of us want to believe that our young people are traumatized by our wars. We don't want to think that as the most advanced nation in the world we send healthy, bright, functional teenagers over there and that they come back broken, changed, lost. We want to think that our national pride, our flag-flying patriotism is enough to keep our children from breaking under the stresses of battle." Francine shook her head.

"We try to make ourselves believe that everything is just fine, so that when they come home and something is wrong, we'd rather believe that it's drugs, or that they're getting in with the wrong crowd, or that they're just not strong enough. It's easier to think any of those things than to face the fact that every time we decide as a country to go in and fight these wars it's our young people we send to fight them who suffer the consequences."

Bernie didn't respond.

"We don't want to know that war causes so much harm." She sat up in her seat. "And my decision to make us run to Phoenix instead of standing up to the FBI agents and telling them what I think about Raymond, telling them that we would protect him proudly, just goes to show you that the real cowards are those of us who don't want to deal with the truth."

"What truth?" Bernie asked, not following her.

"The truth of the horrors of war, the truth of post-traumatic stress disorder, the truth of Raymond's need for treatment and community and care."

"You're sounding pretty fired up there, Francie." He smiled.

"You're damn right I'm fired up, and I tell you what else I am." She shook her head. "I'm ashamed of myself. I should have never put my tail between my legs and made you drive me over to Phoenix. I should have been willing to stay and support Raymond, to go to his accusers and defend him." She paused.

"We know that boy. We love that boy, and so does everybody else in Pie Town. Raymond Twinhorse is no thief, and he does not deal drugs. If he takes them, it's because he's hurting, and he needs his town to stand behind him and get him the help he needs, not hightail it to Phoenix at the first hint of trouble. And what about Trina?" She turned to Bernie.

He waited.

"What kind of friend am I being to her?" She shook her head and turned away. "She would never have taken off somewhere if you were in trouble. She would have stayed by my side. She would have been there for me."

Bernie reached out to her, grabbing her by the hand.

"I am a terrible friend," she added, the tears filling her eyes. "We have to leave here.

We have to go home."

Bernie leaned over, wrapping Francine in his arms. He knew that a decision had been made. "I'll get the suitcase packed." He reached to start the engine, but then paused. "Or do you want to eat first?" he asked.

She smiled. "Well, since we're here, we might as well have supper. They do have good sopapillas."

"Yes, they do," he agreed. "And Francie, you are not a bad friend," he noted. "You've just been absent a few days is all." He grabbed her hand and held it. "Trina knows you care about her, and you can tell her again when we get there tonight." He winked at her.

She dropped her head with a nod. She was glad she had finally come to her senses. She was glad they were going home.

TWENTY-EIGHT

Roger had decided to make another visit to the Silver Spur and find out for himself what Gilbert had been feeding the FBI. When he walked into the bar, he was surprised to see one of the two agents who had been in Pie Town since the robbery sitting at a table near the door. He appeared to be glancing over notes.

"Well, well, I guess the FBI has a more lenient policy about drinking on the job than the state of New Mexico and the local county offices," Roger said, standing near him.

"Hello, Sheriff," the man responded. "I don't think we've had the pleasure of meeting." He stood up. "I'm Kevin Cochran." He held out his hand. "Agent Williams's partner."

Roger took his hand. "Sheriff Roger Benavidez," he responded. "But I guess you knew that."

"Please," the agent said, "have a seat. Join me." He smiled and pulled out the chair next to him. "I figured you'd be in Pie Town," he said.

"This is still in Catron County," Roger noted. "And there is still an open investigation, as far as I've heard." He sat down. He turned to the bar. Gilbert was talking on the phone.

"Yes, yes, that's true," Agent Cochran agreed. "It's nice when law enforcement agencies can unite and work together on some things, isn't it?"

Roger eyed the young man. "Whatever you say, Agent." He glanced around. "Where's your partner?" he asked.

"Somewhere at the other end of your county," he replied. "I think he's taking reports from some of the townsfolk."

"And what kind of reports would he be interested in from Catron County?" Roger wanted to know.

The agent shrugged. "Drug dealing, Raymond Twinhorse's associates, just the usual kinds of questions for folks who know the fugitive."

"Raymond Twinhorse isn't a fugitive," Roger responded. "I want to speak to the young man with regards to a small-time robbery that happened at a place he sometimes frequents. I hardly think that makes him a fugitive." He pulled a toothpick out of his pocket and stuck it between his teeth. "Unless you got some other case you're investigating that you'd like to clue me in on." He studied the agent. He still had not been brought up to speed on what exactly the FBI was doing in Catron County and why they were interested in Raymond. All he knew was what everybody in the county was saying, and he knew most of that wasn't based on any facts.

"We just think there's more going on in your little southwest corner of the state than the Very Large Array antennas and serving fresh desserts."

Roger smiled. "We have a nice festival in the fall. That's pretty exciting. And there's good rock climbing over at Mogollon."

Agent Cochran nodded. "I'll keep those things in mind, but that's not really what we're talking about, Sheriff."

"Then, please tell me, what are we talking about?" Roger asked.

"Drugs," the agent answered. "Meth, cocaine, heroin, the usuals. We got information that there's a nice little connection here to Mexico. Used to be up in Chimayo, and now it's moved down south."

Roger shook his head. "Then you need to

check out the source of your information. Because if there was an operation, it was small-time and it was located at the ranch at Old Horse Springs that I reported almost a month ago and it's now shut down. There's nothing else around here. If there was, I'd have heard about it."

"Without trying to sound disrespectful, Sheriff, maybe your ear isn't as close to the ground as you think." Agent Cochran turned to the bar and held up his coffee cup to Gilbert, signaling for a refill. "You want something?" he asked Roger.

Before he could answer, Gilbert walked over with the coffeepot and an extra cup, which he set down in front of the sheriff. "I hope ya'll ain't planning to stay all day. You sort of cramp my style here, if you know what I'm saying." He poured a cup for Roger. "Folks don't like to drink when the law is hanging around."

"Gilbert, I don't know how to assist you. First you make me come over here so that you can report a robbery, claimed I couldn't get here fast enough. Then you apparently called the feds for reasons I've yet to understand. And now you complain because we're sitting in your establishment, trying to solve the case. I'm having a hard time knowing how to help you." Roger reached for the cup and took a sip.

"I want you to catch that little son of a bitch that robbed me, and I'm pretty sure you can't do it sitting in here drinking my coffee." Gilbert turned and walked away.

"Look," Roger said, getting back to his conversation with the FBI agent, "I don't know what you heard about Alamo. I can tell you that there are no drugs there. And I have known Frank and Raymond Twinhorse all my life. They aren't involved in any drug operation." He put down his cup.

"What I think is that your partner screwed up by busting into Alamo and not finding anything, and he's desperate to have something in Catron County to make up for his stupid mistake. I suspect there's some supervisor somewhere demanding reasonable cause for that search, and Williams is doing everything he can to try and find one. And I'm telling you, there's nothing here."

Cochran sighed. He wasn't going to argue with Roger. "Why don't you tell me about the Twinhorse people. Who are these Navajo who live outside the reservation?"

Roger shook his head. He could tell he wasn't getting through to the young agent. "Not that this information matters, but Frank's people are the Ramah Navajo. They're the largest of the Navajo Indian groups living away from Window Rock. The reservation, north of here, is almost 150,000 acres and covers a lot of territory. The land was settled by the Mormons in the late 1800s, and this group of Navajo had intermarried with the Apache. Most of the Navajo and Apache were exiled to Fort Sumner in 1863 on what's known as the "Long Walk." When they were released or when some escaped, many of them settled in the area around Ramah, one of the places where some members of the group had made homes before. They've been there ever since."

"Why doesn't Frank live over there?" Agent Cochran asked.

"I don't have the answer for that," Roger responded. "He had a falling-out with his people." He studied the agent. "But you should know that by now, shouldn't you? How long do you plan to keep him locked up without having anything to charge him with?"

Agent Cochran glanced away, and Roger could see he was suddenly ill at ease with the direction of the conversation.

"What's happened?" Roger asked.

Agent Cochran turned again to face the sheriff. "Nothing's happened," he replied.

Roger continued to watch the man. He

waited for more of an explanation.

"Okay, the truth is that I'm not happy about that detention either. As far as what I know, we should only be interested in the boy, the son. Williams is the one who seems to think that if we keep his father locked up and Raymond finds out, he'll turn himself in."

Roger took another sip of coffee. "Well, that's actually the only smart plan your partner has come up with. Raymond would never want his father in jail because of something he's being accused of. If he knew Frank had been arrested and detained, he'd be here to clear his name and prove his innocence."

Agent Cochran placed both of his hands on the table, leaned in closer to the sheriff. "Why are you and your town so sure Raymond Twinhorse is innocent?" He pulled away. "That's the one thing that has me so puzzled about you and your little village. How can you be so sure he's not dealing drugs?"

Roger smiled. He relaxed a bit. "You got children?" he asked.

The man shook his head.

"You ever watch a child grow up?"

Cochran shrugged. "I've got a couple of nephews in Texas, but I'm not around them very much."

Roger nodded. "I have a daughter. She's twenty-three, lives out of state." He reached in his wallet and took out a picture to show the other man. "She's our only one."

Cochran glanced at the photo and smiled. "Attractive girl," he commented, unsure of why the sheriff was suddenly talking about his family.

Roger looked down at the photograph. "Angel has had difficulties in the past. Been involved in some stuff she shouldn't have. Ran with the wrong crowd. Got into drugs. I tried everything I could to straighten her out." He shook his head, stuck the picture back into his wallet. "And it took me a long time, but I learned I can't fix her. And let me just tell you, that's the absolute worst thing for a father to have to know."

Cochran was listening carefully.

Roger returned his wallet to his rear pocket.

"Frank raised Raymond side by side with my girl. They're like siblings, the two of them. When they were little, they stayed together night and day. They were inseparable." He stopped, took a sip of coffee, and continued.

"When she was a teenager and it became clear that she had a problem, lots of folks had plenty to say about her bad choices. People who had known her all her life just gave up on her, talked about her like she was trash, like she didn't matter. And when everybody else turned on her, turned on us, neither Frank nor Raymond left her side. They never stopped trying to get her back. They kept right on asking her to do things with them, inviting her over for meals, to go hiking or horseback riding, go camping, four-wheeling." He stopped, took a breath.

"She was dead set on heading down her own path, though. Got pregnant young and just kept falling further and further into her addiction. Lots of other people wanted to keep their children away from her, started treating her and her parents like we had a disease or something. But not Frank Twinhorse, and not his son Raymond."

Roger shook his head. "They never acted like she was ever any different than the little girl who had learned to ride her bicycle side by side with Raymond or sat next to him on the school bus. They never quit believing the best in her."

Agent Cochran shifted in his chair.

"So you ask me how I know this boy is innocent? You want to know how I'm so sure?"

The agent studied the sheriff, waiting for the answer.

"Because Raymond Twinhorse is just like his father. He was a good boy, and he is a fine young man. He is kind and loyal, and I believe the best about him because he is deserving of my faith. He earned it a very long time ago."

Cochran didn't respond.

"He is not involved in drugs. Believe me, I know those signs all too well. And he would never be involved in dealing them to others. He's seen the harm that drugs will do. He's not a thief. If something happened here, if there was some trouble of any kind, it is not about illegal activity, it's about him being in trouble. And in exactly the same way Frank and Raymond were there for me and my daughter, I intend to be there for them."

The FBI agent folded his arms and nodded his head. "Your point is well made" was his only comment.

There was a pause between them.

Cochran hesitated, glanced around the bar to see if anyone was listening. Roger watched as the young agent appeared to be making some decision. There was a long silent pause between them.

"I'm going to give you a bit of information, but if you tell anyone you heard it from me, I'll deny it." He studied the sheriff.

"You got it?" he asked.

Roger nodded.

"If you want to visit Frank Twinhorse, today might be the best day to do that."

Roger seemed confused.

"I can make that happen, but only today," Cochran added.

Roger leaned away from the table. "I guess your partner is busy doing other things."

Cochran nodded. "I suspect he'll be preoccupied for most of the day. Of course, your friends in Pie Town might not be too thrilled about that."

Roger stood up. He knew he should take the agent's offer as soon as it was given. "Good seeing you, Agent Cochran," he said and turned to walk away and then turned back. "So what made you decide to give me this opportunity, to let me see Frank?" he asked. "You growing a conscience?"

Cochran smiled. "Just a sucker for a good story," he replied.

Roger grinned, stuck the toothpick in his mouth, reached for his phone to check his messages, and made his way out of the bar.

TWENTY-NINE

"Something's wrong. I can just feel it." Malene had been trying to reach Trina all morning, and she wasn't answering her cell phone. Malene had already left five or six messages in the last hour and was thinking about calling the dispatcher to send Danny over to check on her.

Roger had gone to Datil. He had explained before they left that morning to go to work that he was heading over to the Silver Spur to talk again to Gilbert. He was hopeful, he told Malene, that he would find some clue about why the robbery at the bar was of such interest to the FBI. Still, she figured he would check his voice mail. She had left a message for him to call her when he was heading home.

Malene had also left a message with Father George, who had responded to the urgency in her voice by coming straight to Carebridge. He was wearing his collar and carrying his Book of Prayer and his Bible because he only understood that there was an emergency and Malene needed him to come to the nursing center as soon as possible. Assuming that one of the residents was in need of a priest, he hurried from the parking lot to the nurses' station where he knew Malene was assigned.

She started explaining as he rounded the corner in her direction. "Trina isn't answering any of her phones, not home or work or her cell. I've tried all morning." She shook her head. "No answer anywhere."

George was surprised that the emergency wasn't of a spiritual nature and didn't have anything to do with the residents at Carebridge, but he clearly saw the worry on his friend's face.

"Wait a minute," he said, trying to catch up. "This is about Trina?" He recalled a conversation he'd had with Malene the previous evening about the young woman. "I thought you said last night that you saw a truck in front of her house?"

Malene had called George just after he returned from Albuquerque because Trina hadn't shown up at her place, as originally planned, and she wanted to see if he knew her whereabouts. When he explained that he had been out of town and didn't know anything, she had told him that she would go looking for Trina. She then later called again to say that she had driven over to Trina's house and everything was fine.

"I saw her truck in the driveway, with another vehicle there too, but I never saw her. I thought maybe she had company or something."

"Did Frieda see her?"

"Frieda told me that she took Alexandria to Gallup yesterday afternoon and stayed longer than she expected. When she didn't get home until after dark, she left messages on Trina's phone to let her know that the baby could stay at her house that night. She just thought Trina had gotten the messages and agreed to the plan. But now it's after eleven o'clock, and Trina still hasn't called or gone over to Frieda's."

"Well, now I understand why you're concerned," he said. He thought about that morning and where Trina might be. "Has anybody seen her at the garage?"

Malene shook her head. "I haven't spoken to anyone else. You were the next person after Roger that I called."

"Do you think she's gotten an infection or something?"

"I don't think so," Malene replied. "She said she was feeling better."

278

George thought about Trina and where she might be. "I'm sure she's fine, probably just overslept. She's been so tired lately. And the truck was probably just somebody in the neighborhood checking on her, Francine or Christine maybe."

He recalled how exhausted Trina seemed the last time he saw her. She was so worried about Frank and Raymond, and she had mentioned to him that the burns kept her from sleeping very well. "But why don't I go to the house and see if she's there? If she's not, I'll also drive over to the garage."

Malene appeared relieved. "Thanks, Father George. I would go, but I'm the only nursing assistant on this floor."

George was getting ready to head back out to his car when he stopped and glanced out the glass door that led to the front parking area. He noticed again the sedan and the man who had been following him since yesterday evening. He had figured out the day before that he was being watched when he pulled into the Holy Family Church parking lot and the car that had been behind him on Highway 60 slowly drove past, went up the road about a hundred yards, turned around, and then stopped, parking on the street across from the church. He had seen the car again in the same place that morning.

"Hey," he said, turning back to Malene, "do you recognize that car?" He pointed out to the sedan in the front lot.

Malene peered out the front door.

"That would be the FBI agents from Albuquerque," she replied. "Williams it looks like. His partner is Cochran, younger, nicer. I don't see him, though." She kept watching. "I met them when I stopped by the diner yesterday morning trying to find Daddy." She paused.

"Wonder why they're here?" she asked. "I don't expect that one of the residents has anything to report." She turned to Father George. "Although Mrs. Henderson is pretty sure that we're an alien agency processing center and that we're doing testing on the residents. Maybe she called."

She smiled at the priest, but he wasn't listening very closely.

George kept staring at the man in the car. He thought about his visit with Frank from the previous day. Remembering that Agent Williams and Agent Cochran had been at the detention center, he suddenly realized that perhaps it was no coincidence that one of them had been following him ever since.

"I saw Frank yesterday," he announced to

Malene. She was dialing Roger to see how his meeting in Datil was going.

"In Albuquerque?"

George stuck his hands in his front pockets. He nodded.

"They let you in?" Malene asked, sounding surprised. She knew that Roger had tried all week to visit Frank Twinhorse and had been denied every time he made the attempt. She hung up the receiver.

"Yeah, Agent Cochran was there and gave the permission." He turned around again to see the man in the car right outside the door.

"How was Frank?"

He faced Malene. "He's okay," George replied.

"Did he tell you where Raymond is?"

Father George hesitated. "I think so." He blew out a breath. "In fact, that's where I was heading this morning. I was packing the car with some things I thought I would need when you called. I figured I'd be gone most of the day."

Malene waited. She could tell George had more to say.

"I think Frank told me in code where to find Raymond. He didn't say hardly anything during the entire visit, and then just before I was leaving he quoted scripture to me."

"Frank knows the Bible?" Malene asked. "I didn't think Frank cared for Christianity or its texts."

"I know," George agreed. "Me neither." He eyed the parking lot again. The car was still parked in the same spot. "I think it was a clue about Raymond's whereabouts. I think Frank was telling me so that I could find him and let him know what's going on here."

Malene nodded. "It sounds like that could be what he was doing. I'm sure he doesn't want Raymond to come into town with no idea about what happened in Datil the night he left."

George glanced up the hall. He could see Malene's supervisor coming up the hall. He nodded in her direction, and she waved to him. "I'm pretty sure we were being watched during the visit," George noted. "And I'm pretty sure they've been following me ever since I left Albuquerque."

"So you think they're hoping that you'll lead them to Raymond?"

George nodded. He suddenly had a sinking feeling that he had become part of the FBI's investigation. It dawned on him that he had been allowed to visit with Frank not because of luck or because of Agent Cochran's respect for a priest. Now it appeared that the visit had been a setup, and it also occurred to him that whoever had been listening during the visit may have also figured out the clue from Jeremiah, was already in Ramah, and had found Raymond. George shook those thoughts out of his mind, deciding to get back to the matter at hand. He would have to deal with Raymond and Ramah and the FBI later. Right now he needed to make sure Trina was okay.

"Maybe I should just get off work and ride by Trina's," Malene suggested, also mindful of the source of her worry. "Maybe you're already in trouble, and if they see you running over to Raymond's girlfriend's house, you'll just have more agents following you."

George thought about the implications of what Malene was saying. He thought about his concern for Trina and how things had changed for him in the previous couple of years. He recalled that when he first arrived in Pie Town things were very different for him and his relationship with the young woman.

Because of what Trina had taught him about a generous spirit and because of what his first year in Pie Town had meant to him, Father George Morris was no longer concerned about what caring for others, being there for others, might cost him. Right now he had not given even a second thought to how his actions might look, or what their consequences regarding Trina or anyone else in the community might be. He did not care how it might appear to FBI agents — or anyone else for that matter — that he would drive over and check on the girlfriend of the young man they kept referring to as a fugitive.

"I don't care if they follow me to her house. I don't care if they stop and question me about what I know and don't know. If Trina's in trouble, then maybe it'll be a good thing for them to be over there."

He watched the agent sitting in the car. "Maybe I should just ask him for a ride." And he winked at Malene and headed out.

THIRTY

Roger checked his messages when he got into his car and saw that Malene had called a couple of times. She was concerned, she said in her voice mail, about Trina. Apparently, there had been a strange truck parked in front of her house the night before, and this morning she wasn't answering her phones. Malene was worried about her, and even though he knew he should be heading to Albuquerque if he wanted to see Frank, he figured he should check on Trina first.

When he arrived at the house, the truck that his wife had said was seen there the night before was still there. He felt himself get a little anxious. Who was visiting Trina from Texas, and had they been invited? Had they stayed all night?

He was getting out of his car when Father George pulled in right behind him. Roger waited until the priest had gotten out of his station wagon and was standing beside him.

"Guess you got Malene's messages?" George was wearing his collar, something Roger had not seen him do except on Sundays.

"You have a funeral?" Roger asked.

Father George glanced down at his attire. "I thought it was a pastoral emergency over at Carebridge when Malene called," he replied.

Roger nodded. He turned to look in the direction of the vehicle parked in the driveway. "You know who drives that truck?" he asked.

George shook his head, but then remembered something. "Wait a minute. I saw that car yesterday, just outside of town, when I was driving back from Albuquerque," he noted. "You think Trina has company?"

Looking through the front window of the house, they could see that there was movement inside.

"Shall we both go in and check on her?" George asked.

"I don't see why not," Roger responded. "We're both here."

They walked to the front stoop. George noticed the dark sedan, slowly driving past them on the street, before he faced the door and rang the bell. He watched as the car continued heading west, away from them.

He was about to say something to Roger about being followed, but then thought better of it. He was tired of thinking about the surveillance.

There was a short wait, and then the door opened.

"Hey," Trina called out. Her face was flushed, and she seemed surprised to see her friends.

The two men waited to be invited in, but she remained standing at the door.

Roger tried to peek around her. "You okay?" he asked.

She nodded. "Perfect." She could see the men were concerned. "Just have a surprise guest is all," she replied, her voice about a pitch higher than usual.

Father George also tried to see around her to figure out who was inside. "Should we make their acquaintance?" he asked. He had never known Trina to be so reticent before, and he wondered who had caused her to act so nervous.

She paused and then pulled open the door, inviting both of them in. She walked in behind them and then passed them in the hallway to move inside and stand near the sofa.

Roger and George walked into the living room and saw a man sitting next to where

Trina had stopped. He stood up with a big grin. He was nice-looking, about thirty-five they both guessed.

"Well, a priest and a sheriff," Trina's guest noted. "That can't be good." He reached over and squeezed Trina on the arm.

Roger introduced himself first. "Roger Benavidez," he said, holding out his hand.

The man nodded and took the extended hand. "Conroe Jasper," he responded. Then he turned to Father George. "Conroe Jasper," he said, offering the same greeting to the priest.

Father George smiled. "George Morris," he answered, taking the man by the hand.

"Well, my goodness, is everything okay?" the man asked. "Should me and Trina be worried?"

"Everything's fine," George replied. "We just wanted to check on Trina."

"Well, how about that? Trina never told me she had made friends with such powerful officials in her new town." He winked at the men.

There was an awkward moment, and Trina motioned for the men to sit down. They all obliged, with Conroe taking his same spot again on the sofa, Roger and George sitting in the chairs situated on both sides of the couch. She remained standing.

"So how do you know Trina?" George asked. He glanced over at their hostess. She was clearly uncomfortable.

"Conroe and I met in Amarillo," she answered for him.

George nodded.

"It's been a while," the stranger added, patting the space next to him for her to join him.

Trina sat down beside him, gingerly, as Roger and George noticed.

"What was the name of that little bar where you worked?" Conroe asked. But before she could answer, he asked another question. "And that bartender, what was his name again?"

"Lester," Trina replied.

"That's right," Conroe noted. "He never did like me," he added.

Roger cleared his throat. "You visiting Pie Town?"

"Funniest thing." He laughed. "A couple of days ago I heard that a girl named Trina was living here. When I heard that, I couldn't believe my luck. So I checked it out, and it was actually my Trina, here in Pie Town. I had a day off, and I just drove up last evening." He winked at Trina. "I think I gave her a start."

"Apparently Conroe ate at Fred and Bea's

a few days ago. Heard my name from Oris and came back." Trina glanced over in George's direction. "He stopped by last night and then again this morning," she explained. "He was just returning to his home in Abilene when you got here."

Roger and George both thought that sounded like a hint for the man to leave, but he didn't seem to take it. He just smiled and nodded. "I can stay a little bit longer."

There was another awkward pause.

"Malene was concerned because Frieda called. She said Alexandria was waiting for you." Roger sat up a bit in his seat.

Trina's eyes darted from Roger to Conroe and then over to George. Everybody could sense her anxiety. It was written all over her face.

"Alexandria?" Conroe spoke up. "That the little girl you babysit?"

Trina didn't answer, and George and Roger both seemed confused.

"Trina told me she watches a little girl in the evenings when she gets off work at the garage." He seemed to be studying the men. "I told her that she sure seemed to have a lot of baby stuff around just to be babysitting."

He waited. When there was no response, he kept talking. "I guess I'm surprised that

Trina chose to babysit is all. She always told me she didn't like children." He turned to the young woman. "You don't want kids, isn't that right?" He smiled.

Trina glanced away.

"Mr. Jasper, do you have a family?" Roger asked, eyeing the stranger, trying to figure out exactly who he was and what he was doing in Pie Town.

The man nodded. "I have two sons, twins," he responded. "My wife and I divorced just a year ago." He glanced over at Trina. She wasn't watching him. "She took the boys to Dallas, so I don't get to see them that often."

"That must be hard," the sheriff responded.

"It is," Conroe replied. "I drove a truck for most of their lives when they were little. And now I only get to see them about once every couple of months." He softened. "That's a difficult thing, to be away from your children."

Roger and George were still trying to understand who Conroe Jasper was and why Trina would lie about Alexandria to him. Something seemed off about the relationship between the two of them, and they were having a difficult time figuring it out.

"I hear ya'll had a lot of excitement here

recently." Conroe decided to change the subject. He was talking to Roger.

"I'm sorry?" Roger responded, not understanding the reference.

"The FBI barreling into some Indian reservation here, a robbery over at the other end of the county, somebody running drugs up here. . . ." Conroe draped his arm over the back of the sofa around Trina. "Ya'll sound like you're having more trouble with laws being broken than they do on the border."

"You sure seem to know a lot about Catron County just to be passing through." It was George making the comment.

"You stop at a bar or a small-town diner and you hear a lot," Conroe responded.

Roger nodded. "I don't think it's anything too dangerous or worrisome," he replied. "We're mostly a pretty quiet little community."

Conroe nodded. "I 'spect so," he said, glancing over to Trina. "But you must have a little something going on or she wouldn't have settled here." He grinned. "Trina likes a little excitement." He touched her on the shoulder, and she flinched.

Father George could see Trina's growing discomfort.

"I was trying to talk her into coming back

to Texas with me when you two showed up," Conroe said, surprising the two other men. "Trina drove long hauls with me. She's as good a driver as anybody I know. We used to have some really good times."

Trina could feel all eyes on her. She fidgeted in her seat.

"You and Trina used to drive together?" the priest asked, starting to understand exactly who Conroe Jasper was.

"Abilene to San Diego, Denver to Las Cruces, Dallas to Tucson. . . ."

And as soon as he named the Arizona town, George figured it out. Even though Trina had never told him the name of the man she left when she came to Pie Town, she had mentioned that he was a truck driver and that she left him in Tucson.

Roger understood it all now too. Trina had told him the same details of her last romantic relationship. Conroe Jasper was the guy who broke her heart. And if Roger was calculating correctly, Conroe Jasper was more than just a former lover — he was also the father of Alexandria. Suddenly, everything became clear to the sheriff.

"Yeah, well, about taking her back to Texas," Roger commented. "We've sort of grown attached to our Trina." He smiled. "We'd have to put up a fight to let her go," he added.

Conroe didn't seem to have a rebuttal to offer, but Roger and George could see him watching Trina. "Yeah, she was telling me that she was happy here." He slid his fingers over his chin and seemed to be thinking. "She was a little vague about why, but the only thing I can figure is she's got a beau." He turned to Roger. " 'Course, I've been around all evening and now this morning and I've not seen hide nor hair of him, so I think she might just be trying to blow me off." He leaned forward, getting closer to the sheriff. "What do you think?"

Roger looked at Trina and then over to Conroe. "Trina's old enough to make up her own mind and tell you what she wants to tell you. Father George and I are just her friends, but we're very protective of her." It appeared as if he was going to say more, but then he just stopped.

Conroe nodded as if he understood the message the sheriff was giving him. "Well, as a friend of Trina's and somebody who cares about her very much too, I'm glad to hear that. And maybe if she'll let me stop by from time to time, you can both get to know me and see that my intentions are honorable and that I can be very protective of her as well." He cleared his throat and then peered down at his watch. He seemed ready to take his leave. "Well, I've got to go check out of the motel in Datil and head over to Abilene."

Everyone stood up with him. Roger held out his hand. "Nice to meet you, Conroe," he said politely.

"Nice to meet you, Sheriff Benavidez." Conroe turned to the priest. "And you, Father George." He smiled.

"Mr. Jasper," George said softly.

He moved closer to Trina and held her by the arms. She stiffened. "I hope to see you again, Trina," he said and bent down to kiss her on the cheek.

Roger and George watched as her face reddened. She did not speak as Conroe made his way out of the house. The three of them watched as he strode to his truck, got in, waved at them, and drove away. The house fell silent.

Trina turned to them both, but didn't speak.

It was George who spoke up. "You want to tell us about that or should we just make a calculated guess?"

Trina blew out a long breath without making a reply and walked over to the phone. "I need to call Frieda" was all she said.

THIRTY-ONE

Father George understood that this was his only opportunity to drive to Ramah to look for Raymond without the FBI agents following him. He hated the thought of not showing up for the meeting scheduled at church that evening, but he felt confident that the worship committee could handle the items on the agenda without him. He also hated the thought of leaving Trina when she was so upset at Conroe's sudden reappearance in her life, but knew that Roger and Malene or Francine and her other friends could help her with that situation.

When Trina had left to go pick up Alexandria, leaving Roger and George standing alone in the living room of her house, Roger invited George to go with him to Albuquerque to see Frank. George explained that he had visited their friend already and that he had a meeting to prepare for. It was then that he suddenly noticed that the FBI agent was no longer following him: the dark sedan was nowhere to be seen up or down the street, the driver parked and watching, nor was it driving slowly past the house. With this realization, he had suddenly understood that this could be his chance to find Raymond.

He had driven home assuming that the FBI agent was likely to be waiting for him at the church. When he pulled up to the rectory and saw no cars in the parking lot and no cars parked on the side of the road, he knew he was free and clear. And then, when he called Malene to see if she had talked to Trina, she said that Roger had come by on his way to visit Frank and told her what had happened. According to Roger, the agents had both left town and as far as he knew were done with their work in Catron County for the day. For whatever reason, George understood, they were leaving him alone and providing him with the chance to get out of town.

He placed a call to the head of the worship committee to explain that he wouldn't be there for the meeting and then jumped in his car. Heading west on Highway 60, he was glad that he had studied the map earlier that morning when he had gotten the call from Malene and driven over to the nursing home. He recalled that at Quemado he would take Highway 36 north to Fence Lake, and then the dirt road to State Road 125 to the Ramah Indian Area, progressing on to Pine Hill. He hoped that there he would find someone from the Twinhorse family who might know where to find Raymond.

As he drove down the highway, checking his rearview mirror and hoping not to see the dark sedan behind him, his thoughts turned to Trina. He wondered what would happen with Conroe if the man was serious about wanting to reconcile with Trina. He wondered what he would do when he found out he had a daughter and why Trina had not kicked him out the night before and had instead even allowed him to come again the next day.

He thought of the possibility that Raymond could return to town and run into this man from Texas, from Trina's past, and wondered how he might react. He worried about the encounter, but George still could not make himself believe that the young man he was just starting to know would resort to something as heinous as intentionally harming another person.

He knew Raymond was capable of violence; he had, after all, seen the burns from the scalding water on Trina. He knew about the trouble in Datil, and he knew that Raymond was a trained soldier who had been deeply affected by what happened while he was in Afghanistan.

And yet, George could not accept that Raymond was the man the FBI agents were making him out to be. He believed that the incident with Trina was an accident and that the outburst at the bar happened only because he was drunk. George did not think Raymond Twinhorse was the *fugitive* the feds were searching for.

George drove on thinking about the FBI agents and how they spoke of Raymond. "The fugitive," they kept calling him, never by his name, always just, "the fugitive."

He hurried as quickly as he could out of Pie Town and recalled a story he once read about a fugitive. It was from a book he had read in seminary, a book by a priest, a renowned scholar and spiritual leader named Henri Nouwen. The story was about a young fugitive running from an enemy and taking refuge in a small village. The people in the village were kind and generous and offered the young man a place to stay. Soldiers who were seeking the fugitive followed him to the village and threatened to burn it and kill all the people unless they turned the fugitive over to them. The people decided to ask their minister what to do, and after a night of reading the Bible to find an answer, he discovered the words: "It is better that one man dies than that the whole people be lost."

After finding these words, the minister closed the Bible, called the soldiers, and turned over the boy. The next day a feast of celebration was held in the village in honor of the minister because he had saved the people. The minister, however, did not join the celebration. He was overcome with grief over what had happened to the fugitive. Later, an angel came to him to explain that the fugitive was in fact the Messiah. When the minister asked how he could have known who the fugitive was, the angel replied — and this part of the story George remembered vividly — "if, instead of reading your Bible, you had visited this young man just once and looked into his eyes, you would have known."

George thought about Nouwen's story and about the unfolding story of Raymond Twinhorse. He thought about the reactions from members of the community to the news that Raymond was a suspect in a robbery and then also suspected to be dealing drugs.

Originally, the priest had expected that the people of Pie Town would cooperate with the FBI agents after hearing their claim that Raymond was a thief and a drug dealer. Even though George knew that Oris had jumped to Raymond's defense, and that Francine and Bernie had chosen not to turn him in when they knew where he was, George had still thought the people of Pie Town would not support Raymond. He had thought that they would choose to give the FBI what they wanted. He even considered it likely that a few of them would help the agents search for the young man, jumping on horseback like members of some posse deputized to assist in a crucial search.

Father George realized as he drove toward Ramah that he had judged the townspeople unfairly. Of course, there were a few who thought the young man was guilty and wanted to see him get arrested, but those few were loyal to Gilbert Diaz and believed everything the owner of the Silver Spur had told them. And those few were actually a very small group. Most everyone he encountered believed in Raymond's innocence and wanted to find a way to support him.

George recalled a meeting held at the church just a few days earlier that had been organized to discuss the annual budget but turned into a gathering of support for Raymond and Frank. It had not been anything at all like he expected.

Francine and Bernie had driven all the way from Phoenix to the church to come to the meeting and announce their plan to support and protect Raymond. They had rushed into the sanctuary, apologizing for interrupting a scheduled meeting, and explained that they were there to talk about Raymond and how to help him. Oris Whitsett had chimed in at that point, standing up in front of the whole congregation and announcing, "Raymond Twinhorse is in trouble, and we need to do something about it."

George had been deeply moved by the townspeople's loyalty to Raymond and their concern for him and his family. One after another, they stood up and shared a story about the young man. One former teacher spoke about his hard work and honesty. Fedora talked about his generosity, how he refused payment when he took care of her lawn while her lawn man was out sick, and Fred and Bea agreed with her assessment of Raymond, explaining that he did chores for them at the diner, never requesting a dime. Another member mentioned his kindness, his quiet way of being, and one young mother explained that to her son, a student at the elementary school, Raymond was a hero, and he had even written a story about him for his class.

"He's our son," Oris had said to the gathered members of the church. "He belongs to us all. His homecoming is no different to me than if it was my Lawrence coming home from serving his country," he noted, speaking of his adult son who had made a career in the military. "And if Lawrence was in trouble, I'd do everything I could to help him." And he vowed his support for Raymond, promising the same kind of care and attention.

Father George knew that even though the FBI thought of Raymond as a fugitive, that label had never been used or even considered by the people of Pie Town. He was one of their own, their son, their hero, and this village, unlike the one in Nouwen's story, would never betray him.

George saw the dirt road ahead and made the turn, heading in the direction of where he hoped he would find Raymond. He wasn't sure what he was going to say if he did find the young man, whether he would tell him about Trina's ex from Texas showing up out of nowhere or his father's arrest. He didn't know what to say about the robbery and the FBI's manhunt for a drug dealer.

All he knew to say was that Pie Town was there for him and wanted to help him. All he knew to do was to take to the boy the love and support of his village. He wasn't sure exactly how he would explain all of this to him, but he would let Raymond know that no matter what had happened, his community cared for him.

Even though he wasn't sure whether or not that information would help the young man, George did know that he would, without pause or hesitation, tell him that.

THIRTY-TWO

"Conroe Jasper." Trina was putting Alexandria to bed for an afternoon nap. She had gone over to Frieda's and picked up her daughter, claiming that she didn't need the woman to watch Alexandria the rest of the day. After the visit from her old lover, Trina decided not to open the garage. With Frank unavailable, she hadn't felt comfortable trying to run the place by herself. The burns on her back and legs were better, but she had difficulty standing for very long or bending over an engine, and sliding underneath a chassis was out of the question.

Besides, the truth was that most of the people in Pie Town preferred Frank's expertise to hers and business was slow anyway; she figured she might as well stay at home with her baby and think through things, make a few decisions about the current issues in her life, about Raymond, about her relationship with him, about Conroe Jasper's recent appearance at her front door.

"Conroe," she repeated to herself, shaking her head as she closed the door to the baby's room. She went to the kitchen and poured herself a glass of iced tea. She sat down at the table, dropping her hands by her sides. "Of all the people to show up this week," she said. Forgetting the tenderness from the burns, she sat back in the chair, then quickly leaned forward.

She thought about calling an old friend from Amarillo, somebody who knew Conroe and knew what he had done to her, just to find out what they had heard about the divorce, if it was really true, and about what he was doing showing up in Pie Town. Once she had that thought, however, she decided against it. She knew that having such information wouldn't really matter. He was there. He knew where she was. And he had made it clear that he wasn't about to leave things alone. Not yet, at least.

Trina was confident that she had kept him from finding out about Alexandria. Somehow he had not been smart enough to figure out that the baby she was supposedly babysitting, the baby who had made herself at home in Trina's house, was actually *at home* in her house. For whatever reason, he hadn't put it together that Trina was a

306

mother. She knew, however, that if he kept coming around, kept showing up, it wouldn't take long before that fact would finally become clear to him. And once he saw Alexandria, learned how old she was, her date of birth, he would know that he was the father.

Trina took a sip of tea. "Maybe he's not bright enough," she told herself. "Maybe he'd believe that some other man is the father." But she knew that wasn't true. Conroe wasn't the sharpest knife in the drawer, but he was no dummy either. He would figure it out. And then what? Would he want some relationship with Alexandria? Would he use the baby as a means to try to worm his way back into Trina's life? Would he want parental rights? Custody? What if he found out about Raymond and the accident and said she was an unfit mother to keep Alexandria around him? It was just too much for her to consider.

She leaned back, gingerly, trying to keep from aggravating her injuries, and thought about their relationship. She had loved him at one time, that was true. She had left everything to be with him and thought he was the man she wanted to live out her life with. She had enjoyed being with him, and most of all, she had trusted him. They'd had some wonderful months together on the road. And then she had overheard a phone conversation when he stepped out of the motel room in Tucson. Standing beneath the balcony, where he had thought Trina wouldn't be able to hear him, he had talked with his wife and his two sons, still waiting for him back in Abilene. Trina had heard what he was saying, the lies he was telling them about working overseas, all alone, and she had walked away. Taken his money, packed a few things, and walked away.

After a number of days, she had landed in Pie Town, and the rest, as far as she was concerned, was history. She had never heard from Conroe Jasper again. When she returned to Amarillo for a few days when she was considering leaving New Mexico and staying in Texas, none of her friends recalled having seen the truck driver. None of them knew where he was, and none of them said he had been around looking for her. They agreed with Trina: it was good riddance that he was gone and out of her life. And she was confident that not one of those friends would have told him that she was pregnant with his child. They were just as angry at Conroe as she had been.

The more she thought about it the more it appeared as if his showing up was exactly what he said it was: a crazy twist of fate. He had stopped in Pie Town and heard her name. And now the life she had written off as history had been standing in her living room. He was back, and he wasn't going away quietly. He had declared his love for her and his intention to have her in his life again.

She drank her tea and placed the glass on the table.

She thought about how it was to see him again. She thought how it was to recognize his face when he leaned up to get close to her while she stood outside his car, how it was to look into those eyes, feel his hand on her arm. It wasn't all terrible, like she had always imagined it would be. It wasn't awful.

She had actually felt a bit of delight when he opened his car door and stood next to her, when he smiled that big smile in her direction. She remembered the way he looked at that moment, the things he went on to say.

"I'm sorry," he had told her as he followed her onto the front porch.

"For which part?" she had asked. And she had opened the door and walked in. He had remained on the porch, watching through the screen, waiting, it appeared, for an invitation to come any farther.

"The lying part," he answered. "Not telling you about my wife and boys."

"Yeah, that was kind of important," she responded. She had not invited him in.

"I was planning to get a divorce when I met you," he noted, still standing there, still waiting. "I was just trying to figure out how to do it." He stopped talking at that point. "Can I come in?" he finally asked.

Trina recalled that she had shrugged and he walked in, slowly moving toward her. He had been close enough to touch, close enough to reach up and touch, and she almost did.

She sat at the table and shook her head. "My God," she said, "I almost did." And then she laughed, remembering how she had stepped away from him, moved into the kitchen, over by the sink, and how he kept talking, making things worse for himself, explaining why he hadn't told Trina about being married, why he couldn't ask his wife for a divorce.

"I knew she would take the boys away from me," he said, reaching out his hands as if he wanted Trina to take them. And when she didn't, he continued. "And I was right, wasn't I? She did just that." He stuck his hands in his pockets. "She took my boys away just like I knew she would."

And for just a second, Trina had felt sorry for him. She had almost walked over to him, almost tried to comfort him. But she had stood firm even as he went on to say that he should have told her the truth and he was sorry, so sorry, but now he was there and single, and after all, he had said with the tiniest smile, wasn't she?

And even though she had told him she wasn't interested, and even though she had acted like a woman in a new relationship, she had never really said that. She had not spoken of Raymond and her love for him. She had only said that she didn't want to go to Texas and that she was happy in her new place. Without meaning to cause harm, Trina, at least in her own mind, had been unfaithful to Raymond and as deceitful as Conroe had been to her. She had not confessed to her former lover the love she supposedly had for Raymond.

"Maybe I should just go back with him," she said out loud, surprising herself. "Maybe it would be better for me and Alexandria to be in Texas, to be with Conroe." And then she shook her head.

She couldn't think those thoughts. She couldn't imagine going back with the man who had lied to her, the man who had been married when he told her he was single, the man who claimed she was his first and only love, the man who got her pregnant and never tried to find her when she left. She couldn't imagine trying to make that relationship work. And yet . . . Trina dropped her head in her hands. It was all so confusing.

Raymond was gone, maybe for good; she couldn't be sure. He had problems, real problems that love and companionship weren't going to heal. Maybe he was too broken to be in a committed relationship. Maybe he was too fragile to be an equal partner. Maybe he was too dangerous to be living with a toddler. Trina thought about Alexandria and how her own decisions about who she dated, who she loved and committed herself to, affected not just her but Alexandria and her well-being too. She was a mother. She had a child to think about now. And even if Raymond got this Silver Spur mess cleaned up, even if he got out of any charges that might be filed against him, he would still have the same problems he'd had before he left. He was still wounded from war, still struggling with demons that were far too powerful for the two of them to handle alone.

She thought about Raymond and then

suddenly recalled a conversation she'd had with Christine and what her friend had said one night when the two of them were enjoying a dinner together at the diner, just a few weeks before the accident, before Raymond came home. The young women sometimes met at the diner while Malene and Roger watched Alexandria. They were close in age and had discovered that they enjoyed each other's company.

They had been talking about Danny and Raymond and whether the two men were similar at all, whether they might like each other, and whether the four of them should go out together when Raymond came home, and out of the blue Christine had mentioned that she was worried about Danny. She just blurted out that he had a problem with his anger and that she had called off the wedding because she was concerned about his temper. Trina had been surprised that Danny had an issue like that and that Christine had been smart enough, she thought, to recognize it and ask him to get help.

"I just don't want to wake up one day and know that I've built my life with a man I'm afraid of." Christine was eating pie and had gotten meringue on the tip of her nose.

Trina was just about to mention it but had been stopped by the sheer force of what her friend was saying.

"You know what I mean?" Christine had said, and then shivered like the thought of living in such fear was too terrible to think about. "I'd rather be alone and living with ten cats in a one-room apartment than be married in a big house to a man who blows up at the least little thing. What kind of life is that?"

Trina had pushed for more. "What's he like when he's angry?" she asked, wondering if he had ever struck Christine, wondering if violence followed the rage, wondering if he was anything like Trina's father.

"It's just scary to me, but he says it's like nothing he can explain, like it just takes over, like his anger suddenly becomes everything he is, everything he feels, thinks, knows. And what's the scariest," she said, lowering her voice to a whisper and glancing around to see if anyone was listening, "is that he says that I've never even seen him when he's really mad. And let me just tell you, that worries me, because the mad I've seen is pretty mad."

Trina had leaned in to hear her friend and then sat back. "Do you know why he's that way? Do you know what made him like that?"

Christine shook her head. "He says he

doesn't know. His dad doesn't have a temper like that. He just says he's always been that way. As a kid, he was always in trouble because of his problem with anger."

After Christine explained that Danny was getting help, going to some anger management classes and talking to a counselor, Trina had asked her friend one last question. It was the one that she thought of as she sat at the table making a decision about Conroe, about going to Texas to see him.

"How will you know if he's better?" she had asked. "How will you decide that it's safe to be with him?"

Christine had taken another bite of pie. "Well, now, that's the million-dollar question, right?" She put down her fork. "And I don't have a clue to the answer."

Trina had thought she had finished and was about to change the subject.

Christine continued, however. "He wants to be better; that ought to be worth something. His getting help isn't just all my idea. He knows he has a problem. And he doesn't like it any more than I do when he loses his temper. He told me that he doesn't like how it feels to be out of control, and he doesn't want to put me through that and be married to him." She shrugged. "So I guess we'll figure it out together. I just hope for the day when he says the spell is broken, the curse is gone, the day when I'm not afraid."

"And what if that day never comes?"

"Then I know that I'm happy in my one-room apartment," Christine answered. "And since I already have made a nice home for two cats, I can always get more." She had then realized that she had pie on her face, laughed hysterically, and moved on to talk about something else.

At the time Trina had agreed with her friend completely, telling her that she was absolutely making the right decision to postpone the wedding and that if she felt pressured to marry Danny before being convinced that he was better at dealing with his emotions, to make sure she went to talk to Trina. "I'll remind you of this conversation and what you've said," Trina told her. "And I won't let you marry a man who scares you." And the two of them had made that agreement.

Trina wondered what her friend would say to her if she were sitting at the kitchen table with her at that particular moment, if she had seen the wounds on Trina's back and knew about the fight the night the lights went out and about Raymond's drinking. She and Christine hadn't gotten together much since Raymond came stateside, and she wondered what her friend would say if she knew what had happened to Raymond in Afghanistan, what had become of him since returning, and how the tables had turned for the two women.

She wondered what Christine would say now that it was Trina feeling so afraid of the man she claimed to love. Would she tell Trina it was worth hanging in there with the relationship, worth the work and the wait?

Trina sat at the table and thought about Danny and Christine and their relationship, Danny's problems, and wondered if the anger management classes were helping and whether or not Christine would eventually decide to marry him, whether she would ever feel completely safe with him.

Trina stood up. She couldn't think about it anymore. She couldn't worry about it anymore. It was all too much for her to consider at the moment. She put her glass in the sink and headed to check on Alexandria.

PART FOUR

THIRTY-THREE

It was not hard for Father George to see that the FBI had figured out the scriptural reference that Frank gave George when he visited him at the detention center. He arrived at the Ramah Indian Area to find that there were agents everywhere. Dark sedans, white vans, men and women with "FBI" plastered across the backs of their jackets. It didn't take a genius to realize who they were, and now that George understood what had happened at the detention center, he knew who they were searching for.

He knew he was spotted as soon as he arrived at the House. Even though he could claim a legitimate reason to be there — Frank Twinhorse's mother attended Holy Family Church from time to time, and Father George was a pastor to the family and had visited there before — he knew every one of the agents suspected him of being there to find Raymond, their fugitive.

He felt many sets of eyes following him as he drove over to Raymond's grandmother's house, and he immediately noticed the car parked at the end of her driveway. He had been used by Cochran and the FBI to bait Frank to share Raymond's whereabouts. They let him make a visit because they thought Frank would give him information that would help them find his son, and they had been right.

The thought of being used in that way made George angry, and he was tempted to walk up to the agents and let them have a piece of his mind. However, just as he was about to exit his car and walk over to the two men parked in the driveway, Maria, Frank's mother, came to her door and opened it, inviting the priest inside. He stared at the two men, hesitated, but accepted the invitation.

"Father George," Maria greeted him. She held open the door while he walked in. "We have many guests on our land today, but only one I recognize. Please come in."

George shook his head. "I'm sorry," he apologized and was about to explain that he was the reason for the FBI's presence all around her house and on her people's land.

She waved off the apology. "Men like them have been here before," she interrupted him. "They'll be gone soon. They've shown up at Ramah before trying to claim something they think is theirs. What I don't understand is why they are searching for Raymond. No one will tell me anything." She made her way into the front sitting room and cleared off a place for the priest to sit on the sofa. "Please, have a seat."

George smiled, thinking that the older woman didn't seem too upset about the agents all around her looking for her grandson, but he decided not to comment. He waited for his hostess to sit in the rocking chair across from the sofa, and then he sat down.

"You have news about Frank and Raymond?" she asked. "I got a phone call from Frank a few days ago that he is being jailed because of this search."

Father George had planned to stop by Maria's and let her know of his visit with her son. Originally, he had intended to explain the clue Frank gave him at the detention center, in hopes of earning her confidence so that she would tell him exactly where Raymond was hiding. With the presence of the FBI, that plan no longer seemed worthwhile.

"I saw Frank yesterday," he answered. "He's fine. They haven't harmed him, and I don't think they can hold him much longer. I don't even understand how they're keeping him detained now. I guess they think if they keep him long enough, he'll tell them where Raymond is hiding."

Maria shook her head. "And why are they searching for my grandson? What has happened?"

"They want to talk to him about a robbery in Datil a few days ago. They think Raymond had something to do with it," George explained.

"A robbery?" she asked, now displaying the surprise George had expected to see when he first arrived. "My grandson had nothing to do with a robbery. He's not a thief." She paused. "And all these men think Raymond is here?"

"Yes," George said.

"Even if there was this robbery, and even if Raymond was involved, why is there so much interest from the government? What kind of robbery was it?"

"It was a bar in Datil, about two hundred dollars is gone."

"This many officers are required for a robbery of two hundred dollars?" she asked.

Father George took in a deep breath. "No, it isn't just about the robbery. They think he's dealing drugs."

Maria laughed. "Raymond?" she exclaimed. "Raymond hates drugs. He's seen what they have done to his friends, to other young people; he would never be involved with drugs."

"I know," the priest responded. "It's just a misunderstanding."

"But that still doesn't explain why they think Raymond is hiding here." She seemed confused. "He has never lived here at Ramah."

"Yes," George said, preparing to share what had happened in Albuquerque during his visit with her son. "I'm afraid somebody was listening to my conversation with Frank. He told me Raymond was here, and I'm sure that's why they've all descended upon you and your family."

Maria seemed surprised. "Frank told you that Raymond was in Ramah?"

"Well, not in those exact words." George wasn't sure he wanted to give Maria all the details just yet.

"Then what did he say?" she asked.

George sighed. He felt it was only right to answer her. "He quoted scripture to me just as I was about to leave. He explained that the prophet Jeremiah was his favorite prophet and that he particularly liked the passage that spoke of the joyful return of the exiles."

"Jeremiah 31," Maria said, nodding. It was a passage she recognized.

Father George was a little surprised that Frank's mother would know the chapter so quickly. He knew she was a devout Catholic who studied the scriptures daily, but it embarrassed him a bit to realize she knew so quickly the location of the passage while he'd had to search for it.

"My people know that Book of Consolation well," she explained, seeing the surprise in the priest's face. "My great-grandfather, even though he rejected the Catholic Church, spoke of reading that scripture when he was released from Fort Sumner."

George knew a bit of the history of Frank's people. He recalled that most of the Navajo and Apache had been exiled in 1863. By December of the following year, over eight thousand Navajo and over four hundred Mescalero Apache had been confined there. When they were released, or when some escaped, many of them had settled in the area around Ramah, where some of the exiles had lived before.

He remembered readings that some of the Navajo had intermarried with the Apache and did not return to the Big Reservation, the Navajo land around Window Rock. He didn't know the history of the name of the area where this group settled, Ramah, only that it was the same spelling as the town mentioned by the prophet Jeremiah in the Hebrew scriptures.

"So doesn't it seem that Frank was giving me a clue if he told me this passage? Doesn't it seem that he thinks Raymond is here?"

Maria smiled. "My son and I have not always seen eye to eye on matters of religion. He is like my great-grandfather and believes that the faith of those in the Catholic Church is narrow and oppressive."

George nodded. He recalled the many conversations he had had with Frank about religion. Frank was never shy about expressing his disapproval of the history of Christianity and the Catholic faith.

"Still," George noted, "he knew the prophet. He mentioned the passage."

"My son is very suspicious of the ways of white people." She rocked in her chair.

Father George was having a difficult time following her. This statement wasn't a surprise to him either. He waited for her to explain, but she seemed to have nothing more to add.

He waited and then, suddenly, he understood.

"He knew they were listening," George

surmised. "Frank knew they were taping the conversation, so he told me about the Jeremiah passage to throw them off." He nodded, taking in the realization. "To send the FBI to the place where he knew Raymond wasn't going to be."

Maria rocked in her chair and laughed.

Frank dropped back in his seat on the sofa. It was funny, and it was also humbling. He had been just as gullible as the FBI agents eavesdropping on the conversation. He had been so sure that Frank was giving him a clue that it never occurred to him Frank knew more about what was happening during the visit than he did.

"So it was just a ruse," he said, taking it in.

Maria raised her eyebrows. "Perhaps," she responded. "What exactly did my son tell you as you were about to leave?"

George tried to remember the conversation in detail. He leaned against the back of the sofa and closed his eyes, reliving the visit he had in Albuquerque. "He said that Jeremiah has always been a favorite of his and that he especially liked the prophet's words about the joyful return of the exiles." George sat up and stared directly at Frank's mother.

"And then he said . . . and I remember

328

this now because I thought it was an odd thing for Frank to say . . ."

Maria stopped rocking and leaned forward.

". . . He said, 'I like that they go back to where they started.' " He thought for a few minutes about Frank's parting words. "Rachel weeps for her children in Ramah. That was the hill country in the north of Judah where many of the exiles were from. Ramah, New Mexico, is the place your people were thought to have lived formerly." He shook his head. "I still don't understand. It still seems like he was pointing me here."

" 'I like that they go back to where they started,' " Maria repeated. "Perhaps he was not talking about the people of Ramah, not about the Israelites, and maybe not even about the Navajo."

George listened carefully. Suddenly his eyes lit up. "Go back to where Frank started!"

Maria began rocking again.

"Frank had started searching for Raymond at a ranch near Pie Town. I told him that I had talked to the ranch owner. I figured the FBI was listening, so I didn't explain that I knew that Raymond had been there, but I'm pretty sure Frank understood what I was saying." George nodded. "I told him how I had been hiking and camping around the area. Frank knew that I was aware of where Raymond had last been seen, where he left Pie Town and took off, where he started his self-imposed exile." It was all coming together for him. "Raymond isn't anywhere around here."

Maria shrugged, appearing very innocent.

"He's where he started." George shook his head. Everything had become clear. He turned to Maria, suddenly figuring out something else — the reason for her calm demeanor.

"But you knew that, didn't you?" he asked, watching her carefully. "Did he come here and leave?" He wondered why he hadn't found Raymond earlier in the week when he searched the area around Techado after hearing from Francine.

She didn't answer right away. She rocked and peered out the front window. "I am Catholic, Father George," she said softly. "But I am also Navajo. Raymond was in trouble, and I gave him help." She faced the priest. "He is better now because he has been given the appropriate blessing, the blessing to heal him of the wounds of battle."

Father George knew about the rituals of the Navajo people. He had learned the history of the ceremonies from Frank, but he had also done a lot of research. He appreciated the means of blessings used by the Navajo to heal and protect their people. There were several classifications of the blessings, or chantways, and he understood that Maria was probably referring to a sing — a ceremony used for men returning from war.

He also understood that this ritual had been carried out in the presence of the Ramah people and officiated by a diagnostician, a kind of priest or medicine man who had learned the chants and the proper way to hold the rituals. George wasn't sure that the time was right to hold such an event for Raymond — he thought he remembered hearing that this blessing could only occur after the late spring planting. But the medicine man must have known what he was doing in conducting the sing as required.

"I think when you find Raymond he will be ready to return to Pie Town." His grandmother smiled. "And I am confident that the FBI will soon learn that my grandson had nothing to do with this robbery and that he has nothing to do with dealing drugs."

Father George stood up, more at peace

331

than when he had arrived, ready to take his leave, ready to find Raymond. He glanced out the window and realized that he probably didn't need to worry about being followed. These agents were not assigned to him. They would stay exactly where they had been instructed to stay, at Raymond's grandmother's house in the area where they were sure the fugitive was hiding.

He said his good-bye, walked to his car, smiled and waved at the agents still parked in the driveway, got in his car, and headed back to Catron County. He would go home, get some rest, pack some supplies, and make his trip to Bernie's ranch the next day.

THIRTY-FOUR

It was not everything he needed to be healed, to be better, but for that moment, that day, that week, it was enough.

Raymond Twinhorse crossed over Highway 36 just a few miles east of Fence Lake. He was heading home, back to Pie Town. He glanced down at his watch. It was just after lunch, and he knew he had at least four more hours of walking.

A couple of cars passed him while he was on the road. One stopped, and the driver asked him if he wanted a ride. Raymond politely said no. He wanted to keep walking. He needed to keep walking.

In the days since he had left Pie Town, the days he had been wandering the desert, it was the walking that had felt the most restorative. The movement of his body, the stride, his gait, the leaving one spot to go to another, somehow it helped. It kept him grounded, centered. There was something very important taking place within himself as long as he was moving. He figured that in the seven days he had been gone he had traveled a hundred miles. He had walked and hiked and crawled across the entire northwest corner of Catron County. He had started walking, and he hadn't stopped.

He headed off the paved road and into the wilderness. He would head east a few miles more and then turn south toward Highway 603, going the same way he had come, across Bernie King's ranch, the land he knew best, the land he was used to working, fencing, hunting. Heading along in that direction, he would make it home by dark. He would stay at his dad's trailer, call Trina, and see if she would agree to see him.

It wouldn't have to be at their house, he would tell her. She wouldn't have to be alone with him. They could go to the diner or the church, wherever she felt comfortable. He just wanted to see her, tell her he was sorry about what had happened, explain that he was wrong to be drinking, wrong not to get help, and wrong to put her and the baby in harm's way. He would explain that he was staying at his father's place until he could get things worked out at the VA. He hoped that he could get a room, be an in-patient and get a good counselor, get the help he needed.

He stopped for a minute and took a drink from his canteen. His grandmother had given it to him when he told her he didn't want her to drive him to Pie Town, when he explained he would rather walk. She had found it in a closet, said it was his dad's, and she had filled it with water, well water from Ramah, packed a few sandwiches in a pouch, and sent him on his way. She had seemed worried at first, when he arrived, but not when he left. When he left, she was radiant, confident, at peace.

He had only seen his grandmother once since he returned from the war. His father had driven him out there around the third or fourth day he was home. Raymond knew his dad didn't like going to Ramah, that it brought up too many unpleasant memories of the time when he left. But telling his son that he needed to see his grandmother, Frank had driven him to Ramah.

Raymond had realized a number of years before that he would never really understand his father's break with the Navajo people, that it was something his dad didn't want to discuss, but he could see in the reunion with his grandmother that his dad was more at ease with his family than Raymond had ever seen before. His dad seemed to have a peace about him while they visited with the family. He told his son that he had been back a couple of times since Raymond had been away, that the experience of Raymond being at war had somehow brought them a little closer.

Raymond put the top on his canteen and kept moving. There were no longer any highway sounds, no passing cars or diesel trucks, just the noises from the desert, the whistle of a hawk, the sounds of a lizard darting through dry grasses, the cry of a coyote from far off. He loved the sounds, loved the silence. And with the week of cleansing, of being alone in the hills, of having nothing between himself and the earth, he felt better than he had in a long time.

He climbed up a hill and peered behind him. He thought of the old man, the shaman, the healer who had performed the sing on his behalf. Raymond knew the man from his childhood, remembered him from the few family functions and festivals he had attended. He had been at the receiving end of the man's treatments a couple of times before. He had taken herbs the man prescribed, had drunk his teas. He wasn't sure he actually believed in the ceremonies or treatments, the blessings, the chants, but once he arrived in Ramah, once he found his way to his grandmother's house, he was in such a bad place, such a lost and broken place, that he would have tried anything, taken anything, prayed to anybody. He'd had nothing left to lose.

Raymond could see the smoke from small fires off in the distance and could also smell the faint odor of ash and burning trash. He hoped that the fires were well contained and presented no threat to the people of Catron County. Watching the rising smoke, he thought of the danger of fires in the desert and immediately remembered the dream that had haunted him since he left Afghanistan, the dream that for some reason had not shown up the previous night, the dream that he hoped was gone for good.

It began simply enough, Raymond recalled, with a light conversation with his buddies, members of his company. They were driving along, laughing at Boxer, the private first class from Chattanooga, Tennessee, called that because he was always in a fight with somebody. He was rapping, making up some crazy song about soldiers in a truck, plowing through the desert; and the others on board, the five men returning to base after "shithole patrol" — what they called the assignment of checking caves for Taliban members — were laughing at the horrible rhymes, laughing at this skinny white kid from Tennessee who thought he could be a rapper.

"You are so far from being black," Dawg said as he pulled off his helmet to scratch his head. Dawg was the only man in the unit who had come from a big city. He was tall, lanky, a basketball player from the Bronx. He was sitting near the window, on the opposite side from Raymond. He was the first one blown out of the truck, the first one Raymond had seen die, the first man Raymond had ever seen take his last breath.

In the dream, just like the real event, the explosion seemed to have come from nowhere. There were no warnings, no time to change course, no time to calculate or evaluate. They were just driving along, laughing, cutting up with each other, thinking about dinner, thinking about mail call and whether they had gotten a letter or a package from home, and then everything went white, a sudden blast that left the truck and the company in pieces spread across the barren desert floor only a couple of miles from their destination. So close to home, Raymond dreamed, so close to marking off another day of combat duty, so close to calling it a day and feeling nothing out of the ordinary except maybe a little gratitude that they were one more day closer to getting out of the war.

The nightmare played out every memory Raymond had of the explosion: Boxer's moans as he lay dying, the screams from the captain trying to create some semblance of order, the cries, the metal popping in the fire, the blinding pain that caused Raymond to come and go out of consciousness, the smell of gas and oil and burning bodies, the last explosion that silenced the commanding officer, and the smoke. Always, Raymond saw and dreamed about smoke.

He took another sip from his canteen, turned, and kept walking.

It had actually been his father who suggested he go to Ramah. Frank had found him just above the ranch the day after he had left. Raymond had been surprised to see him. Frank had explained that he had seen Trina and that she was injured but okay. He also explained that he knew things were worse than Raymond had let on and that it was time he figured out what he needed to do. And that had been just about all that Frank had said about the situation.

They spent one day and one night together, catching dinner, a rabbit that somehow happened upon their camp, getting water, a long walk to a small spring, without any more conversation about what had happened, what was needed. Then, when Frank had awakened Raymond out of the recurring nightmare as they slept under the stars near Techado Mountain, he finally said to his son: "Go home. Go to our people," he added, surprising the young man. "Go and have the sing."

And that had been the end of it. His dad had promised to stay away and to keep everyone else away for a week, but after seven days, Frank said, he expected Raymond to return to Pie Town and face the consequences of what had happened the night the lights went out. He expected his son to come back and talk to Trina and make it right. But first he had made the suggestion to go to Ramah, to go home.

Raymond now realized that his dad had been right. The ceremony had helped. It had not alleviated the wounds, and it had not done away with the fear and anxiety and rage he had felt since returning from Afghanistan. But he had experienced one full night of sleep, and that had given him hope, given him some small sliver of light in his otherwise dark and clouded mind. It was only a very little, but it was enough.

Raymond pushed toward Pie Town, remembering the sing, remembering his

father's departure, remembering the shaman's blessing, remembering his grandmother's knowing eyes, remembering the
light way he felt just for a second, and he
kept walking, feeling glad. Glad for what he
had, glad for rest and hope, glad for where
he had been, glad for the small flicker of
light, the respite from the smoke.

He quickened his stride, knowing he was
making good time.

THIRTY-FIVE

"She just said that she was going to Texas to see him." Malene was recounting the story she had heard from Trina early that morning. She and Roger were meeting for lunch. Trina had called her at work a few hours earlier.

"Hey, Daddy," she called out to Oris, who was walking over to his seat at the counter. He had been in the restroom when she arrived.

"Baby girl," he responded without turning around.

"You want to sit at the table with us?" she asked.

Roger answered for him. "Already asked," he explained. "He said he couldn't stay long, has to run an errand."

"What errand?" Malene asked, pulling the silverware out of her napkin.

"I don't need to tell you my business," the older man replied.

Malene faced Roger, who just shrugged. "Suit yourself," she said, placing the napkin in her lap.

"Okay, so why is Trina going to Texas to see him?" Roger wanted to know. He had ordered for them both when he arrived first. Bea had already brought them drinks.

Malene shook her head. "I don't know," she answered. "Maybe she just wants to come clean about Alexandria. Maybe she thinks she owes him that information. Or maybe she's thinking about giving him a second chance." She opened a packet of sugar and poured it in her tea.

"I think that's a very bad idea," Roger said. He was having coffee.

"I tried to tell her that," Malene responded. She shook her head. "But she's a stubborn one, that Trina Lockhart."

Roger nodded. "She is that," he agreed.

"You hear anything else from Frank?" she asked, knowing that her husband had enjoyed a very long visit with their friend after the agent made arrangements for Roger to see him. "Are they letting him out?"

"The attorney says they don't have any grounds to keep holding him, but they just keep making things up to satisfy the laws."

Malene waited for an explanation.

"They've accused him of being involved

in some Mexican cartel, of running drugs. They even dug up some old outstanding arrest for him that I know happens to be false. Seems like there's another Frank Twinhorse somewhere in the country who likes to write bad checks. When they found out that bit of information, they claimed they could keep him locked up until they straighten that out." He blew out a breath. "According to Agent Cochran, who agrees with all of us about Frank's detainment, if the federal government wants to keep a person jailed, they've got about all the power and authority they need. They just use the words 'a threat to national security' and they can hold a person for as long as they want."

"Seems to me somebody over there needs a good butt-whipping." Oris was listening to the conversation.

"I thought you didn't want to join us," Malene noted.

"Well, if you're going to talk loud enough for everyone to hear, you ought to expect comments." He still had his back to them while he finished his meal at the counter. He demonstrated his annoyance by noisily folding and slapping the newspaper he was reading.

"Still . . . ," Malene said, trying to ignore her father but dropping the volume a bit,

"there ought to be something you can do."
She studied her husband. "Can't you talk
to Agent Cochran again? Can't you talk
sense into somebody in the agency?"

"I'm afraid not," he replied. "I've shaken
every tree I know to shake. They aren't letting Frank go until they find Raymond."

"I heard that the gun they found in the
Dumpster was his," Malene said.

Roger seemed surprised, and then he nodded knowingly. "Christine?"

"None other," Malene responded. "She
knows more about crime in Catron County
than you. Maybe you should just put her on
the payroll."

Roger laughed. "Danny thinks that telling
her stuff about his cases makes him seem
more interesting to her." He shook his head.
"Yeah, it was Raymond's. But that doesn't
mean anything," he added. "Maybe he just
got smart and decided to get rid of it.
Although the Dumpster isn't really the best
place for that."

Bea brought the two plates and set them
before her customers. "Two specials," she
announced. "You need anything else?"

The two shook their heads.

Roger took a bite and then asked, "So
what do you think Trina will do?"

Malene was adding hot sauce to her dish

of chile rellenos. She shook her head. "I don't know. All she told me was that she needed to talk to Conroe Jasper and that she didn't think Raymond would care."

"She didn't think Raymond would care?" he repeated. "Of course, Raymond will care."

Malene took a bite and shrugged. "I don't know, Rog. Even though I tried to talk her out of going, what she said actually made a lot of sense."

Roger drank a sip of coffee. "What?" he asked. "What did she say?"

Malene recalled her phone conversation with Trina earlier that morning. "Just that she thought that Raymond would be disappointed if she took Alexandria and moved back to Texas, but that he wouldn't stand in her way. She said that he had told her numerous times since he got home from the hospital that she would be better off without him."

Roger kept eating. He had heard the same thing from Frank when they had their recent visit.

"She said she figured she would have to fight with George and you and me about her decision to leave Pie Town, if she made that decision, but she knew she would never have to fight with Raymond. She said that he would not stop her from going back to Conroe. And that was the hardest part for her as she tried to make up her mind. In spite of Raymond's scars and demons, she said that she wanted to know that she and Alexandria were worth a fight, worth a commitment from him to be with them." Malene took a breath and then finished eating.

Roger understood that, for Trina, not having that fight from Raymond, that drive to keep the relationship alive, that desire to keep her there in Pie Town, to keep her in the relationship with him, would be the single worst loss she could encounter in the man she loved. He knew that in the letters they exchanged when he was overseas, in the calls they made to each other, his love for her had been obvious. Roger knew because Trina had confided in him that Raymond had spoken of his desire to be with her and Alexandria, to build a life with them, to protect them, take care of them. And he also knew that since Raymond had come home hurt and changed and broken, he had told both Trina and his father that he was incapable of loving her the right way, caring for her the best way, protecting or taking care of her and her little girl.

Malene took a swallow of her tea. "She thinks that at least Conroe seems willing to put up a fight for her, that he at least seems devoted enough to make a stand for her. And I suppose that even though it was late in coming, at least she thinks it's there."

Bea walked over to the table and refilled their cups. She had been listening. "Well, I think it's a crying shame if she leaves that boy to go back to that lying dog."

Malene reached out and patted the woman on the hand. "I know, Bea, but it's not our decision to make."

Bea nodded and returned to the kitchen.

"Still, I can't believe she would just leave like that and go see that man. Didn't she talk to anyone about her decision?" Roger asked.

"I guess she thought this was one choice she had to make for herself," Malene replied.

As Roger and Malene finished their lunches, they could hear Bea make an announcement. "Oris, your pie is ready."

Malene turned to her father.

"You want me to box it up?" Bea then asked.

Malene added sugar to her fresh glass of tea. "Why did you buy a pie?" she asked her father.

"Again, it's not any of your business, and yet, as usual you just can't stop yourself worrying about other folks." He had been eavesdropping. "But if you must know, I ordered it for somebody else," he explained.

"He got a pie to take to Albuquerque," Bea answered.

"Now, nobody asked for you to be a part of this conversation," Oris said, sounding irritated at Bea.

She just shrugged and walked behind the counter.

Malene was surprised. "Who are you taking a pie to in Albuquerque?" She remembered that his neighbor Millie Watson had been in the hospital, but Millie was home now. Malene knew that because the older woman was receiving rehabilitation over at Carebridge.

"I think it's for the FBI agents," Bea said. She was cleaning up the plates on the counter and grinned at Oris. "It's a new recipe for Francine."

Malene waited.

"Mud pie," she said with a smile. She clucked her tongue. "You can say a lot about your daddy, but he does have a sense of humor."

Malene glanced at Roger, who was laughing. "What?" she asked.

"I haven't said a word," he replied. He took a sip of coffee. "But mud pie, after they got stuck out there chasing Trina? You do have to admit that's kind of funny."

"Hilarious," Malene commented. She turned in her seat to look at Oris. "Daddy, you can't take that pie to Albuquerque to those agents. You'll just make them mad." She waited for him to turn to face her. "You'll just make things worse for Frank."

Oris finished his lunch, wiped his mouth, slid off his stool, placed some bills at his plate, and waited for Bea to finish bussing the counter and bring the pie box from the kitchen. When he got it, he walked over to where Malene and Roger were sitting.

"Last time I checked, giving a pie was a nicety." He smiled. "I just wanted to show our appreciation for the entertainment we've enjoyed, compliments of our government officials."

Malene turned to her husband. She was hoping Roger would say something to Oris. They just stared at each other. Roger only shrugged. He wasn't getting into this conversation. He knew when to leave his father-in-law alone.

"Exactly who are you giving the pie to?" Malene asked. She wiped her mouth, dabbed on some lipstick.

"Well now, that is a bit of a problem since I don't know the names of those fine officers who got lost on our fair county roads, but I figure I can just leave this mud pie at the front desk with a note of apology from the good folks of Pie Town and somebody will figure it out." Oris had a twinkle in his eye.

Roger finally spoke up. "I thought it was a thank you-gesture."

"Thank you, apology. . . . I don't really think my note will matter all that much." Oris opened the box and peered in at the dessert. "I've always heard that a good slice of pie is worth a thousand words." He closed the box. "This will say it all." He turned to walk out of the diner.

"Tell Francine thank you," he called out to Bea. He turned to his daughter. "I'll be home by supper." And he was gone.

Malene was going to try to talk her father out of his silly prank, but she knew he had already made up his mind. She turned around, shaking her head.

"Well, it looks like you might have to make another trip to the detention center in Albuquerque, only this time it won't be for Frank."

Roger agreed. "I suppose bailing your dad out of prison is just part of our marriage contract." He took a last sip of coffee, and

the two of them slid out of their booth to
return to work.

THIRTY-SIX

Father George parked at the north end of Bernie King's ranch. He reached behind him and pulled out the supplies he had packed earlier that morning before his pastoral visits and before the morning mass. He had been called to the nursing home for a death before he left and was still wearing his collar, his short-sleeved black shirt, and his black dress pants.

He worried that he was not where he should be. He didn't know what was going on in Pie Town since he had come home from Ramah, and he wondered whether or not Trina was okay. He felt somewhat guilty for being unavailable during what he was sure had to be a difficult time for his friend. He hadn't contacted Roger since seeing him at Trina's, and Malene hadn't been at Carebridge when he was there. He figured the FBI agents in Ramah had informed the two men in charge of his whereabouts, but whether or not they were still searching for him, George wasn't sure.

He got out and checked the car, then realized he had kept a pair of hiking shoes in the back of the station wagon. He changed shoes and wished he had thought to bring something more comfortable to wear but soon realized that he was just going to have to head out into the desert in his priestly attire. Stepping away from the car, he laughed when he remembered how he had come to Pie Town with only black pants, shirts, and dress shoes — only the orthodox clothing. It was Trina who had told him that he shouldn't wear black in the desert and that he needed boots, and it was Oris who had bought him his first pair. Once he returned to Pie Town and started building the new church, he wore the collar and the black attire only on Sundays or during pastoral emergencies, as he had done that day. Most of the time he dressed like everyone else. He knew that the priest in Quemado didn't care for his casual ways, but the people in his parish didn't seem to mind at all.

George glanced down at himself and thought that even though at the moment he looked exactly as he did when he first arrived in Catron County, he was nowhere close to being the same man. He grabbed his small pack, the bottles of water, and a pair of binoculars and locked up his car. He was confident that he had parked in a remote and safe location; the only person who might notice his vehicle, he figured, would be Bernie King. But George knew that Bernie and Francine, having offered their full support for Raymond, wouldn't care if he was on their property searching for the young man. He didn't think anyone else would be driving out past the ranch. It was well after lunchtime, and he knew that hikers and hunters would have come and gone by this late hour. Taking a deep breath, he headed up the path that led to Techado Mountain and out past Adams Diggings.

It was the second time in a week that he had been hiking near the King ranch, and he remembered how incredible he had thought the area was. Before that week, Bernie King had often tried to get George to walk his property, bragging about how beautiful the ranch was and especially how popular that northern area had become. George knew that Adams Diggings was a favorite destination for folks coming to Catron County. For years rumors had swirled that a miner named Adams had found gold on Techado Mountain and that before he cashed in his findings he buried his gold somewhere in the area but then died before being able to retrieve it or tell anyone the exact location. The whereabouts of the treasure remained a mystery.

Lots of people brought shovels and picks and dug everywhere around the vicinity for the buried treasure. People in Pie Town had confessed to him that they had gone up to the diggings more than once. He had heard about people's dreams and premonitions telling them, they believed, the location of the gold. He had even been asked to bless some tools for digging, but to date, no one had admitted to finding anything more than fossils and old bones.

He walked the path along the desert floor, and as the sun was creeping west, he began to realize he was heading up an incline, that the path was climbing, twisting and turning up the mountain. He paused for a moment, looked at his watch, and realized he had hiked for an hour. He kept going along the same path he had walked earlier in the week, but not at all sure he was in exactly the right place to find Raymond. He did know that once he arrived at the summit of Techado, he would have a great view of the entire area. Even if he wasn't on the right path, perhaps he would still be able to see a tent or small fire that might point him to where Raymond had camped. He was hopeful, like the gold-seekers at Adams Diggings, that this time he would find his treasure.

As George walked, he felt his body relax. His thoughts turned to Trina, and as his concern about her rose, he said a prayer for her. He thought again about Raymond and the possibility that the FBI agents were right: maybe he was hiding out somewhere because he was guilty, maybe he was not just troubled or wounded but a thief and a drug dealer.

George thought about Trina and the day she had explained to him why she fell in love with Frank's son. The two young lovers had not actually spent much time together before he was deployed to Afghanistan. She had gone with Frank to Raymond's boot camp graduation, enjoyed a few meals with the young soldier, and spent only a couple of evenings alone with him. George knew they couldn't have spent too much time together because it wasn't too many days after the graduation that Trina and Frank were back in Pie Town and Raymond was on his way to war.

Over the year or more that they spent apart, she had confessed, they wrote hundreds of letters, talked on the phone at least once a week, and used computers to communicate. It had been, she had told the priest, a very different way to learn about and love a person. Father George had asked her later what she meant when she said that. How had she learned about and come to love Raymond even though they were thousands of miles and more than a few lifetimes apart?

She had just put down Alexandria for a nap when he posed the question. It was after the explosion, and he had stopped by to find out from Trina the latest news on Raymond, when he was coming home, how he was doing with his surgeries and rehabilitation. She had walked back into the room, sat down, and seemed to be thinking about his question. George had waited for her to respond.

"It's easy to fall in love when a person is doing his best to impress you. You get all dressed up and you go to some fancy restaurant, and you watch how easy it is for the guy to order wine or how vulnerable he is because he's never done it before, and either way you're charmed by what he's gone through to capture your attention. And you're making sure you don't show the wrong parts of yourself too quickly, and both of you are somehow pretending to be something you're not."

George stopped walking, leaned against a

large rock, drank some water, and thought about that afternoon when Trina had taught the priest what she knew about romantic love.

"And by the time you've fallen in love, you aren't sure who you are or who the other person is, but it's too late, your heart is already convinced that this is the one. And by that point in the relationship, you've invested so much time and energy in making sure that he's pleased with you that you don't want to throw it all away even if you find out that he's not the person you believed him to be. And so, even if it doesn't feel natural, you make yourself fit into his ideal of you, and you pretend that he fits into your ideal of him."

George recalled being somewhat confused by the young woman's ideas of romance. He had asked her, "But if it's easy to keep from revealing yourself when you're with a person every day, seeing them, being with them, isn't it even easier not to reveal yourself when you're only exchanging letters and emails? Can't you be even more careful about your words and how you appear?"

Trina had agreed that was a reasonable question, but then explained, "Yeah, but in all my letters and phone calls and videos,

359

the emails, I haven't tried to be anything I'm not. I figure it's a real gamble anyway that anything will work out for us, so why not just be myself when we talk or when I write?"

George had then pushed her farther. "So you fell in love with Raymond because you can be yourself around him?"

And he remembered how she smiled, how serene she was when she said, "I fell in love with Raymond because we met each other when he was going to war and I was going to have a baby. What we shared in our letters and in our phone calls was about these things we're both dealing with, these new and hard and unpredictable and scary things. And he's not trying to win me like a prize, and I'm not trying to convince him that I'm anything other than what I am. As weird as it sounds, the not being together while we were facing the things we've had to face has somehow allowed us what we need to be completely honest."

George stood up from his resting position and started walking north. He knew he wasn't far from the summit, but he was concerned about the late hour. The sun would soon be setting, and he wasn't sure he wanted to be out on the path when night fell. He might have a couple of hours of daylight left, and this was the time when he needed to start heading back down to his car. He wasn't sure he could make it to the crest of Techado after all.

He kept moving forward, hoping to find a place where he could get a good look at the valley below him and at least feel like he had conducted a worthy search. George wasn't sure when he could make another trip out to the area, and he worried that this was his one chance to find Raymond before the young man returned on his own to Pie Town, before he faced the FBI agents.

Thinking about what had happened since Raymond left town — the night lightning striking the transformer, shutting off the power in Pie Town, Trina's accident, the robbery at Datil — he realized that it had been exactly seven days since Frank had admitted to George and Trina that he had found his son and that Raymond had said he needed one week alone in the wilderness and then would return to Pie Town. George thought about Maria and her idea that her grandson would be ready to go home and face whatever he had to face, that he was better now and could handle whatever was happening in Catron County. He could only hope that she was right.

George soon came upon a resting place, a

place with a view, and he stopped. He slid the backpack off and pulled out his binoculars to take a look around. He moved his eyes from left to right, seeing the plains, the vast desert. He could even see as far as the lava beds and Cebollita Mesa. He could make out a small herd of antelope, a couple of ravens circling above, miles of empty washes snaking across the land below him, the sunlight streaking across the sky, but he saw no sign of human life. No tent, no campfire, no man walking toward town.

Looking down, he could see the path he had taken, and he remembered walking past Adams Diggings and the miner's loot that had been buried there somewhere.

"The kingdom of heaven is like a treasure hidden in a field," he said, quoting from the New Testament. He pulled the binoculars away from his face and dropped his hands to his sides.

"Some search for gold while others search for lost soldiers," he said aloud. Sighing, he began packing up the binoculars and turning to walk back to his car.

"And which is worth more?"

The voice and the question startled the priest so completely that he turned around too quickly and almost tripped and fell. He could hardly believe his eyes, and he had to blink a few times to make sure what he was seeing was real.

"What are you doing out here, Father George, and why are you wearing your uniform?"

The priest smiled because it was real. Standing right in front of him was Raymond Twinhorse.

Thirty-Seven

Trina glanced over at the letter on the passenger's seat in the truck. The envelope was opened, but the one piece of paper was still folded and stuffed inside. She didn't have to take it out to read it again. She knew what it said, knew who wrote it, and knew what it meant.

"Come to Texas," he had written. Nothing more. No explanation. No pleading. No apology. Just those three words.

He had left the note in the front door sometime after he had been to visit. She wasn't sure when he had stopped back. She didn't know if he left it while she was home and inside with Alexandria or when she was away, at work or at the diner visiting with friends, over at Malene's or the church. She didn't know if he was hoping she was there and planned to ask her in person to come to Texas, or if he had decided to leave the invitation written in a note, not to make his plea in person. She didn't know when he left it or what he was thinking when he did. She only knew that it had been enough.

She had read it, put it away, pulled it out, and read it again. And she had done that a hundred times. And then, after that one hundredth time, she had made a few phone calls, arranged to leave Alexandria with Frieda, packed a few things, read the note again, and was planning to leave when Francine arrived at her front door, all excited about the town's plans to free Frank and get Raymond pardoned.

Trina reached over for Conroe's note and stuffed it in her front pocket. As she drove east, she kept thinking about her conversation with Francine, how it was to see her friend, see her disappointment, experience her disapproval. Trina sped up as she passed the diner, hoping no one was seeing her drive away, and recalled what Francine had told her about some church meeting she had just attended, a meeting in which the people of Pie Town had made some decisions about how they intended to support Raymond. Francine had been the only person she had seen before leaving town.

The people of Pie Town were rallying together, Trina realized, and organizing themselves on Raymond's behalf. She knew that one impromptu meeting had been held just as Francine and Bernie returned from Phoenix, but the older woman had explained to Trina that it was more of a pep rally than a strategic planning session. At this meeting, which was supposed to be the worship committee meeting to discuss the church calendar and was supposed to include Father George, real plans had been made. Tasks were assigned. Roles were given. And everyone present decided that how Pie Town handled the FBI's treatment of the father-and-son duo, Frank and Raymond, was going to change.

Trina smiled when she thought about what Francine had told her. Oris was planning to collect money to pay Gilbert back whatever had been stolen from him and to urge him — and this was the part that made her smile — *as delicately as possible* to withdraw his robbery charges against Raymond. Francine had told Trina that a petition was floating around Catron County that was a sort of protest against the Silver Spur, and the plan was for Oris to tell Gilbert that a boycott of the bar would go into effect if he refused the money and refused to drop the charges.

Bernie was organizing a group to go to the detention center in Albuquerque where

Frank was being held. He was planning a peaceful protest and getting together a list of everyone willing to ride over there and gather in the parking lot. He was collecting food and bedding and urging everyone who intended to go to prepare to stay at least one or two nights. He was trying to contact the news stations as well as a freelance videographer because he wanted to make sure he had media coverage of the protest. Members from the Ramah reservation as well as Navajo supporters from Big Rock had been contacted and were also planning to attend. It was going to be a big rally of support for Frank and for Raymond.

Even Fedora Snow had gotten involved by finding a screen printing company in Las Cruces to make T-shirts. SEE FRANK TWIN-HORSE was printed across the fronts and backs of three hundred shirts, more than enough to clothe all the residents of Pie Town. Fred and Bea had agreed to pay the costs and had only noticed the mistake — the slogan should have been FREE FRANK TWINHORSE — when they were giving the shirts away to everyone who came by the diner. This had caused a bit of embarrassment for Francine, although she didn't elaborate while talking to Trina, only promised that the mixup would be fixed by the time of the rally. Trina had not asked any questions. She was in kind of a hurry to leave. But Francine still had more to say.

According to her friend, the entire town, the entire county, was supporting the plan to get the FBI to leave Frank and Raymond alone. Every citizen of Pie Town and beyond was doing something to promote this endeavor to get Frank released and all charges dropped against Raymond.

Trina switched on the vent in the truck. It was warming up in the cab. She thought about how excited Francine was when she was telling Trina the news. The older woman was shouting the information, talking about how much they all owed Raymond and how much they were going to do for him. She was so glad that she had returned from Phoenix, so glad that she was doing the right thing, and she apologized again for her departure.

Francine had gone on and on about how proud she was of the residents of Pie Town, proud of their support for Raymond. In her excitement, she kept talking for more than fifteen minutes about the rally in Albuquerque and the T-shirts and the phone calls and the pies she was baking for all the protesters before finally noticing Trina's suitcases packed and sitting by the front door.

The older woman had turned to her young friend at that point. She had stopped talking and just stared at Trina. "You going somewhere?"

Trina rolled down her window, checked the clock on the dashboard, and realized she wouldn't get to Abilene until after dark. She thought about Francine, how disappointed she had seemed when Trina explained that she was going to Texas for a few days, that she needed to work through some things while Raymond was gone.

"I heard he was here," Francine had said, taking a seat on Trina's sofa even though there had been no invitation. Bea had told her that Conroe stopped in town after she figured out the identity of the trucker who came by the diner for pie.

"This isn't about him," Trina had responded, and she felt Francine's eyes on her.

"Then who is it about?" Francine wanted to know.

"Me, I guess," Trina said.

There had been a long and uncomfortable pause in the conversation. It was as if the two friends had nothing more to say to each other. Before too long, Francine had left. She had appeared dejected and very saddened by the news of Trina's plans, but she hadn't tried to change her young friend's mind.

"You've got to do what you've got to do" had been all she said.

Trina knew there was a lot more that Francine wanted to say. She could see it as Francine stood at the door, trying not to leave. There were all kinds of reasons she could give Trina for staying, but she knew that Trina understood them all already. Trina had already told herself every one of them.

She had already asked herself every possible question about her loyalty, her commitment to Raymond, her faith in the man she claimed to love. But in the end, she just felt like she had to see Conroe again. She couldn't sort through everything just by being back in Texas, but she needed to talk to her baby's father, give him a chance to know he had a daughter, give him a chance to say what he wanted to say about the two of them getting back together. She thought that since he had found her, looked her up, and sought her out, since he had taken the time to come by the house again and leave that note, she at least owed him that.

Francine didn't have to say anything

because Trina had already said it all to herself. And even though she felt like she was abandoning Raymond — which she didn't think she was going to do — and even though she felt like she was letting everyone in Pie Town down by driving away at the very moment they were deciding to put themselves on the line for Raymond, she just had to go to Conroe. She had to talk to him, hear what he had to say, give him a chance with Alexandria. Still, Trina realized, while the others were gathering and organizing support for Raymond and Frank, coming together on their behalf, she was turning aside and walking away.

She glanced at herself in the rearview mirror and quickly looked away. It was not her finest moment.

THIRTY-EIGHT

"I don't understand these messages." Raymond replaced the receiver in the cradle and turned to Father George. They were at Frank's trailer, and Raymond had picked up the phone to call Roger when he heard the beeps that signaled there were messages. He thought he would listen to them to see if his father or Trina had made a call, perhaps trying to reach him. Even though he lived in town with Trina, he still often picked up messages from his father's place.

George and Raymond had driven over to Frank's trailer. Raymond wanted a shower and a change of clothes before turning himself in to the sheriff. He had agreed to drive Raymond over to Frank's, hoping that the FBI agents he had seen parked there earlier in the week had left that original post to go to Ramah. George was satisfied that no one had followed him as they left Bernie's ranch, but he took the back roads just to be sure as he drove to the small trailer several miles out of town.

He had driven around the property a couple of times, making Raymond hide in the back of the station wagon, before finally parking behind a grove of cottonwoods near the trailer, where the car was hidden from the main road by the trees. Raymond had a key to his father's place and had gone inside to change clothes and get something to eat. After finding a pair of jeans and a T-shirt, he had gotten some crackers from the cabinet and a soda from the refrigerator. He had offered food and drink to George, but the priest had refused. He waited outside for Raymond, trying to figure out the best place to go to find Roger and avoid the FBI and how much more he needed to tell Raymond before taking him to town. He was too nervous to eat.

"Who left them?" the priest asked, coming inside after Raymond told him about the phone calls. He wondered if the calls were from FBI agents to Frank's phone in the hopes of having Raymond answer.

"Francine," he replied. He held out the phone so that George could listen.

"Whoever is there, if you get this message, you've got to call me. I've got to talk to somebody about Trina. I really need to talk to Frank or Raymond. She's making a very bad decision." Francine sounded more and more upset with every message she left.

George listened to the time of the calls and realized that the last one had been made just after noon that day. He glanced at the clock on the wall. More than six hours had passed.

He hung up the phone and wondered if the FBI had bugged it, if they had heard what he had just listened to and were somewhere around the trailer, ready to take some action.

"What is she talking about?" Raymond asked. "I thought you said Trina was okay. What bad decision is she making?"

Father George wasn't sure he knew the answer. He had not talked to Francine either. He had not talked to anyone about Trina since he had returned from Ramah. He didn't know what the messages meant, but he did know that he hadn't told Raymond everything as they made their way to Frank's.

"Sit down, Raymond. I need to tell you a little more about what has happened since you left." George waited while the young man took a seat on the sofa, then sat down in a chair across from him.

During their walk down the mountain and

on the drive to Frank's, Father George had already explained about the robbery and why the FBI had been searching for Raymond since the night he left. He had also explained about the FBI's suspicions that he was a drug dealer. He had told Raymond that Frank was arrested after he returned from finding him a week ago and that now the agents were searching the area around Ramah because they were convinced that was where Raymond was hiding.

"Father George, I didn't steal anything from Gilbert, and I have never dealt any drugs. When I get to town, I plan to set that right with Roger. I left the Silver Spur, threw my gun in the Dumpster, and drove down to Apache Creek and then to the ranch." Raymond had shaken his head. "I don't know anything about a robbery at that bar."

George had believed the young man. He just didn't think Raymond should show up in Pie Town right away. He didn't know how he could contact Roger without the FBI agents finding out. And George had known that he needed to tell the young man about Conroe showing up in town to see Trina, but he hadn't had a chance. He wasn't sure what the phone messages meant, or why they were left at Frank's, but he knew he needed to tell Raymond about Trina. He couldn't keep that information away from the young man any longer.

"I don't know what those calls are about." George thought he would start with that. He took in a deep breath and exhaled. "Raymond, something has come up for Trina."

Raymond jumped from the sofa. "What? Is it what I did to her?" he asked. "Did I hurt her really bad? I got to get to her." And he started heading for the door.

George stood up and grabbed him by the shoulder, stopping him. "Wait, Raymond, sit down a minute. This isn't about the accident. She was burned that night, but she's okay."

Raymond sat down. The relief showed, but so did worry. "Then what?" he asked, glancing up at George. "What happened to her?"

"This guy stopped in town a couple of days ago at the diner." George smiled nervously. "You know, for pie?"

Raymond waited. He shook his head, not understanding.

"While he was there, somehow Trina's name was mentioned. I don't really know that part," he explained. "But anyway, this guy knew her. And it turns out, he came back later to see her." Father George waited.

"Who is he?" Raymond wanted to know.

There was a pause before the answer.

"Conroe Jasper," George said.

Raymond turned away. He knew the name well. Trina had spent a lot of time explaining to him who Alexandria's father was, how they had met and fallen in love, and then why she had left him. He knew that Trina had been very wounded by the relationship and Conroe Jasper's lies. She had also told Raymond that she had not been sure for many months that she would ever be able to trust any man again. And he had explained that he would wait for that trust from her. He would prove himself to her and wait.

Raymond rubbed his eyes, trying to take in all the information that had come to him since running into the priest while he was returning to Pie Town. He was a suspect in a robbery. His father had been arrested for refusing to tell anybody where he was. His grandmother and the people in Ramah were being watched and harassed, and now he was hearing the news that Trina was in contact with her former lover, the father of her baby.

"Do you think she's gone back to him?" Raymond asked, glancing at the phone. "Is that what Francine was trying to tell me?"

George shook his head. "I don't know."

He stopped.

Raymond didn't ask another question.

Father George thought about the suggestion. He recalled again the messages he had heard. It did make sense. Trina had seemed unraveled by Conroe's appearance. She had seemed to be very unsure of herself.

"She may have made a decision to go see him again," George agreed.

"Then I guess there's nothing I can do," Raymond responded. "If that's her choice, and I certainly don't blame her for that," he added, "then I have to let her go."

"That's it?" George asked, appearing surprised. "You have to let her go?" He shook his head. "First of all, you don't even know what these messages are about, and second, that's it?"

Raymond didn't answer.

"Tell me that you care more about her and Alexandria than that?" George asked. "Tell me that you'd put up more of a fight for them than that?"

"What do you want me to say?" Raymond asked, shrugging. "Did you see what I did to her? Do you know what I am capable of? She's better off."

"With a man who lied to her about being married? A man who had two children and a wife and pretended he was in love with her? A man who got her pregnant and then when she left never even tried to find her, never even wanted to make sure she was okay?" George ran his fingers through his hair, a habit when he was anxious. "She's better off with *him*?"

Raymond slid down onto the sofa. "I don't know if I can ever be with anyone," he confessed. "I'm not the man she wrote letters to, the man who wrote letters to her. I'm not the man she fell in love with. I'll never be that man again."

"Then be the man you are," George argued. "Yes, you've changed. Yes, you've seen and experienced things that have made you different, but that doesn't mean they have to make you less than who you were before. These things, this war, doesn't have to make you worse. We break and we heal. We lose and we find new ways to open our hearts. We hurt, but we get better." He hesitated. "Show her the man you can be. Show yourself the man I know and the people of Pie Town know that you can be."

Raymond closed his eyes.

Father George waited.

"I'm not sure I know who that man is" was all he could say.

THIRTY-NINE

Malene was worried. Since Trina had left for Texas, nobody had heard from her. Father George had taken off; apparently he had left town without telling anyone, missing a church meeting, and no one had seen him. Roger had returned once again to the Silver Spur to try to talk Gilbert out of pressing charges and give him the money collected from the people of Pie Town to pay back what was taken. And one of the FBI agents, Agent Williams, kept hanging around the diner, where Malene was planning to talk to a news reporter from Albuquerque who was covering the story of the arrest of Frank Twinhorse.

She wasn't sure that Agent Williams knew about the interview, and she hoped she could meet the reporter out in the parking lot and go somewhere else before he had the chance to figure things out. She didn't really want to give him the opportunity to say anything, make up some bogus story about what he believed about Raymond and Frank; she wanted the full attention of the reporter.

She planned for the story to be about Frank Twinhorse, the upstanding citizen of Pie Town, the well-loved and well-respected business owner who had no prior criminal record and who was being held without proper cause. She intended to make sure the reporter knew about the unsubstantiated charges and the illegal detention, and she didn't want an FBI agent present while she was giving her take on what was happening. "Let the reporter speak to someone in Albuquerque, not to the agent who's been harassing everybody in Catron County," she thought to herself.

Malene didn't like Williams, and it wasn't just because of the things her husband had told her about him. She knew he had bungled the drug bust in Datil. She knew he thought Raymond Twinhorse was guilty of dealing drugs and that he saw no wrongdoing in keeping Frank locked up. She knew that he thought the older man was guilty as well. She had lots of reasons not to like the lawman; he was rude and insensitive, and he kept showing up at the diner and the church, filling up the entire room where he sat watching everyone. There were plenty of reasons not to like Agent Williams, but the main reason Malene had lost all charity for him was the way he treated the people of Pie Town. He used every opportunity he could find to belittle the citizens.

She had heard him on the phone calling the protests about Frank "a horde of hicks raising a stink for some Indian" and talking about their concern for Raymond as "a waste of time and emotion on a drunk and a junkie," so convinced was he that the young man was guilty of both robbing a bar and being involved in drug trafficking. Agent Williams kept hanging around Pie Town asking the same stupid questions of everyone, questions like, "You heard from Raymond Twinhorse?" "You know where that boy liked to hang out?"

He harassed every person he ran across in Pie Town. And that day it had been no different. He had already spoken to Francine, making all kinds of threats against her and Bernie if she was keeping information about Raymond's whereabouts from him. And ever since Malene had stopped by the diner after work, Agent Williams had been staring at her, listening to every phone conversation she had and watching every email she sent while she tried to get protesters ready for the trip to Albuquerque on Frank's behalf. He had overheard Roger tell Malene to call him if Father George contacted her, and Malene knew that Agent Williams remained convinced that Father George would be the one to lead the FBI to Raymond.

When George did call her on her cell phone just after the news reporter pulled into the parking lot, and just before she could explain that they needed to find a better place to talk, she did everything she could to keep Williams from knowing it was George on the other end.

"Malene here" she answered the phone.

"It's George," he replied.

And she immediately glanced around the diner. Agent Williams was watching the reporter, who was sitting in his vehicle in the parking lot, apparently talking on his phone. She turned around in her chair at the table, her back to the agent, hoping he wouldn't figure out who the stranger was or realize that she was talking to the priest. She knew it was a lot to hope for.

"Where are you?" she asked, talking as softly and as hurriedly as possible, glancing out at the parking lot. "We were about to send somebody to search for you!"

"I had an errand to run," he replied.

"An errand?" she asked.

He didn't explain. "Has anybody talked to Trina?" he asked, not really expecting good news after the messages he had heard on Frank's phone, the messages from Francine frantically trying to get Raymond to talk to his girlfriend.

"No," Malene answered. "I guess she's gone to Texas. Nobody's seen her all day." She turned back to see Agent Williams. "Of course, the FBI is here. Maybe I can make the suggestion and they'll go look for her."

"They're there?" George asked.

"Only the rude one," she replied, turning away from Williams. She thought he had ordered dessert and was no longer paying attention to her. "I really need to talk to Roger," Father George said.

"He's in Datil," she said. "He thought he could talk Gilbert into dropping the charges. Oris collected two hundred dollars to pay him back for the money he's missing." She noticed the reporter starting to get out of his car.

"Does he have his cell with him?" George asked.

"Sure, do you need the number?" Malene knew it by heart.

"Thanks, yes."

As Malene called out the number, she

384

could hear George reciting it to someone else, someone, she assumed, who was writing it down.

"Where are you?" she asked, wondering where George had gone and who was with him.

He cleared his throat before answering. "I found Raymond," he replied.

"What?" her voice was raised. She glanced around and didn't see Agent Williams sitting where he had been before. She turned and could see that the reporter was still in his vehicle, back on his phone.

"Look, don't let the FBI hear you." George tried to quiet her. "I figured out where he was and found him this afternoon. He wants to talk to Roger before the FBI gets to him."

He continued. "I don't want you to get in trouble, so I'm going to hang up and call him. But if he calls you first, let him know I need to talk to him. I'll have my cell phone with me in the car. You've got that number, right?"

"But where are you now?" Malene asked. "And is he okay?"

She was waiting for an answer when she felt the phone being grabbed from her hands.

"Raymond's fine" came the answer. "He's

385

been out near Techado all week, and he doesn't know anything about any drugs." He paused.

"Malene? Are you still there?"

Agent Williams had the phone and had heard enough to know that Father George was with his fugitive. "You need to stay where you are," he instructed the priest, and then heard the phone disconnect.

He held the cell phone so that he could read the screen and smiled. He turned and showed it to Malene, and she read the information about the number that she had entered into her phone when she first purchased it: FRANK'S HOME.

That was all Williams needed to know. He handed Malene the phone and headed out the door, leaving her shaken in his wake.

FORTY

By the time Williams had arrived at Frank's trailer with at least six other agents in tow, Raymond had gotten out of Pie Town and was driving toward Datil. It was dusk, and Father George was alone, waiting inside the trailer and expecting the worst. He had never been arrested before, and he didn't really relish the thought of having it happen right then, but it was the way, he believed, things had to be.

Remaining at the trailer had been his idea. George had reached Roger and told him that he was with Raymond. The young man wanted to talk to the sheriff and get the mess cleaned up. He wanted to get his dad out of jail, and he wanted to figure out the best way to talk to the FBI agents.

Roger was the one who suggested to George that they drive as quickly as possible to Datil, to the Silver Spur, where he would wait for him. He said that he would talk to Raymond and to Gilbert, and then call Agent Cochran, who he thought was in Albuquerque. He explained that he believed Cochran was fair and would be the best person from the FBI to see.

When George had put Roger on hold and told Raymond the plan of action, Raymond had asked the priest if he would drive him to the bar. And that was when Father George had the idea that Raymond should go alone and that he would wait at the trailer for Agent Williams to arrive. That way, he realized, there would be time enough for Raymond to get to the sheriff and do what they thought would be best. In a moment of clarity, George decided it was the right thing to do.

He would delay Williams in his search by being uncooperative while Raymond was given the time to get to the sheriff. And once the decision was made, neither Raymond nor Roger could talk him out of it.

"He'll threaten you with everything," Roger had explained when Father George got back on the phone, just a few minutes before Raymond left. "He's going to be very angry," he added. Later, when Father George heard Williams speeding down the dirt road with horns blowing and sirens blaring, it proved what Roger had said after finally agreeing to the plan: Williams liked a show.

Father George was listening carefully to the sheriff. "What are the consequences of aiding and abetting a fugitive?" he had asked, starting to feel a little nervous.

Roger had been silent a few moments before replying, "He'll likely throw you in jail." And then he had commented once again that trying to stall an FBI agent wasn't the best idea.

"Father George," Roger had said, "I don't think you should do this. If you leave now, we should have time to make this work."

There had been no response from George.

"If you stay, I'll do everything I can to make sure you aren't detained long, but I can't guarantee anything, and I don't know exactly what will happen after Raymond gets here. Right now, Gilbert is still planning to press charges. I can't get him to change his mind or take the money. I'm hoping that if he gets to talk to Raymond, he'll be convinced that something else happened, but I don't know that for sure. So you see, Williams might still get to Raymond anyway. So think about it," he had said.

Father George didn't know what to say. The news that Gilbert wasn't cooperating was not surprising, but it was also not what he had hoped to hear. He didn't want to give Raymond that bit of information.

"You saw what Frank is facing. It'll be the same for you."

There had been such a long pause that George almost thought Roger had hung up the phone, but then the sheriff spoke his final words. "Think about it before you make this choice. You can get Raymond to drop you off somewhere or you can walk along the creek bed, over to Bernie's, and take one of his vehicles back to the church. They probably wouldn't find you out there, and we'd still have time to figure this mess out. You have to consider the fact that making the decision to stay and face Williams will cost you."

And George knew Roger was talking about his relationship with the diocese, his standing as a Catholic priest.

At that point, he had glanced over at Raymond, who was waiting there beside him in the trailer, so broken and lost, so misunderstood, so determined to do the right thing, and while studying the boy, Father George had made his choice. He had put the phone down, sent Raymond to the car, and began preparing himself for what lay ahead.

He had already done a few of the things that Roger had told him to do. He had deleted the messages from Frank's voice mail and tried to get rid of anything that could show that Raymond had been there recently. When he hung up from the call to Roger, he had given Raymond information about his cell phone, which was in the car, and the clothes Raymond had been wearing to take with him to Datil. He wanted there to be as little evidence as possible that Raymond had been in the trailer.

And then, after explaining to Raymond that the keys were in the glove compartment of the car and that it would be safer and quicker for him to avoid Highway 60 and head south on the forest road to Aragon, then east on Highway 12 to Datil, he had sent the young man on his way. He then gave Raymond Roger's number and told him to call the sheriff when he got closer to the Silver Spur. All George knew was that Roger was trying to convince Gilbert to drop the robbery charges and working with Agent Cochran to try to figure out where the rumors of drug dealing had come, and that they were both working on getting Frank released before some big rally was held in Albuquerque.

Looking around the trailer, the priest awaited his fate. Nowhere in Frank's home could he see any harmful evidence that Raymond had been there. He knew that if the FBI found any fingerprints of Raymond's, he could argue that they had been made long before lightning struck and everything came unraveled in Pie Town. He wasn't sure exactly what story he would tell about where he had been, what he had said to Malene on the phone, or where his car was, but he knew he had to come up with something.

Checking his watch and waiting for Williams, he thought that he probably had time to make a phone call if he wanted to, but then decided there wasn't anyone he wanted to call. He wouldn't really know what to say to his mother, with whom he actually had little contact. His father was dead, and he had no siblings. Of course, there was the diocese in Gallup, George realized, but why would he want to call his superiors? Besides, he wasn't sure what he would say to them.

Father George knew that Roger, in speaking of the costs involved in his decision, was referring to his professional standing as a priest in the Catholic Church. However, since returning to Pie Town and rebuilding the community church, his relationship with the diocese had not been a very strong one anyway. The strain had begun when he was sent back to Catron County and given permission to rebuild the church, but offered no financial or contractual assistance.

George had been told not to expect any help, but once the building began, he had hoped there might at least be some assistance from the diocese with the required permits and county licenses. The diocese had been firm, however, in providing no help at all. And even though Father George had claimed that he didn't want or need that help and that his superiors' decision was not troubling for him, he knew there were a few hard feelings. Therefore, when the first service was held in the church and his superiors called to make arrangements to be in attendance, Father George had offered no invitation. "It was a community project," he had told the secretary in the office at Gallup, who was calling to secure the date, "and it will be a service only for the community." That had created a very chilly relationship with the Gallup Diocese.

George was also well aware that all the other local priests had heard of or spoken about his unorthodox ways — how he didn't wear the proper attire, how he cavorted with women, and, worst of all, how he offered Communion, the sharing of the Elements, to Protestants. He knew reports had been filed.

Father George Morris had not yet been cast out by the Bishop, but he had remained as far out on the periphery of the Church as a priest could be. He was sure that once an arrest was made, once he was accused of aiding a suspected drug dealer, searching for and finding him without giving proper notification to the authorities, turning over to the boy the car that had actually been a gift from the diocese, and lying to officials, any semblance of a tie he had with the Catholic Church would be severed immediately.

He heard the cars screech to a halt outside the trailer. As he calmly sat on the sofa, he remembered the story of the fugitive and the minister and thought about how sad that story had always made him. He recalled the meeting at church and the way the people of Pie Town had rallied around Raymond and Frank, refusing to believe that Raymond was guilty of robbery, refusing to believe that he was involved in drugs, refusing to allow FBI agents to force them to turn in one of their own. He took in a few deep breaths. Bolstered by the resolve he had seen in the people of Pie Town, he was proud to be a part of the community. He thought he should pray, for guidance and wisdom, and try to recall any appropriate scripture, but all he could think about was what Raymond had said before he left.

"Raymond Twinhorse." The voice on the loudspeaker sounded to George like Agent Williams's. "We know you are in there, and we have the place surrounded. Come out the front door with your hands up now."

For the longest time, Raymond had stood outside the door of the station wagon before driving off, just watching the priest. It had seemed as if he was offering some prayer or blessing of his own, and George was about to hurry him along when the young man finally spoke.

"My unit commander in Afghanistan always claimed that it wasn't courage or honor that defines a soldier," he had said, and George had stood silent.

"He said it was the sacrifice."

And then the priest lowered his eyes. When he looked up again, the boy was already traveling down the dirt road in the direction of Datil.

George rose from the sofa, crossed himself, and opened the front door of the trailer. A dozen guns were aimed right at his head.

FORTY-ONE

Deputy Danny White was parked off Highway 60, down along the forest road that twisted and turned from Datil to Old Horse Springs, listening to the police scanner and eating a sandwich. It was a favorite spot of his when he was on duty and needed to park and take a break. He had a good view of the highway and any speeders he might want to stop, and it was a good hiding place where he could just rest and stay out of the line of sight of all the folks in the county who enjoyed telling the sheriff every location where they had seen his deputy.

Learning that lesson had taken a few years, but after hearing Roger repeat the story of Danny hanging out at the diner in the middle of the afternoon, or the deputy waiting in the parking lot in the evening for his girlfriend to get off work, he decided that being out of town and off the road was the best place to spend time when there was nothing to do. Besides, he liked being outside and alone. He enjoyed the freedom of being parked off-road in the squad car, the space to ponder, to listen to chatter on the police radio, and to think about things, especially things with Christine. And in recent months, there had been many things to think about when it came to his fiancée.

She claimed that she was going to marry him, claimed that she loved him and wanted to make a life with him. But after watching as Danny almost beat Rob Chavez to death when he thought Rob had hurt his sister, Christine had said yes to the engagement but refused to set a date until Danny found a better way to handle his temper.

She had been right. Danny knew he had problems with anger long before he started dating her. He had been involved in so many fights as a young man that he had been warned by the high school principal that if he didn't figure out another way to settle his problems, he would surely end up fighting the wrong man and getting either killed or arrested. He had started trying to control his behavior after that conversation, but he had never learned how to control his anger. He just knew how to back away from a situation before he blew up. He knew how to walk away, but he didn't know how to keep from getting to that boiling point. Much to his surprise, though, his anger management classes and the one-to-one sessions with the instructor were helping. He was learning things about himself he hadn't known. For example, he was learning that he had real problems with being out of control, but that in fact life was mostly about being out of control. He was surprised that he was learning skills he would need for the rest of his life.

Danny rolled down his window and stuck his arm out. He slid down in the driver's seat and closed his eyes. It was late in the evening, not too much going on in Catron County, and he had three more hours left on his shift. It was still warm, his belly was full, and he thought he might take a nap.

"All deputies, please be on the alert that there is an APB out on Raymond Twinhorse," the announcement came across the scanner. "He's driving a 1979 Chevrolet station wagon, white with brown panels. He was last seen near Highway 603, just outside Pie Town, destination is unknown. The suspect is considered by the federal agents who are tracking him to be armed and dangerous."

Danny reached up and turned down the scanner. Raymond Twinhorse, he thought.

They're still after Raymond Twinhorse. He yawned and rubbed his eyes. He didn't understand all this attention being given to a guy suspected of robbing a bar. He didn't understand why this guy Williams seemed to have such a need to find someone who had no criminal record and had never been in any trouble with the law.

He leaned back and recalled his conversation with a new deputy who was coming on duty when Danny was going off. As his most recent experience with uncontrolled anger, he guessed, it was the incident he would likely bring up in his next session with the class instructor.

"Feds catch that Indian yet?" the officer had asked.

"Not today," Danny had answered.

"Why don't they go over to the reservation at Window Rock? They take care of their own, you know." The deputy had laughed at that.

Danny had not responded.

"I heard he went over there to Iraq and came home crazy, that he tore up the Silver Spur and threatened Gilbert that he was going to kill him and all his family." The deputy was looking over the daily records and grinning.

"I was at the Silver Spur," Danny finally

replied, taking a few clothes out of his locker and placing them in a small duffel bag. He was planning to do laundry. "It was not torn up, and Gilbert didn't say anything about a threat of violence." He closed his locker and was about to walk out the door. "And it was Afghanistan, not Iraq," he said. He wasn't really interested in defending Raymond Twinhorse, but he did have a soft spot for veterans.

"Afghanistan, Iraq, what the hell difference does it make? That war is a waste of our money. And those guys that go over there can't handle their shit. They go for a year, see a little action, and come home all messed up. They beat their wives, shoot each other, take drugs; they shouldn't let them go to war if they can't handle it."

"Oh, and you're so much better than that?" Danny had asked. He had never liked the new deputy, who had transferred in from Las Cruces.

"Hell, yeah," the young man had answered. "I'll go over there, raise hell with those desert rats, show them who's boss, clean up the mess, and come home a hero."

"Well, last I heard, they're still taking names down at the recruitment station in Socorro. Why don't you run over there and put your money where your mouth is?"

Danny had asked as he was walking away.

"Why don't you?" the other deputy replied. "Oh no, wait," he added. "From what I hear, you're already messed up and the only action you've ever seen in this county is that dog that bit its owner on the ass and a little old lady speeding home from church." He laughed. "I guess you don't have to go to war to find out you can't handle your shit."

With that, Danny had calmly placed his bag on the floor where he was standing, walked over, and punched the deputy in the face. The young man had not fought back, had instead screamed some obscenity and run out of the locker room. Danny remained surprised that he had not been called to the sheriff's office to talk about the incident. "Maybe I'm not doing as well as I thought," he said, laughing to himself.

He sat in the car and thought about Raymond. He wondered if the young man's problems in coming home from the war were anything like the problems Danny faced without ever having left New Mexico. Did Raymond struggle with rage and the loss of control the way he did, even though they hadn't faced similar experiences? He wondered how Raymond would fare if he was picked up by the FBI and thrown in prison. How long would he survive that kind of environment?

Danny didn't really know Raymond Twinhorse at all. He was eight or nine years older than the young veteran, and they had never run in the same circles. Danny had been a jock in high school and had remained close with the other athletes, even those from different classes. They still met to play ball on the weekend and often attended high school games together.

Raymond, Danny thought, had been kind of a loner in school, sociable but probably not all that popular. He had heard that the boy was smart and won a lot of awards for his grades, and he remembered that Raymond had always been in ROTC, the group of kids the football players loved to harass. He helped out Bernie King when he was a teenager, working on the ranch, and he was often seen hanging around the garage with his dad. But in all the time they had lived less than a few miles away from each other, Danny had not spoken more than a sentence to the boy. He wasn't even sure he'd recognize Raymond if he ran across him, although lately there had been more than one photograph of him floating around the station.

Danny had actually not seen Raymond Twinhorse since he returned from his tour in Afghanistan. He had been away for a buddy's wedding the weekend of the homecoming party, and since then, even though Christine had tried to organize a double date with Trina and Raymond, they had not gotten together. And yet, he had not pushed for an introduction. He had not been thrilled about meeting the guy. The truth was that he didn't really think the two of them would have anything in common. And since Danny might be called upon to arrest Raymond, now a suspect in a robbery and in drug dealing, he was glad the double date never worked out. He was glad Christine had been unsuccessful in getting them together since he didn't like socializing with men he had to drag to jail.

"All officers. . . ." The sudden announcement made Danny jump. He had gotten quite comfortable in the silence of the afternoon. In fact, he was almost asleep.

Danny turned up the volume as the county dispatcher continued. "It is believed that the suspect in the white station wagon is now heading east on Highway 60 in the direction of Datil. If you see the vehicle, please contact FBI Agent Lewis Williams," and then she called out a phone number. There was some static and then the words, "Do not approach the suspect alone. He is believed to be armed and dangerous. Call the FBI if you see this vehicle or the suspect, Raymond Twinhorse."

Danny sat up, placing his hand on his revolver. "Where are you going, Raymond?" he asked out loud, and then, just as the words left his lips, a white station wagon came speeding around the curve behind him, snaking and swerving down the dirt road, heading squarely in his direction.

■ ■ ■ ■

PART FIVE

■ ■ ■ ■

FORTY-TWO

Father George wasn't sure what was happening. The guard escorting him out of his cell and through the main exit wouldn't explain anything. He had shown up that afternoon, barking orders at the priest to get out of bed and walk to the cell door. When George did as he was told, sliding out of his cot and moving toward the front of the cell, shuffling his feet in the flip-flops that he had been given, the guard opened the door and placed handcuffs on his wrists. He started walking away and glanced back at George, who was still standing at the door. "Let's go," he instructed. And without knowing where he was going or what awaited him, Father George had followed.

The arrest, the processing, the almost twenty-four hours he had been jailed at the detention center in Albuquerque, none of it had been as bad as he expected, but then again, he had expected the worst. The previous evening, just as the sun was setting, George surrendered to the FBI agents who had surrounded Frank's home. He walked out of the trailer, his hands high above his head, and was immediately thrown to the ground by Agent Williams.

George was sure that he had a few bruises on his back from the agent's knee grinding between his shoulder blades, and his arms were sore from being yanked behind him. But aside from being handcuffed and then grabbed by the shirt collar and forced down to his knees, there had been no other physical mistreatment to endure. Far worse had been the mental struggle the priest faced, his struggle with dread and fear.

Williams had been so angry about Raymond getting away and the priest refusing to answer his questions sufficiently that George was convinced that more physical harm would be coming to him at the federal officer's hand. He tried not to be overcome by his fear of Williams, but the hostile agent was a big man and it was clear that none of the other officers present for the arrest would have stopped him if he wanted to rough George up.

After he had been handcuffed, he was ordered to sit against the rear wheel of a car while they searched the trailer. Two armed agents stood in front of him. When the exhaustive search had been concluded and it was clear that George was alone, one of the agents had yanked him up by his shirt collar and dragged him over to Williams, who was waiting by the trailer steps. The priest had been forced to his knees, with the two agents still behind him and a gun at his back, while being interrogated by Williams, who loomed over him.

"Where is Raymond Twinhorse?"

George shook his head. "I don't know."

"I'll ask you again, Father. Where is Raymond Twinhorse?" Williams's voice had been calm but very sharp.

"I don't know. We were here, and then he left." He had decided not to tell the lie that Raymond had not been with him.

"Where did you find him?"

"Up near Techado Mountain."

"You were in Ramah earlier?"

George nodded.

"How did you know where he was?"

He had shrugged. "Just a lucky guess." When he looked up at Williams, he had wanted to ask for a lawyer and be done with this very uncomfortable interview, but he had known that the longer his conversation with Agent Williams went, the more time Raymond would have to get to Roger.

"Where is Raymond Twinhorse now?" Williams had asked again, leaning into George, his face close to the priest's.

George shook his head, trying to pull away from the agent. "I don't know," he had answered again, feeling the barrel of the gun jammed into his back.

"You left Techado Mountain together, you drove to Frank's trailer, you called Malene Benavidez, and then he stole your car and left you here?" Williams paused. "Is that what you're saying?"

And George had sat back on his heels and stared up at the agent, his confidence growing a little. "No, that's not what I'm saying," he had replied.

"You gave him your car?" Williams demanded, lording over the priest.

"I did," George answered.

"And where was he going in your car?" The agent would not give up.

"Again, Agent Williams, I don't know where Raymond Twinhorse went in my car," he had lied.

Williams had immediately pulled his cell phone off his belt and made a call. He gave a description of the car that was already on file — since he had been following Father George for a while — and reported that it was likely to be somewhere in the area of

Pie Town.

Straining to see the watch on Agent Williams's wrist, George had just been able to make out the time. It had been almost half an hour since Raymond drove away, and Father George was hopeful that he'd had enough time to get to Datil and that Roger had come up with some plan for his release. He had waited, his head bowed.

"You think you're smart, don't you?" Williams had sneered.

Father George didn't answer, kept his head bowed.

Williams had kicked him, not hard but forcefully enough that George winced.

"You and these hillbillies from *Cartoon County,* you all think you're above the law, but I'm here to tell you I can lock you up for a very long time. I got obstructing justice, aiding and abetting a fugitive, hindering the process of prosecution, and a whole list of laws about national security at my disposal for assholes like you that can get you in the same prison as terrorists. And the funny thing is, there's not a damn thing you or your Mexican sheriff or your dumb-ass rancher church folks can do about it."

Father George had not responded. He knew it was best just to keep quiet. He certainly had not wanted to antagonize the

411

agent any further. Williams had kicked him again, calling him a name that George didn't remember ever being called before. And that had been the extent of his interview. One of the agents behind him had jerked him up to a standing position, walked him over to a car, and thrown him in the backseat. "Take him to Albuquerque" was the last thing he had heard Williams say.

About twenty-four hours had passed since that encounter, and the only human contact George had had since his arrival at the detention center was a guard bringing him his meals: dinner after he had been in the cell for what seemed to be about five hours, breakfast before the sun rose, and a sandwich just before he had been ordered out.

"Where are you taking me?" he asked the guard, walking at a brisk pace, trying to keep up. "I don't know a lot about the law, but I'm pretty sure I have a right to an attorney." He followed the man.

The guard said nothing. The two of them moved through a number of corridors, several large steel doors magically opening and closing as they passed through.

"I demand the opportunity to make a phone call," George said, his voice a little louder this time, but still there was no response.

The guard led him through a final door, and George recognized where he was. He had arrived in the front of the center, the same place where he had started when he came to visit Frank. He glanced around and saw no one. At the desk the guard picked up a manila envelope, and George was given his personal belongings — his watch, a ring, his wallet and shoes, a crucifix necklace, and rosary beads. The guard unlocked the handcuffs and pointed to the front door.

"You are free to go," he said, then turned and walked away.

As George made his exit with no understanding of what had just happened and what he was allowed to do, he heard a familiar greeting.

"Buenos dias, Father."

George lifted his face, felt the warmth of the sunshine, and took in a deep breath. "Buenos dias, Roger," he replied, glad to be outside, glad to be free. He stood for a moment, enjoying the outdoors, his eyes closed. When he opened his eyes and looked around, he saw that the parking lot was filled with people. It appeared as if everyone from Pie Town was standing there to greet him, and when they saw him approach they immediately let out a loud cheer.

The sheriff slapped George on the back

and opened the rear door of his squad car, and as the priest started to get inside he noticed someone in the front seat. He saw the long black hair, now twisted in the traditional Navajo bun, and he smiled.

"Hope you don't mind another rider," Frank Twinhorse turned and said.

"Not at all," George responded. "Not at all." And as Frank turned to shake his hand, the priest crawled into the backseat, gripping the hand offered to him.

FORTY-THREE

"Well, look who's here!" Francine called out as Trina walked in the diner carrying Alexandria on her hip. "You sure are a sight for sore eyes," she added, reaching over to take the baby from Trina.

"Hello, Francie," Trina said, placing Alexandria into the older woman's arms.

The little girl laughed as she received a big hug from Francine.

Trina smiled. "Somebody's happy to see you," she commented, noting her daughter's exuberance at being in the arms of their friend.

"I'm pretty sure somebody's happy to see you too," Francine responded, tilting her head in the direction of the back of the restaurant.

Trina glanced over to where Francine was motioning and saw Raymond sitting alone, watching. He raised his chin in greeting.

"Let's go see what Uncle Fred has cooking in the kitchen," Francine said to Alexandria as she headed around the counter, leaving Trina alone in the front of the diner with Raymond.

Trina slowly moved over to his booth.

"You want something to eat?" he asked.

She shook her head. "We had a late breakfast," she acknowledged.

He nodded. "I'm glad you came," he said, watching as she slid into the booth opposite him.

"Glad you asked," she responded.

There was an awkward pause.

"Guess a lot happened while I was away," Trina said, glancing around the diner. There were no other customers yet, but she knew that would change soon. Lunchtime was fast approaching.

"Dad's out of the detention center," Raymond said. "All the charges were dropped." He shrugged. "Turns out, there weren't really any charges against him. The FBI just claimed he was 'being processed.'" Raymond shook his head. "I guess that's how they do things these days."

"Yeah, I guess so," Trina noted. "How did they finally get him cleared?"

"One of the agents who was around here looking for me, Agent Cochran, he did it."

"With a little help from Roger's persuasive

nature, I imagine." Trina knew the sheriff was not going to stop until he got Frank out of jail and Raymond out of trouble.

"Apparently, he made quite an impression on Agent Cochran," Raymond noted. "Got him to check out his suspicions about a drug operation at Old Horse Springs and kept him from arresting me."

"But there was that other agent, Williams. Wasn't he the one determined to see you locked up?" Trina had met the FBI agents before she left for Texas.

"Father George and I ran into each other over at Techado. We were at Dad's trailer and Agent Williams found out, but by the time he got to the trailer looking for me, I was already gone. That's why Father George got locked up, for covering for me, for not turning me in."

"Father George got locked up too?" This was news she hadn't heard.

Raymond nodded.

"Wow, I did miss a lot." She shook her head. "So where did you go when you left the trailer?"

"Datil," he replied. "The Silver Spur, to try and fix things with Gilbert."

"And that FBI agent didn't find you?"

"It was a while before Williams actually figured out where I was. He was pretty mad, took it out on Father George, I imagine. Anyway, I had time to get things straightened out and Cochran had time to get Dad out of jail."

"George was able to stall the agent?" Trina asked. "How did he do that? He's a terrible liar, you know."

"Well, he kept the agent busy for a little while, but it seems there was also an official report filed that wasn't quite accurate," Raymond answered.

Trina waited for the rest of the explanation.

"Danny called the FBI and said he had seen me and George's missing vehicle way in another part of the county."

"Danny White?" Trina asked.

"The one and only," Raymond replied.

"Danny called in a false report?" Trina was surprised.

"Well, I don't think Roger wants to have his deputy accused of that." Raymond grinned.

"Wow, well, that's pretty impressive," Trina responded. "I guess I had pegged the deputy all wrong. Looks like I need to talk to Christine and tell her what a good guy she's actually got."

"Of course the FBI wasn't too thrilled about the wild goose chase, and Roger and

Danny both got their asses chewed out by Williams. But in the end it was very helpful not to have Williams in Datil or at the detention center throwing his weight around because it gave Agent Cochran and Roger enough time to get everything sorted out."

Trina nodded. "Wow, what a story!" She paused to think about everything Raymond was telling her. "But what about the whole drug thing? Were there really drugs in Catron County?"

"Roger and Cochran were in Datil when I got there. Agent Cochran finally listened to what Roger had thought was happening all along. So the agent went to Albuquerque to check on what had really occurred that morning in Alamo. It turns out the other guy, Agent Williams, had made such a mess of things on the pueblo land, acted on some bogus information and made the bust without having any cause, that he was searching for any way to save his reputation. So when Williams got wind of the Silver Spur robbery, he talked to the bartender and just made the leap that I was the one he was really after."

"So it was like Roger thought all along," Trina commented. "It was just a matter of a federal officer trying to clean up his mess and save face."

Raymond nodded.

"But was there ever any drug trafficking?" Trina asked. "Didn't Roger think there was something going on down at Old Horse Springs?"

"According to Danny, not anything that amounts to a real operation. Some guy in prison made the story up just to get his sentence reduced. The suspicious activity that the sheriff called the feds about down at that old ranch was just a couple of guys selling pot. The fellow in prison knew about it and thought he could make it sound bigger than what it was. So he made up a lot of stuff and then gave the agents a wrong address."

"And Agent Williams took it from there." Trina was filling in the blanks.

"I guess he was hoping this would lock in a promotion for himself," Raymond suggested.

Trina had to laugh. "Well, I hope that's no longer in the works," she said.

Raymond shook his head. "Agent Cochran told Roger that his partner has been assigned to White Sands."

"White Sands?" Trina repeated. "There's nothing in White Sands."

"I think that's the point," Raymond responded with a grin. He slid his hand over the top of his head. "Well, I'm just glad Dad and Father George and Roger are okay."

"Yeah, me too," Trina said, smiling.

The two stopped talking and glanced around. A couple had just made their way into the diner. Trina didn't recognize them. She assumed they were tourists traveling through.

"What about you?" Trina asked when she met Raymond's eyes again. "You okay?"

Raymond smiled. "I'm better," he replied. "All the charges were dropped against me." He paused. "Turns out, the bartender's brother had deposited the money in the bank before leaving on his camping trip. He returned to Datil and cleared things up about the same time I got there."

"All this trouble and the bartender's brother had the money the whole time?" Trina asked. "Man, it seems to me like they should arrest him for making a false report."

Raymond shrugged. "He thought he was robbed. He was just mad because he thought his money was stolen."

"Still, he caused a lot of people a lot of trouble. Didn't he talk to his brother at all?"

"Guess there aren't any phones where he goes camping. And he had left a note, Gilbert just never found it. He saw the empty cash register and jumped to a conclusion about what had happened."

Trina looked at Raymond. "Did he even apologize to you?"

Raymond shook his head. "Not really," he said. "But it's okay. I was a real jerk that night I was in the bar."

Trina glanced away. She listened as Bea came out of the kitchen and answered the couple's question. She smiled as Bea gave them the list of available pies.

"I'm the one who owes everyone an apology," Raymond said softly and then turned away. "Especially to you." He turned back and faced Trina. "I'm so sorry for what happened that night, for the drinking and for causing you to get burned." He shook his head. "I am really. . . ."

"It's okay," Trina interrupted him. "I know that you're going through a really difficult time. I know that whatever happened to you over there in Afghanistan is way more than what showed in your X-rays at the hospital."

Raymond nodded. "I know that now too. And that's part of the reason I wanted to see you today."

Trina waited.

"I'm going to Albuquerque this afternoon. Dad's taking me to the VA Hospital." He hesitated. "To the psych unit," he added. "I'm checking myself in as a patient." He dropped his face. "I know now that I need some help."

Trina reached across the table and took his hands.

"I'm glad for you, Raymond," she said.

There was another long pause as they listened to Fred and Bea and Francine playing in the kitchen with Alexandria.

Raymond smiled and then slowly pulled his hands away from Trina.

"How was Texas?" he asked.

Trina sat back in the booth. "Big as always," she answered, knowing full well what he was asking.

"You going there to stay?"

Trina blew out a long breath. "Well, here's the thing." She cleared her throat. "Turns out Conroe has his hands pretty full trying to pay child support and share custody of his other two children. He's not real interested in playing house with a woman and her two-year-old." She tried to smile, but it was obvious that what had happened in Abilene had been a difficult experience for her.

"I'm sorry," Raymond said.

"I'm sorry too," Trina responded. "I should have waited and talked to you before I left to go see him. I should have let you know what I was doing."

"Well, it's not like I was around to give you a listening ear," he noted. "And it's not like the last time we were together instilled any confidence in me or in our relationship."

Trina shook her head. "I doubted you. I doubted us."

"I'm pretty sure that's my fault," Raymond said.

"Maybe," Trina replied. "But I gave up pretty easily, and I was way too quick to think about going back to Conroe."

Raymond didn't respond. He glaced away and then faced Trina. "Look, I asked you to come here today because, besides saying I'm sorry, there's something I need to say to you."

She listened.

"While I was away I had a lot of time to think. About me, about the accident, the stuff that happened over there, you, us." He leaned forward. "I want to say that I finally realize and accept that I'm not the man I used to be, the one I think you fell in love with, but while I was up in the hills, away from Pie Town, away from you, someone helped me see that even though I might be different, that doesn't have to be a bad thing." He hesitated. "Maybe it's actually a good thing, because maybe I can be better

— you know, be an even better man."

Trina smiled and nodded. "Sounds like you spent some time with Father George," she said.

He laughed. "Yeah, we had a few hours together. He's a good guy."

"Yeah, he actually is," she agreed.

"I want to say to you that I want to be a better man for myself, but I also want to be a better man for you and for Alexandria." He took in a deep breath. "I love you, Trina, and I want us to be together, the three of us, and I am willing to fight to get better because I want to be with you and with that little girl in there."

Trina felt the tears standing in her eyes. "I'd like that too," she said. "I'd like that very much."

"I'll be gone about a month," he explained. "I don't know what will happen."

"We never do," Trina said. "But you know, that's what makes life so interesting." She reached out her hands.

He took them.

"What you can count on is that Alexandria and I will be here when you get back, and we can try again."

Raymond nodded.

Both of them turned just as Francine was making her way over to their table. "You two look like you could use some pie." And she placed two small plates in front of them and handed each of them a fork. "It's a new recipe, and I think you'll like it. I'm calling it Stay Home Pie."

"Yeah?" Trina said, wiping her eyes. She stuck her fork in the slice in front of her. "And what made you call it that?" She took a bite and nodded in approval.

"Well, I'm glad you asked. You see, I'm hoping it's so good that our friends will never leave. I'm counting on it being so tasty that you'll both never head out of Pie Town again. 'Cause even if a relationship hits a bump and a person is thinking about taking the fast train out of here, or motorcycle or fancy truck, well, maybe at least this pie will make that person want to stay home." Francine winked at Trina. "It's really just tomato pie," she whispered.

The two women watched as Raymond took a bite from his slice and grinned.

"Well, Ms. Francine, it works for me." He put down his fork. "I was just telling Trina that I'm going away for a little while, but when I get back, as long as you teach me how to bake this pie, I plan to be staying at home for a very long time."

And Francine clapped her hands together and headed back to the kitchen.

FORTY-FOUR

Father George had stepped out of the rectory to pick up the morning paper out of Glenwood, which he received once a month. He had been up before dawn and was glad to see that the delivery person had gotten the papers out early. He opened it as he stood on the porch and read the monthly headlines that told the story of false charges made some time ago against a Catron County resident and the reaction of the Federal Bureau of Investigation to the protest rally held at the detention center that was really more like one huge party.

There was a picture of Oris standing next to a Navajo shaman. The two of them were grinning and eating pie. George laughed.

"Good story?"

George glanced down from the porch to see Raymond Twinhorse standing near the steps. He was surprised, since he hadn't heard or seen a vehicle in the parking lot of the church or anywhere close by, and also because he hadn't heard that Raymond was home from the hospital.

"Raymond," he said. He glanced around. "How did you get here?" he asked.

The young man smiled. "Walked," he replied.

"From Albuquerque?" The priest sounded surprised.

"From Techado," he answered and then had to laugh. "I love to walk, but not that far," he said.

George nodded, realizing his mistake. "Right," he said.

"Just north of Mr. King's ranch." Raymond looked behind him. "I got home yesterday, and then I drove out there a couple of hours later and started walking. I couldn't sleep. I just feel better when I'm outside."

George thought about the area where he had searched for Raymond and knew that it was much more than five miles away. He figured the young man had walked at least ten or twelve miles to get to the church. "You want to come in for some breakfast?" he asked. "Coffee?"

Raymond turned to face the priest. "I wanted to come see you," he said.

George sensed that Raymond preferred to

stay outside, so he walked down the steps to stand closer to him. He left the paper on the porch railing.

"I haven't had the chance to thank you for what you did," Raymond said.

George shook his head. "It was Roger who was smart enough to handle everything so well. He got that agent to check out the story about the drug dealers. He's the one who got the charges dropped against you and got Frank and me out of jail. He's the one you need to thank."

"I have, and I will keep thanking him. Roger is a good man and an excellent sheriff. And Danny, he kept the FBI from finding me. I can't forget the deputy."

George sat down on the steps while the young man remained standing. He was glad to see Raymond. "I hear you've done well these last couple of weeks at the VA. I tried a couple of times to see you, but they told me you couldn't have visitors."

Raymond nodded. "It was pretty intense what they put me through, but I think it helped. And I'm going to stay in a support group, take new meds for depression. I think I'm better."

George smiled. He was glad to hear that.

"I wanted you to know that I had a lot of time to think before I went to the hospital."

He sat down next to the priest. "And then, of course, I had a lot of time to think while I was there," he added.

George looked ahead. "Yeah, I had my own time of reflection and contemplation. They don't call it 'serving time' for nothing." He leaned into Raymond, making a small joke.

Raymond nodded.

The two were silent for a while. They were enjoying the rising sun coming over the mountains.

"I'd like to confess."

George was surprised. He had never known Raymond to make a confession. He hesitated. "Oh, okay, let me go get the room ready, and I'll meet you over there." He pointed with his chin toward the sanctuary and started to get up.

Raymond shook his head. "No, I'm fine to do it here," he replied.

"But I don't have my vestments," George said, "or my prayer book," he added, thinking he should go inside to get them. He stood up.

"I don't need all that," Raymond noted.

There was a pause.

George nodded. "Okay," he said and sat back down.

Raymond stayed seated on the steps

beside him.

"Forgive me, Father, for I have sinned," Raymond began. He stopped and turned to Father George. "Is that right?" he asked. "I've forgotten what to say."

"That's fine," George said.

Raymond nodded and continued. "Forgive me, Father, for I have sinned." He hesitated.

The priest turned to face the young man to make sure he was okay and to help him along if he needed it.

Raymond spoke quietly. "I thought I could shake the demons I faced as a soldier by myself. I thought I didn't need help."

There was a pause.

"And in my arrogance and in my decision not to get the help I needed, I have harmed the people I love and brought danger to them."

George wanted to interrupt. He wanted to tell the young man that his actions were consequences of what he had endured in war, but he didn't stop him. He knew that Raymond needed to relieve himself of the burden and that his job as priest was to allow that to happen. He waited as Raymond continued.

"I confess that I have wanted to die."

Father George closed his eyes.

Raymond took in a breath. "I've thought

a lot about what happened over there, and I've thought that since I was so damaged, so, you know, broken, that I would only be able to damage or break the people around me." He hesitated.

"I have wished every day since I got back that it had been me who died in that desert and not everybody else in my company." His voice shook a bit. "I don't know why I'm the one who lived, why it's me and not any of them."

There was no response.

Raymond continued. "And for the longest time, I haven't been able to think anything else other than that."

Father George felt heaviness, a weight upon his chest.

"But when I was out on the mountain, out near Techado for the seven days, I felt something else, something different. I don't know." He waited. "I started to feel like maybe I could be okay."

Father George kept his head bowed.

"There were lots of things that helped. Talking to the hospital shrink has been important. The sing was good," he added, referring to the ceremony his people and the medicine man had held for him. "Dad coming out and being with me, that helped too. What you said about fighting for Trina, about fighting for what is important, that helped. And the place. . . ."

Father George smiled.

"The desert, the silence at night, the beauty I saw every day, that made a difference."

The priest nodded. Having been where Raymond had been, he understood.

"But what I think helped the most was this town, these people, Roger, Trina, Malene. . . ." He turned to the priest. "You."

George glanced up.

"I guess I figured that if this many people. . . ." He paused, recalling the responses from the members of the community. "Did you know that every day I was in the hospital somebody from town wrote me a letter, that there was a list of folks who tried to visit and were turned away because I couldn't have guests? I had more requests than anybody else." He paused. "Frankly, after a couple of weeks I could have had visitors, but I just couldn't take all that company." He rested his hands on his legs. "Did you know that Mr. Whitsett called his son, an officer in the army, and made sure I got the best care at the VA that was available? And did you know that he even offered me his Buick to drive when I need a car?"

George shook his head. Of all the reports about the people of Pie Town, that bit of information was the hardest to believe.

"Danny has invited me and Trina to hang out with him and Christine. Mr. King said I could work on the ranch if I needed a job, and he wants to give me an old Cadillac he has. And his girlfriend, Francine Mueller, is going to teach me how to bake pies. She says I have the hands for baking." He held out his hands in front of him.

George watched as the young man seemed to be studying his hands. Maybe he was still surprised at what good they could do, he thought.

"Did you know that three hundred people showed up at the detention center in Albuquerque to get them to release Dad? Three hundred people?" he repeated. "That's twice as many people as live in Pie Town!" He shook his head in amazement.

Raymond continued. "They were all standing out there when Roger and I came out from the interview. All of them out in the parking lot, wearing these crazy T-shirts that somebody ordered with the wrong words on them, holding hands, singing crazy songs from the civil rights era. Have you ever heard that song, 'We Shall Overcome?' "

434

George had to laugh. "Yes, I have, and they sang it like they meant it. Of course, the T-shirts were pretty funny. *See* Frank Twinhorse instead of *Free* Frank Twinhorse? I got one as a souvenir."

"I know . . . crazy, right?" Raymond laughed too. "Anyway, I guess I figured if this many people cared about me, cared about my dad, believed me when I said I didn't steal any money or deal drugs, I guess I thought that if they were willing to stand by me, stay with me, I must not just be the damage. I must be something more than what happened over there. There must be more to me than that. And I guess I owe something to the men who died. Being a drunk or a suicide is a poor way to honor those who didn't make it." He shrugged. "So, I don't know." He turned back to Father George.

The priest was watching him.

"I guess I'm not doing this thing right," he said, referring to the confession he had started. "What I really wanted to say is that I'm sorry I couldn't see what everybody else saw and what I want, what I need, is to be able to see myself like they do."

George waited. He lifted his face, glancing toward the horizon, where the sun was now full and high in the morning sky.

The priest took a breath and quoted the words of Jeremiah that he had memorized since his trip to Ramah and since his return home from the detention center.

" 'Thus says the Lord; a voice is heard in Ramah, lamentation and bitter weeping. Rachel is weeping for her children; she refuses to be comforted for her children, because they are no more. Thus says the Lord: Keep your voice from weeping and your eyes from tears; for there is a reward for your work, says the Lord: they shall come back from the land of the enemy; there is hope for your future, says the Lord; your children shall come back to their own country.' "

Father George turned to the young man and made the sign of the cross above his head. "You are absolved of the errors of your way. Go and sin no more." And then he bent down and grabbed some dirt from the ground and poured it into Raymond's open hand.

He nodded with a smile and simply said, "This is your land, Raymond Twinhorse, the land that raised you, the land that healed you. Welcome back, son. Welcome home."

Forty-Five

"Daddy, did you spike this?" Malene had just taken a sip of punch.

Oris smiled. "I may have added a few extra ingredients to sweeten it up." He winked.

"Daddy!" Malene rolled her eyes. "The punch is spiked," she announced to the group gathered in the diner for a party celebrating Raymond's return from the VA Hospital in Albuquerque and the engagement of Bernie King and Francine Mueller.

"Well, hallelujah!" Father George headed to the table, causing everyone to laugh. "What's a party without having a little Oris Whitsett adventure?" George poured himself a glass and took a swallow. "It's almost as good as the birthday party punch, but not quite."

He was speaking of the first party he had attended in Pie Town, a birthday party for Roger and Malene's grandson. The priest had been unaware of the spiked punch and ended up getting very drunk.

"You go easy there, Father George. I think we're still expecting the late Mass this evening at church." Fedora Snow was sitting at the booth near the window.

Father George smiled and took another swallow.

Trina immediately pushed her cup of punch away from Alexandria. "Bea, would you get us some milk, please, and a soda for Raymond?"

Bea walked behind the counter and poured the little girl some milk in a cup and grabbed a soda from the cooler. She walked back and handed the cup to Trina. She smiled at Raymond, who was seated next to Trina, and handed him the other drink.

"Well, Bernie, Francine," Roger decided to change the subject. "Why don't you tell us about your wedding plans?" He got a glass of punch and returned to the table where he had been sitting.

Everyone hushed.

Bernie cleared his throat. "Well, since we're of a more mature age . . . ," he started.

"You mean since you're almost dead," Oris yelled out, interrupting the groom-to-be.

"Thank you, Oris," Bernie commented.

"Since we're older," he said with a smile, "Father George has released us from the six weeks of premarital counseling."

"Hey, that's not fair!" Danny stood up from his seat. "You're making us go through all the workshops, plus we have to do a retreat in the fall."

Father George shrugged.

"Don't lose your patience, Danny," Trina said, glancing over at Christine. "I'm sure you'll be hearing your own wedding bells soon enough."

Danny sat back down, and Christine reached for his hand. He turned to his fiancée and mouthed an apology, and then he glanced over at Raymond, who was wearing a big smile. The two men had become friends after all.

"Do you really think that's such a good idea?" Oris asked, changing the direction of the conversation back to Bernie's announcement.

"What do you mean, Oris?" Father George wanted to know.

"Shouldn't they at least take the sex class?"

Millie Watson elbowed Oris so hard that he spilled his punch.

"Well, I don't know why I shouldn't bring it up. We all know that Bernie King doesn't have any idea about how to please a woman." He pulled away from Millie, afraid she'd elbow him again.

"Oh, and like you do?" Fedora Snow wiped her mouth. She had just taken a swallow of the punch.

"Now, Fedora, don't you sit over there and pretend I can't make you bark like a dog."

"Daddy, please!" Malene spoke up. "We have children in the room."

"Oh, sorry, Raymond." Oris winked at the young man.

"Could I please get back to our wedding?" Bernie asked.

The room was quiet.

Bernie cleared his throat. "We're planning a nice ceremony at the ranch late September, to which you're all invited." He turned around. "Except you, Oris."

Everyone laughed.

"Serves him right." Fedora Snow drank the rest of her punch and sat up in her chair.

"We'll have a big spread, and Roger and the boys will play the music. Father George will officiate, of course."

The priest lifted his cup and nodded in agreement.

Bernie grinned and turned to Francine. "And it will be the happiest day of my life."

A chorus of "ahhhs" filled the diner. Francine blushed.

"There will, of course, be a wedding pie," Fred announced. "The bride and groom will serve both chocolate and pecan. Their favorites." He smiled at the couple. "And Bea and I will be preparing all the food."

"Well, now I'm not so disappointed that I'm not invited." This time Oris elbowed Millie, almost knocking her over.

"It sounds lovely," Trina responded, smiling at Bernie and Francine.

"So everybody take your glasses of punch." Roger had stood up from his seat. He paused. "That is, if you're of age," he added. "And let's toast the soon-to-be bride and groom. To Bernie and Francine."

"To Bernie and Francine," everyone called back.

"And now for the other reason we're here." Roger was still standing. "We celebrate the release of Frank and Father George from the detention center in Albuquerque. . . ."

"Here, here!" Bernie shouted, and everyone applauded.

Father George bowed from where he was standing next to the front table, and Frank lifted his hand in acknowledgment. He was at the table with Trina and Raymond and

441

the baby.

"Lord knows, if they were still locked up we'd be faced with a lot of unhappy Catholics and a few broken-down cars." Roger smiled.

"Not my Buick," Oris noted.

Roger ignored him. "And we also celebrate the homecoming of Raymond Twinhorse, our hero, our son."

Everyone lifted their glasses again. "To Raymond," they all shouted.

And the young man watched as the citizens of his town toasted him. He smiled at Trina and looked down. It was obvious that he was at a loss for words.

"And now," Bea announced as she returned from the kitchen, "there is pie!"

Everyone got their slices and began eating.

"Francine, this is your best yet." Malene had her mouth full.

"This is excellent," Roger agreed.

"Well, Francine, even I have to give my stamp of approval and take away every bad thing I've ever said about your baking. I may have to wrestle Bernie for you if you can bake pies like this." Oris had eaten his in three bites and was already going for a second slice. "What do you call this?" he asked.

"Heavenly Chocolate Pie. But I didn't bake it," Francine responded.

"What?" Malene asked. "Bea, did you start baking?"

Bea shook her head. "Nope, not me either."

"Then who?" Christine asked. "Because I already want to place an order for my birthday party. Who needs cake when you can have Heavenly Chocolate Pie?"

"I guess now is as good a time as any to make my announcement." Francine moved away from the counter and stood in front of the group.

She smoothed down the front of her dress. "I have decided to leave my job here at the diner," Francine said to the group, glancing over at Bernie. "I'd like to be able to spend as much time as I can with my husband on the ranch."

"I told you they were near death," Oris said to Millie.

"Then who will make the pies?" Danny asked.

"The person taking my place is the one who baked the pie you're eating," Francine replied.

Everyone glanced around the room trying to figure out who was such a good baker and who was going to work at the diner.

A throat was cleared, and everyone turned to the table where Trina and the baby were sitting with Raymond and Frank.

Raymond stood up. "Francine taught me a lot since I've been back," he said. "It's really more about the crust than it is the filling."

"Well I'll be damned," Oris exclaimed. "Our hero can bake pies."

And everyone at the diner cheered.

EPILOGUE

The old man walked to the top of Techado Mountain. The sun was setting, but the desert air was not yet chilled. Autumn had arrived, but the summer was unwilling to release its hold on the earth and the air was hot and dry. He walked slowly, his cane guiding his steps until he reached the peak. As he stood above the land of his ancestors, the only place he knew as home, he cast his gaze to the south, in the direction of the place he had come to bless: a large ranch with a house at the far north end.

He could not see the celebration that had begun in the late afternoon. He could not make out the faces of those who gathered, the smiles of the well-wishers, the quiet tears of a man promising himself to a woman. He could not make out the hands that slipped into others or the close way lovers danced. He did not hear the music or the laughter, the words of a prayer given by a priest, words beckoning the spirit of love to fall like rain upon the couple and upon those gathered. He did not recognize the shouts announcing that another marriage had been made. He could not see or hear the wedding, but he knew that love and life were rich below him. He knew that a man and a woman had joined themselves together and that a boy had been reunited with the earth, with his home.

The old man smiled as the clouds gathered and a low rumble of thunder could be heard from the mountains far away. He saw a few flashes of heat lightning dance across the western sky, but he was not worried. He knew the storms of yesterday could not threaten the bonds forged today.

He bowed to the east and the west. He bowed to the north and then, turning again to the south, in the direction of the gathering of the people of the little Catron County village, he opened his small pouch, the corn pollen falling through his fingers, and quietly said the words of a blessing for the people.

He finished his prayer, made his four bows again, and headed back to his home. His job was done for the moment. The boy, the town, and the gathering of those below the mountain had found their hope in this ceremony of love, their courage in the choices made by friends for friends, and their strength in the power of the bonds between them. On this day, he knew, no storm cloud or rain, no harsh winds or fierce lightning, no violent hail or scorching sun, on this day, this good day, no enemy would prevail against them.

The old man laughed as he walked off the mountain. "This is a good place" you would have heard him say if you had been there, listening. "This place they call home. This place they call Pie Town."

CINNAMON COFFEE CAKE

Topping
1/4 cup sifted all-purpose flour (sift before
  measuring)
1/2 cup brown sugar
1/4 cup butter, room temperature
1 1/2 teaspoons cinnamon

In a small mixing bowl, combine all of the
topping ingredients. Blend with a fork until
crumbly and then set aside.

Cake
1 1/2 cups sifted all-purpose flour (sift
  before measuring)
2 1/2 teaspoons baking powder
1/2 teaspoon salt
1 egg, beaten
3/4 cup sugar
1/3 cup melted butter

1/2 teaspoon vanilla extract
1/2 cup milk

Sift the flour with the baking powder and salt into a medium bowl. In another medium bowl, beat together the beaten egg, sugar, and melted butter. Add the vanilla and milk. Stir in the flour mixture and mix well. Pour the cake batter into a greased and floured 9-inch layer-cake pan or an 8-inch square pan.

Sprinkle the topping crumb mixture evenly over the batter. Bake at 375 degrees for 30 minutes, or until the cake tests done. Allow the coffee cake to cool partially in the pan on a wire rack before cutting it into squares. Serve immediately.

TRI-BERRY PIE

1/2 cup white sugar
3 tablespoons cornstarch
2 cups fresh strawberries, halved
1 1/2 cups raspberries
1 1/2 cups fresh blueberries
9-inch double pie crust

In a large mixing bowl, stir together the cornstarch and sugar. Add the berries and gently stir until the berries are coated. Line a 9-inch pie plate with one crust. Stir the berry mixture, then transfer it to the pie plate. Top with the second crust. Seal and crimp the edge. (To prevent overbrowning, cover the edge of the pie with foil.) Bake at 375 degrees for 25 to 30 minutes when using fresh fruit, and longer, 45 to 50 minutes, when using frozen fruit. Remove foil. Bake for an additional 25 to 30 minutes, or until the top is golden. Cool on a wire rack.

BROWN SUGAR PIE

1 stick (1/4 pound) butter
1 1/2 cups dark brown sugar
1/2 cup light brown sugar
3 eggs
Pinch of salt
9-inch pie shell

Cream the butter and sugars. Add the eggs, unbeaten, with the salt. Bake in an uncooked pie crust for 45 to 50 minutes at 350 degrees.

CHOCOLATE PECAN PIE

2 eggs
1 cup white sugar
1/4 cup cornstarch
1/2 cup melted butter
1 ounce praline liqueur
1 cup finely chopped pecans

6-ounce package semisweet chocolate chips
9-inch unbaked pie crust

Beat the eggs slightly. Combine the sugar and cornstarch and add gradually to eggs, mixing well. Stir in the butter. Add liqueur, pecans, and chocolate chips. Pour into the pie shell and bake at 350 degrees for 45 to 50 minutes. Cool. Top with whipped cream or vanilla ice cream.

MUD PIE

1 stick (1/4 pound) butter
2 ounces unsweetened chocolate
3 eggs
1 1/3 cups white sugar
3 tablespoons white corn syrup
1/2 teaspoon vanilla
9-inch graham cracker pie shell

In a saucepan, melt the butter and chocolate, stirring often, until blended. Beat the eggs; stir in the sugar, corn syrup, and vanilla. Add the chocolate mixture to the egg-and-sugar mixture and blend well. Pour the filling into the prepared pie shell. Bake 35 to 40 minutes at 350 degrees. Make sure filling is set. Serve warm with whipped cream or ice cream.

STAY HOME PIE
(AKA TOMATO PIE)

2 cups grated Monterey Jack cheese

4 or 5 medium ripe tomatoes, peeled and sliced

4 green onions, chopped

1/4 teaspoon salt

1/2 cup mayonnaise

2 tablespoons dried basil

1 teaspoon dried oregano

1 teaspoon black pepper

9-inch deep-dish pie shell (baked at 350 degrees for 10 to 12 minutes and cooled)

Sprinkle 1/2 cup of the cheese on the bottom of the baked and cooled pie shell. Top with salted tomato slices, allowing them to overlap in a circular pattern. Mix the mayonnaise, basil, oregano, pepper, green onions, and 1 cup of the cheese and spread this mixture over the tomatoes. Sprinkle the remaining cheese on top and bake at 350 degrees for 35 to 40 minutes. Serve cool.

HEAVENLY CHOCOLATE PIE

1/3 cup cornstarch

2/3 cup white sugar

1/4 teaspoon salt

4 egg yolks

3 cups milk

2 tablespoons butter
1 tablespoon vanilla
2 cups dark chocolate chips
9-inch deep-dish pie shell (baked at 350
   degrees for 10 minutes and cooled)

Stir the cornstarch, sugar, and salt in a large pot over medium heat. In a mixing bowl, combine the egg yolks and milk and then gradually spoon the egg-and-milk mixture into the ingredients on the stove. Stir constantly until the mixture boils, then continue stirring for two minutes. Remove from heat and add the butter and vanilla. Stir in the chocolate chips until they melt and the mix is well blended. Pour into the pie shell and cool for two hours. Add whipped topping and serve.

TRIPLE CHOCOLATE DECADENCE (AKA BROWNIE PIE)

Pie Crust
1 1/3 cups all-purpose flour
1/2 teaspoon salt
1/4 cup + 3 tablespoons lard
3 to 4 tablespoons ice water

Brownie Filling

1 cup granulated sugar
2 eggs, slightly beaten
1/2 cup melted butter
1/4 cup cocoa powder
3/4 cup all-purpose flour
1/4 teaspoon salt
1/4 teaspoon baking powder
1/2 teaspoon vanilla extract
1/2 cup white chocolate chips
1/2 cup milk chocolate chips
1/2 cup dark chocolate chips

Topping

1/2 cup white chocolate chips
1/2 cup milk chocolate chips
1/2 cup dark chocolate chips

Preheat oven to 375 degrees.

In a large bowl, mix the flour and salt together, then cut in the lard until the mixture is crumbly. Sprinkle 1 tablespoon of ice water over the dough and mix in with a fork. Keep adding water until all the flour is moistened and the pastry almost cleans the side of the bowl. Form the pastry into a ball and flatten with the palms of your hand. Dust a clean surface with flour and place the ball of dough in the center. Flour a rolling pin and then roll out the dough to 2 inches larger than an inverted 9-inch pie plate. Fold the crust in half gently, and then fold in half again (so that it's folded in quarters). Put the pie dough in the pie plate and press firmly against the bottom and sides. Trim the overhang to about 1/2 inch, fold underneath crust on rim, and use your knuckles to flute the edge. Prick the bottom of the pan with a fork and bake for 10 minutes.

Mix together the sugar, eggs, melted butter, and cocoa. Add the flour, salt, and baking powder and blend well. Stir in the vanilla and baking chips. Pour the batter into the pie crust and bake for 20 minutes (or until a toothpick comes out clean). Let cool completely.

Put the milk chocolate chips in a microwave-safe container. Microwave for 15 seconds and stir. Continue until chocolate is smooth. Pour into a sandwich bag and press all the chocolate to one corner. Standing close to the pie, snip the corner of the baggie just a little, so that the chocolate will flow out in a thin stream. (Make a practice line on wax paper.) Draw a thin line on the top of the pie by starting at the top and working your way back and forth until you get to the bottom. (Go off the pie and then back on so that the crust is covered as well.) Rotate the pie by one-third and repeat with the white chocolate chips (melted the same way). Rotate once more and cover in the same way with the dark chocolate. Let cool at room temperature.

Submitted by Barbara Duck
First runner-up at the
Pie Town Festival Pie Contest, 2010

READING GROUP GUIDE

1. The book starts with a Navajo medicine man. How does the medicine man add to the story? What do you know about shamans in the Native American cultures? What stories have you heard about medicine men and women? In what other books have you encountered this role?

2. When Raymond returns home he certainly demonstrates signs of PTSD (posttraumatic stress disorder) with his out-of-control drinking, inability to sleep, and issues with anger. Family members and friends who recognize the personality changes nevertheless don't push him to get help. How might Trina, Frank, Roger, and George have handled things differently when Raymond first came home?

3. After she is injured, Trina must make a decision about staying with Raymond, and one of the issues she considers is whether Alexandria should live in the same house

with him. What do you think she should have done? Do you think she should have forgiven Raymond for what he did?

4. Why is Francine surprised to find love with Bernie King? How is their relationship different from those of the younger couples in Pie Town?

5. Why is Roger angry about being the last one to find out about what really happened between Raymond and Trina? Was Malene right not to tell him the truth? Should people in a relationship tell each other everything?

6. Father George acknowledges that he did not expect the town to be so supportive of Raymond. What about you? Did it surprise you to see how they rallied around one of their own?

7. Raymond claims that it was the support of his hometown that had the biggest impact on his healing. How important is it to have a community stand behind you when you're in trouble or in need?

8. Why is Raymond labeled the town "hero"? What do you think makes a hero?

9. How much do you know about PTSD? What is being done in your community to help young veterans who may be dealing with PTSD? What do you think should be done?

10. Do you think the novelist Thomas Wolfe was right when he wrote the famous line, "You can't go home again"? What does it mean to "go home" if you have experienced a trauma? How do communities help or hinder people when they come home?

ABOUT THE AUTHOR

Lynne Hinton is the award-winning author of fourteen books, including the Hope Springs series, featuring the national best-seller, *Friendship Cake*. She has also written a mystery series under the name Jackie Lynn. An ordained minister in the United Church of Christ, Lynne is available for speaking engagements and offers writing and spirituality retreats in New Mexico and across the country. You can contact her at www.lynnehinton.com. You can also find her on Facebook at Lynne Hinton Books. Lynne lives in Albuquerque, New Mexico, with her husband, Bob Branard.

The employees of Thorndike Press hope you have enjoyed this Large Print book. All our Thorndike, Wheeler, and Kennebec Large Print titles are designed for easy reading, and all our books are made to last. Other Thorndike Press Large Print books are available at your library, through selected bookstores, or directly from us.

For information about titles, please call:
(800) 223-1244

or visit our Web site at:
http://gale.cengage.com/thorndike

To share your comments, please write:
Publisher
Thorndike Press
10 Water St., Suite 310
Waterville, ME 04901